Death in the tropics . . .

"Those poor dumb bastards," whispered Hubert Boston.

"They're walking right into it!"

The Death Merchant waited. When the first wave of Brazilians was 90 to 95 feet from the dike, Camellion held the radiotelephone close to his mouth and said, "Now!"

A few seconds later four grenades sailed over the dike and exploded among the first line of Brazilian soldiers. There were screams of agony. Arms and legs were torn off. A few decapitated heads shot skyward. Bodies were pitched into the air and, amid a shower of dust and broken rocks, crashed back to earth and lay still. The Brazilians not killed or wounded either turned and attempted to retreat, or else flung themselves down in a frantic effort to find safety in the rocks.

But there was no safety. . . .

The Death Merchant Series:

#27 in the incredible adventures of the

DEATH MERCHANT
THE SURINAM AFFAIR

by Joseph Rosenberger

PINNACLE BOOKS   LOS ANGELES

This is a work of fiction. All the characters and events portrayed in this book are fictional, and any resemblance to real people or incidents is purely coincidental.

THE DEATH MERCHANT #27: THE SURINAM AFFAIR

Copyright © 1978 by Joseph R. Rosenberger

An original Pinnacle Books edition, published for the first time anywhere.

ISBN: 0-523-40119-1

First printing, March 1978

Cover illustration by Dean Cate

Printed in the United States of America

PINNACLE BOOKS, INC.
One Century Plaza
2029 Century Park East
Los Angeles, California 90067

This book is dedicated
to
Moonwatch–7

"Those who play the world's most dangerous game never concern themselves with winning. Success takes care of itself. But the true realists in counterintelligence always prepare for failure. . . ."

R.J.C.

Chapter One

The chant of the *Pai y mae de Santos*, the "Father and Mother of the Saints," was low but vibrant, the tonality of the young black priestess containing only a hint of the religious frenzy that would diabolize her completely before the rite of possession was completed. The five drums were in tempo with her unusual chant, which she half-sang and half-spoke in a vernacular called *Sranan tongo*, or "Surinamese," the widely used hybrid language of Surinam.

With scores of other tourists who were visiting Surinam, Richard Joseph Camellion stood and watched the ceremony of the Lemanja cult that, like all the rest of the South American-Afro sects, was a hodgepodge of Roman Catholicism, voodoo, European spiritism, and West African religious beliefs.

This particular ritual, on this particular March night—an invocation to the West African god *Boca Suja*, or "Foul Mouth"—was being held in Watermolenstraat Park, just off the busy Dominestraat, the "Broadway" of Paramaribo, the coastal capital of Surinam.

The government always permitted the various cults to perform their religious ceremonies in parks and in other public places, not only for the pleasure of tourists but also because there wasn't any logical way to suppress the weird sects without risking riots on the park of the highly superstitious blacks, who composed 50 percent of the population. The government realized it was wiser to let the cults perform their religious rites unhindered than to incur the hatred of the members and have them become anti-government. Cult activities held in public enabled the police to keep a watchful eye on the proceedings and to act instantly should possession lead to violence, should some of the members become overly possessed and go berserk. The police could also prevent tourists from being mugged and robbed and perhaps murdered; foolish tourists who, otherwise, would have gone to where a

1

Lemanja or a Xando or a Candomble ceremony was being held in secret.

There was order in this Lemanja *hoki*. The *Pai y mae de Santos*—now chanting louder, her dance movements more sensuous—moved within a large red circle painted in a 60-foot square of green canvas. Hundreds of black men, women, and children formed three sides of a square. Their colorful clothes had a definite West Indian skirt-and-blouse form, the material a bright mixture of cotton prints. The hats were fashioned of large, printed handkerchiefs, pleated to form a wide band over the forehead and widely flared at the back. Both men and women wore earrings, bracelets, and numerous strings of colored beads. Many wore a crucifix and religious medals side by side with voodoo charms and sacred trinkets of the Lemanja cult.

The Death Merchant wasn't surprised by the clothes worn by the blacks, for he knew that Surinam's population was one of the most ethnically varied in the world. Because of the early importation of slave labor from Africa and contract labor from Asia, there were more than just thousands of blacks in the nation that had formerly been known as Dutch Guiana; there were also thousands of Indonesians, Chinese, Creoles, Hindustani, various European minorities, and slightly over 10,000 native Indians, hundreds of whom were deep in the unexplored interior and were very savage. The total population was not quite 400,000.

Nor was Camellion the least bit intrigued by the Lemanja ritual, although this was his first visit to Surinam. In his various travels, he had seen similar ceremonies in other South American cities. Now he was only killing time, waiting to meet Godfrey Gell the next morning for the second and final time. Their first contact at Konfrie Airport had been brief, involving only enough time for Gell to give Camellion a suitcase containing a makeup kit, accessories, two SIG Neuhausen autoloaders, and two boxes of 7.65 Luger cartridges. The final item in the suitcase was a Veskin bullet-proof vest—as light and as thin as an undershirt, but as strong as steal. Not even a .44 Auto Mag slug could penetrate a Veskin B-Vest.

The only thing that Camellion had been able to smuggle aboard the KLM plane had been a box of candy given to him by a CIA "street man" in Belize, the former capital of British Honduras in Central America. Inside each chocolate that was covered in red tinfoil was a thimble-sized contact

2

bomb of DP gas; inside each green-wrapped piece of candy was the antidote, each triphenylmaleate capsule effective for twenty-four hours. Camellion had taken the first capsule that night after dinner at the Surinam Torarica, the hotel at which he was staying. He had then returned to his room, opened the makeup kit, and gone to work. An hour and a half later, he had slipped—unnoticed, he hoped!—from the hotel, disguised as a slightly stooped man in his sixties, silver-gray hair showing under his Brisa Panama, his mouth and chin framed by a silver-gray mustache and neatly trimmed silver-gray beard. Tucked inside his belt, on the left side in a waistband clip holster, was one of the SIG automaics. A special pocket inside his coat contained four extra magazines.

Ever on guard and keeping in the light, he had taken a stroll around downtown Paramaribo. Its wide streets and buildings were distinctively Dutch, with the exception of some of the religious buildings, which, according to the guidebook, included a Moslem mosque, a Hindu temple, and even a Jewish synagogue. He had also read with interest that ". . . tourists can arrange to see Indonesian parties or weddings in Hindu temples. Cars can be rented in Paramaribo for visits to some of the bush villages of the Djukas that have road connections with the capital. Other Djuka and native Indian villages may be visited by launch. At Joden-Savannah, one can see the ruins of Synagogue Berachah Ve Salom and the graveyard of one of the oldest former Sephardic Jewish settlements in the Western Hemisphere."

The Death Merchant had smiled when he read that ". . . Tonee's Travel and Tour Bureau, Surinam Airways, Ltd., Surinam Safaris, and Gell's Sightseeing Tours can arrange sightseeing trips into fifty miles of the jugle interior. English-speaking guides are provided. Among the tours that are provided are a day's trip by car and boat to the bush Negro village of Montigron on the Saramacca River. Gell's Sightseeing Tours also has a two-day trip to Afobakka, site of the hydro-electrical works of the Surinam Aluminum Company."

Godfrey Gell was the president of Gell's Sightseeing Tours. The tall, friendly Britisher (who wore a beret and loved to give the impression he was an alcoholic) was also the agent-in-residence of S.I.S., the British Secret Intelligence Service (formerly M.I.6).

It was unfortunate that Gell's tours did not include a hop, skip, and jump through the wild, mostly unexplored area

3

around the Wilhelmina Gebergte in southwestern Surinam. It was in the area of the Wilhelmina Mountains that WINK-EYE-1 had crashed. The thought was chilling: WINK-EYE-1, Uncle Sam's most advanced satellite, was at the mercy of the jungle of Surinam. Even worse was the fact that the Soviet Union probably had a good idea where WINK-EYE-1 had fallen. Therein lay the danger: that the Soviets would get to the satellite before U.S. intelligence agents did.

Camellion had finally wandered into Watermolenstraat Park to watch the Lemanja *hoki*. He had scanned the crowd of Occidentals. Hmmmmm. At no time since his arrival in Paramaribo had he seen anyone who even faintly resembled an agent of the Soviet Union. Camellion felt like laughing at himself. Ridiculous! What did an agent of the *Kah Gay Beh* or *Geh Eh Ru* look like? What was he or she supposed to look like? The answer was simple—like anyone else! For that matter, any of the non-whites in the crowd could be a *nash*[1]*

Richard was positive of some facts, one of which was that the Soviet intelligence officer represented the species homo Sovieticus in its unalloyed and most successful form, the final and extreme product of the Soviet slave state, a perfect but hideous example of the Soviet mentality. In spite of the many flaws in the Soviet system, the Soviet intelligence officer was well-trained and blindly dedicated to the cause and the world ambitions of Communism.

Camellion often thought of the fantastic paradox that was the Soviet Union. In the entire country one could not buy a simple ballpoint pen! Russian methods of commercial merchandising were so inefficient that it was common for people to stand in line for hours to buy as little as a single loaf of bread, wrapped in coarse brown paper. The average citizen did not even have access to an ordinary telephone book—as if telephone numbers were meant to be a carefully guarded secret! Yet the Soviet Union had one of the finest intelligence gathering organizations in the world, the KGB, a first-rate apparatus that, while not more efficient than the American Central Intelligence Agency, was every bit as good. The Death Merchant had not a single doubt that he would meet Soviet

[1] Literally, "one if us" or "ours"—one who works for Soviet intelligence, but is not a member of the KGB or GRU. The plural is *nashi*.

agents in the jungle of Surinam; special *Zapvboyakh*—emergency—teams would be flown in from Havana, Cuba.

Another bit of irony! The Soviet military machine did not have a choice. The Russians would have to try to find WINK-EYE-1. They couldn't ignore the tapes, the recording unit, the laser, and its "brain."

The dancing of the *Pai y mae de Santos* had become faster, more frantic, her arms and legs glistening with perspiration, twisting, jerking like striking snakes. Her entire body jerked with fantastic rhythm, as though she were in the grip of a maniacal seizure that was continuing to grow in intensity.

Dressed entirely in white, she moved in no particular pattern within the red circle; somehow her bare black feet avoided the lighted candles and the bottles of *cashasa* resting on the canvas. Like a wild woman, she danced all around the card-table altar filled with numerous objects. A large lithograph of the Sacred Heart of Jesus was propped up in the center of the square card table. Next to the picture was a two-foot-high statue of the horned god *Boop*, the sex god of the Lemanja cult, and a foot-high clay statue of Baron Semedi, the voodoo spirit of death. Arranged around the lithograph and the statues were *govi*, small clay jars that were believed to contain the tortured souls of *pretos velhos*—old blacks, the souls of slaves who had not received a proper burial.

The beat of the drums increased, the throbbing in tempo with the bizarre gyrations of the *Pai y mae de Santos*, as were the high pitched notes of the *rondador*, a pan pipe made from a series of bamboo reeds and played by a tall, concentration-camp-thin black who appeared to be exophthalmic—pop-eyed—due to goiter, although his neck was as skinny as a chicken's!

"*Boca Suja! Boca Suja! Boca Suja! Humda Gui Vo Suja Wik!*" screamed the priestess. Her howling and the hypnotic effect of the drums and *rondador*, created in the hundreds of bush blacks an emotional state on the brink of mania.

Some of the police, looking uncomfortable in their starched gray uniforms, shifted nervously and fingered their black plastic batons. The tourists shuffled restlessly.

"She must have joints made of rubber!" a young woman whispered to her husband. Standing only a few feet to Camellion's left, she clutched her husband's arm and stared in fear-

5

ful fascination at the black priestess, who appeared to have lost all control, not only of her body but of her mind.

A relaxed smile crossed the Death Merchant's face. *Yes, macabre! Like a beautiful sunset over Auschwitz, in 1944.* But he knew what the majority of other tourists did not know: the cults served as an emotional safety valve for the blacks of Surinam, who were at the butt end of society. As the underprivileged, cult members looked up not only to their saints and various gods but also to each other. The cults gave them confidence to live an existence that otherwise was hard, filled with 365 days of misery, of fighting to stay alive. The self-esteem that ritual returns is also restored through the mythology of the cults, which reasserts the value of the undervalued. Reduced to nothing by poverty, the individual is rebuilt by the experience of possession, with the priest or priestess being like a favorite neighbor, doctor, psychiatrist, and parent —all rolled into one.

Camellion thought of what anthropologists refer to as the Law of the Retarding Lead—still another incongruity of these poor, ignorant blacks. According to this law, the best adapted and most successful nations have the greatest difficulties during transition periods in adapting and retaining their lead in world affairs; conversely, the backward and less successful societies are more likely to adapt and lead in the transition process.

His icy blue eyes on the priestess, who had almost reached the peak of her obsession, Camellion stopped smiling. *In medieval times, it was the affluent and sophisticated Chinese empire that proved too set in its ways to change its values and institutions, while the primitive frontier society in Western Europe, because it was so backward, was free to evolve a new civilization that still dominates the globe. Too bad that World War III will shortly bring down the final curtain on our Western society!* Laughter floated through the halls of his mind. *As if the Universe gives a damn!*

By now, scores of men and women cult members were shaking and twitching and trembling. Many were still on their feet. Others were lying on the grass, rolling from side to side on their stomachs or backs, every muscle in their bodies quivering with the delirium of momentary madness, with possession by "Foul Mouth." Some barked like dogs. From other men and women—and even children—came yelps, screams, screeches, and a various assortment of howls and yells.

The *Pai y mae de Santos* was down on her knees, her head

flung back, her arms outspread and twisting. Her white turban had become unwound and now lay on the canvas, freeing her hair.

The Death Merchant had a very uneasy feeling. Intelligence agents are not only trained, they are born. Early in life such individuals develop a suspiciousness bordering on paranoia. This type of forever-watchful personality, polished with intense training, results in a first class "street man," a rarity in any intelligence service. Just as blind people somehow know when an object is directly in front of them, an expert in the clandestine service can sense extreme danger.

In spite of the screaming and yelling blacks, the Death Merchant had been constantly vigilant. A chill raced through the center of his spine. He was positive—*Behind me and very very close!*

He was about to step to his right and turn around when he felt the sudden and severe pinpoint pressure in the region of his left kidney. Instinct and the type of pressure told him the rest. Someone, standing behind him, had just tried to shove a blade into his kidney, but the lower part of the Veskin B-Vest had saved him.

The Death Merchant spun around with such incredible speed that the would-be assassin didn't have time to pull back on the knife and try the second time. Instead, the sharp blade freed itself by ripping through Camellion's brown sportscoat and tan shirt as he turned.

There was a twinkling of an instant in which Camellion saw the man who had tried to kill him. An Oriental, either Chinese or Japanese, the fortyish slant-eyes wore a dark suit, white shirt and inoffensively patterned tie which made him look like a bank clerk; in the white glare of the park's lights, his skin was the color of rancid butter. On the face of the man was a dumb look of astonishment, his eyes asking, *Why aren't you dead?*

Recovering from his amazement, the Oriental attempted to bring up the boot knife in his left hand, a movement that was instantly blocked by Camellion who grabbed the man's left wrist with his right hand and twisted. The knife was still falling to the grass, and Isamo Fukuda was still gagging with pain when the Death Merchant speared him in the throat with a deadly *Nihon nukite*. Some of the tourists and two of the policemen saw the one-sided fight but didn't know what was happening. It didn't make any difference to Fukuda. The devasting double piercing finger strike had crushed the top

7

of his trachea and he was choking to death. Making gurgling sounds, he clawed frantically at his throat in a desperate effort to get air.

The pretty young woman, who had been to Camellion's left, screamed and swayed against her husband. Very quickly, he pushed her behind him, fear falling all over his own face. Two cops, thirty feet to Camellion's left, started toward him. While one blew a whistle, the other took the lead and used his baton to shove aside tourists blocking the way. In the meanwhile, the black Lemamjaists were becoming more hysterical, screaming and jumping all over the place. Only the priestess was quiet; she had swooned by the altar and was unconscious.

Not taking any chances, other men and women in Camellion's immediate vicinity began to move back.

"I think they were fighting!" a man behind Camellion said in a loud voice.

"That Jap on the grass!" a woman exclaimed. "Look how he's jerking!"

And I think I had better make like the Invisible Man. To do that, I've got to make this crowd move in a hurry! Camellion reached underneath his coat, pulled the Swiss SIG automatic and thumbed off the safety. With his other hand, he reached into one of his coat pockets for one of the DP "marble" bombs. Just as he was removing his hand and about to fire a shot into the air, a young muscular man in a white Palm Beach suit tried to rush him.

Tch! Tch! All guts but no common sense! Camellion, holding the SIG with the muzzle pointed upward, pulled the trigger and, at the same time, let the stud have a savage Goju-Ryu karate *Kekomi,* a downward kick given with a corkscrew motion. The right heel of Camellion's foot smashed into the left kneecap of 'Mr. White Suit,' who howled in pain, tumbled onto his left hip next to Isamo Fukuda, grabbed his shattered knee with both hands, and began to moan. He wouldn't be able to walk for six weeks. Still, he was luckier than Fukuda. Fukuda was dead.

The Death Merchant spun around, crushed one side of the plastic marble and tossed it at the two cops who were only ten feet away, their 9-millimeter Browning pistols drawn; yet neither man could fire. If they missed their bullets could hit one of the innocent tourists.

The tiny bomb of compressed DP gas fell on top of the head of a bald tourist and bounced to the ground. The last of the six seconds went by and the miniature bomb began hissing out yellowish gas.

Diphorisorisine was developed by the U.S. Bureau of Prisons in 1962. Essentially a nonkilling nerve gas, DP-3 works on the hypothalamus, which, as a "brain with-in a brain," controls the entire autonomic nervous system. A few sniffs of DP-3 and the hypothalamus of the victim becomes short-circuited for an hour or so. The victim feels that he is unable to breathe. He can't talk properly. His vision blurs. The senses of smell, taste, and hearing vanish. With his senses cut off, the sufferer becomes frantic and thinks he is dying. Unable to use his legs, he falls. He tries to move his arms one way, but they move another.

All this happened to the two policemen and dozens of tourists as they inhaled the gas, the number of victims increasing with each second as Camellion, moving constantly, threw the remainder of his DP bombs—seven in all—spacing them out in a wide circle around him. Within a few minutes tourists, police, and blacks—several hundred people—were flopping and rolling around on the grass, strange sounds pouring from their throats. Those tourists on the fringe of the crowd ran before the drifting gas, thinking they were saving their lives.

Still holding the Swiss SIG, the Death Merchant looked all around him, his concern twofold—escape from the park and the backup team of the rice-eater who had tried to butcher him with a boot knife. *No backup? There has to be! A KGB assassination without a B-team is like a Southern breakfast without grits!*

Camellion didn't expect to find the team before it went into action; he intended to flee from the park before the support *Boyevaya Gruppa* could put the second plan into operation. Yet see them he did! As he was turning, he saw a man in the very process of aiming down on him. Standing by a tree, the man had "pig farmer" written all over him! There he was, 100 feet to the northeast, in an area free of tourists who had not been touched by the DP-3. The tourists had scattered to the south and the southeast and were fanning out across the park, in an effort to get to Keizer-straat, to the east, and Knuffelsgracht, to the south. There were two other men and a woman with the Russian who, with both hands on the butt of the pistol, had just completed his firing stance.

Ducking down, Camellion moved at an angle to the south, wondering if the man had fired the silenced pistol and, if he

9

had, where the bullet had gone. Weaving as best he could, the Death Merchant raced across the grass, jumping over or skirting around those men and women whom the gas had reached, who were writhing on the ground from the effects.

How did they know me? How did they see through this disguise? Not even Gell knew about it!

A hundred feet from where he had started, Richard darted behind a large palm tree, dropped down and looked around one side of the tree. He was just in time to see two men and the woman, who had started after him, drop to the grass. The Death Merchant smiled. *They thought I was getting set to fire on them. I will, but not yet. But where's the third joker?*

He got his answer in the form of noise to the northeast—a motorcycle engine roaring into life. To the northeast, a single headlight winked on. Then the cycle roared off, the beam of light pointing east.

There was a smacking sound as a bullet struck the other side of the palm treee, not more than a foot from Camellion's face. Another slug tore through the crown of his Panama, knocking the hat from his head. The Russians had spotted him.

Damning the silencers, Camellion jerked back behind the tree. Now the two men and the woman would spread out in a hurried attempt to whack him out before more police arrived. Richard looked around him. Between Camellion and the two streets bordering the east and the south sides of the park were trees and bushes. A quarter of a block away, in the southeast corner of the park, was a large tool house where the park workers stored their tools and power mowers. Camellion decided to move in the direction of the tool shed, his strategy based on the premise that he wouldn't be able to trick the Russians into thinking he was moving east. The tool shed would slow them down. They would think he was planning an ambush.

The Death Merchant leaned around the palm tree, fired three quick shots, turned and, just as quickly, blew apart two park lights sixty feet to the east, the loud roars of the SIG echoing all through the park. Not bothering to pick up his Panama—*Another $50 wasted!*—he started toward the tool shed, running first at one angle and then another. If the Russians were firing at him—if they even saw him—he didn't know it.

Charging around bushes and dodging between trees, he had not forgotten the man who had roared away on the motorcy-

10

cle. He could hear the Russian gunman on the machine charging along Keizerstraat. He didn't relish what his common sense told him. The Kremlin stooge was going around the block to intercept him when he came out of the park.

Halfway to the tool house, he ducked behind a jacaranda tree and strained his ears in an attempt to hear if anyone was moving through the brush behind him. In spite of the noise of traffic from both streets, the whispering of the leaves and the rustling of the palm fronds in the moderate breeze, the Death Merchant could detect those faint kind of sounds that are made when someone in a hurry brushes up against bushes, particularly bissana bushes. The Russians were not too far behind Camellion. It was no surprise. Richard hadn't thought for a single moment that he had tricked them. KGB assassination experts were the best the U.S.S.R. had to offer and were not easily fooled.

Camellion didn't fire the last cartridges in the SIG at the KGB men and the one female Marxist idiot. He didn't know where they were—and why reveal his own position? He shoved a full magazine into the pistol, sprinted the remaining distance to the tool house and then crept along the east side of the green-painted concrete block building. Ten feet in front of him was the sidewalk, then the narrow parkway, called a boulevard in all South American countries, then Keizerstraat and its traffic. To the south, at the same distance from the shed, was Knuffelsgracht.

One way wasn't as good as another. Camellion chose the east. He could see there was a divider strip, about eight feet wide, running down the middle of Keizerstraat. Through palm trees planted in the divider strip he could see a church on the opposite side of Keizerstraat. It was an architectural classic of the seventeenth century—adobe, with a fat bell tower built onto the front right side of the main building.

The plan ran smoothly through his mind. Would the Russians be desperate enough to come after him? Sure they would! Wasn't one kill-specialist stupid enough to be using a motorcycle? A silenced rifle with a night-vision scope would have done the job much better. Poor, worried pig farmers! The *Zapyboyakh* were improvising for the same reason that he had hurried from Mexico City to Belize City in Belize, the former British Honduras[2]: the KGB, like the CIA, had not

2 See *Death Merchant #26: The Mexican Hit.*

11

had time for any meticulous planning. The KGB in Moscow had not expected WINK-EYE-1 to crash any more than the CIA experts in Langley, Virginia, had anticipated the disaster.

He switched on the SIG's safety, shoved the autoloader into its waist holster, and hurried to the front of the storage house. Keeping the shed between himself and the park, Camellion made a dash across the sidewalk, deserted except for a group of people half a block away, and in a few steps came to the curb at the edge of the parkway. Sirens not too far away! Expecting a bullet in his back at any moment, he looked up and down Keizerstraat, at the headlights moving in both directions on the wide avenue. With only a sprinkling of luck, he would be able to reach the Catholic church on the northeast corner of Keizerstraat and Knuffelsgracht.

Hoping that there wasn't a hot rodder coming at him, Camellion judged speed and distance, then moved out into the traffic, running and weaving between cars. Some drivers, fearing they might hit him, jammed on their brakes, a few coming to a rubber-burning stop. Many yelled obscenities at him, in various languages.

Ignoring the angry drivers, the Death Merchant reached the divider in the center of the wide street and stood to one side of a palm tree with a trunk not more than a foot in diameter—*Better than no protection at all!*—and looked over at the park as he heard a motorcycle roaring around the northeast corner of Keizerstraat. On the south side of the storage shed, he saw a man and a woman, each holding a pistol. The second man was on the north side of the shed, holding the pistol with the silencer in both hands, trying his best to zero in on the Death Merchant between the moving cars. The Death Merchant dropped to one knee, pulled out the SIG, and turned his attention to the agent on the motorcycle. By this time, the man and the bike were less than 150 feet from Camellion, who now saw that he had been wrong. The hog the man was riding was not the product of that self-taught Japanese genius, Soichiro Honda. The Russian was on a Kawasaki KZ1000, a bigger and faster machine than a Honda. Hunched low over the handelbars and moving in the Death Merchant's direction, he started to bring the bike to a stop. Camellion spoiled his plan by putting two 7.65-millimeter slugs into the front tire of the Kawasaki. *Bang!* The tire blew, the Kawasaki veered to the left, the front wheel struck the curb and the motorcycle did a backward somersault, taking the Russian with it, while the drivers of cars behind the motorcycle attempted to stop their own vehicles. The driver of the first car did not succeed. His car hit the Russian with a loud *smack* and pitched the body ten feet. At the same time, the Kawasaki sailed over the hood and crashed onto the pavement of the next lane, barely missing the rear end of a minibus. The driver behind slammed on his brakes and skidded just as the Kawasaki exploded into a ball of orange flame. Another half a dozen loud noises sounded as cars rammed into each other.

The Death Merchant glanced in satisfaction at the Russian, who lay as limp as a bag of macaroni crushed by a bulldozer. A tug and a rip at his left shoulder—a bullet had almost found flesh! Camellion jerked to the right, ducked down and saw, between cars that had slowed on the other side of the boulevard, that one Russian agent—the woman—was still by the shed. One of the men was standing at the curb, as if undecided what to do.. The Ivan with the silenced pistol was trying to slip between cars and get to the center divider. Camellion fired a single round at him but he ducked a split second before the Death Merchant fired. The Russian jumped back to the sidewalk and dropped flat, as did the two other Russian agents. Meanwhile Camellion moved out among the stopped cars on the other side of the median strip. He darted between a British-built Austin and a Brazilian Novo and reached the curb. Amid the frightened stares of people who ducked away when they saw the SIG in his hand, Camellion headed for the church. He had passed judgment on himself, and if he had guessed wrong about the Russians the verdict could be death. . . .

Chapter Two

The doors of South American churches are seldom locked, so the Death Merchant had no trouble getting into Saint Sebastian's. All he did was open the single massive door in the center of the front of the building and slip inside. Once he was cloaked by the partial darkness, he felt safe for the moment, yet out of place, out of contact with reality.

Camellion crept past the holy-water font and the life-size statue of a saint. In front of the statue were a dozen rows of burning votive candles, which illuminated the rear of the church. The only other light came from the sacristy lamp to the left of the main altar and from six tall candles in massive brass holders, two on the main altar and two on each side altar. A small oil lamp burned close to each confessional at the ends of the communion railing.

Shadows flickering over him, the Death Merchant paused and looked down the single aisle. There wasn't anything unusual about the church. In South America there were thousands of such churches all built in a similar style. The front, with the main door through which he had just come, was gabled with corbiesteps. There were two sections of wooden pews on either side of a wide center aisle. Stations of the Cross stood on the side walls. Small cinquefoil windows of stained glass were placed high in thick adobe walls that supported the barrel-vault ceiling, filled with crude murals of heavenly scenes—like a poor man's Sistine Chapel.

Suppose there were worshipers in the church? *Ignore them!*

The Death Merchant raced down the center aisle, vaulted the communion railing, and rushed through the door of the sacristy. He blinked several times, adjusting his eyes to the darkness, and went to a door that opened to the outside. He checked the large brass knob over the decorative handle. Good. The door was unlocked. He took a position by the side of the door and, with his back against the wall and the scent of incense in his nostrils, he tensed his muscles and began the

14

wait, thoughts tumbling through his mind. In hide-and-find hit situations such as this, the logic of replacement could not be applied. The variables were too numerous. All three Russians might use the front door of the church. Or all three might use the door to the sacristy. Or they might not come into the church at all. The Russians would have to take risks, because time was working against them. Very often the Death Merchant had found himself in the predicament now confronting the three Ivans. He, too, had been forced to race against time and take risks. He was gambling that the Russians would consider the fastest and most logical way—split up and come in after him. At all costs, they couldn't wait outside the church. They couldn't afford to be around when the police arrived, any more than he could.

Several minutes passed. Holding the SIG in his right hand, the Death Merchant waited, relaxed, breathing evenly. At length, he heard a very slight sound: the knob of the door being turned very slowly! Just as slowly the edge of the door moved gently inward, until the space between door and wall had widened enough to admit entry. In the darkness, Camellion saw the dim otuline of a foot appear. The lower part of a leg! Then, as the Russian moved forward, there was the rounded end of a Gronskovitch noise suppressor. As though the KGB agent were walking on very thin ice, he stepped into the darkened sacristy.

The Death Merchant, who had placed his SIG autoloader on the floor, struck with fantastic speed. His left arm shot out, the fingers of his hand clamping like a steel vise around the thick right wrist of Alexi Kovasin, who snarled in anger and surprise. Camellion pushed the Briansk machine pistol away from him, the sudden movement causing Kovasin's finger to pull against the trigger. The muzzle of the noise suppressor pointed upward and the Briansk went off with a soft popping sound, the 7.65-millimeter slug coming to a stop in the ceiling. Simultaneously the Death Merchant slammed Kovasin across the face with a *Gyaku Shuto* reverse chop.

The Russian grunted in pain. His senses dazed from the blow that would have turned off the consciousness of the average man, Kovasin instantly showed why members of the KGB *Spetschasti*[3] were feared by the intelligence services of other nations. The huge Russian—built like a junior bull, his

[3] Special Department

arms and legs like a grand piano's—immediately reverted to *Sambo*, the Russian version of judo and karate. Not only did he attempt to snap his gun arm free, he also tried to knee Camellion in the groin and to sore-throat him with a bunched two fingers and thumb strike. The only thing wrong was that Kovasin was trying it on the world's deadliest fighter in hand-to-hand combat.

Ducking both the knee and the axlike edge of the hand, Camellion tightened his hold on the Russian's wrist and quickly went to work on Kovasin's washtub of a face with a series of *Hira Ken* blows. The joints of his knuckles first broke the nose of the Russian, staggering him. The second *Hira Ken* shook his skull like a bone-quake. The third went to Kovasin's philtrum, directly below the nose. The fourth and fifth blows landed on his windpipe. Choking, Kovasin began to sag, his head jerking with such intensity that his gray felt hat fell off. Two *Shuto* sword chops to the Russian's neck finished him off. Unconscious, he started falling to the floor, his fingers going limp around the butt of the Briansk MP. Camellion caught the machine pistol before it could fall to the wooden floor and make a racket. For several moments he looked at the Russian, who lay sagged against the door. To make sure the Russian would remain unconscious, Camellion kicked him in the chin with the top of his foot.

Time! Time! Time! He bent down, picked up the Russian's hat and put it on. The hat was slightly too large, but it would have to do. He went over to the SIG, picked it up, and shoved it into its holster. Lack of time prevented him from giving a full check to the machine pistol. The other two Russians right now might be creeping around the communion railing. Camellion pushed the hat back on his head. Unless the other two Russians came within 10 feet of him, it was possible that, the dim light, he might fool them for four or five seconds. His sports coat and the suit coat of the Russian were about the same color. The Russian outweighed him by 75 to 100 pounds, but they were the same height. The Russian's pants were a shade lighter than Camellion's—*but all I need is four or five seconds.*

Fully cognizant of the 50-50 chance he was taking, the Death Merchant went out into the church and walked to the communion railing, stopping when he was before the center of the main altar—all the time very careful to keep his back to the glow coming from the sacristy lamp.

The machine pistol held loosely in his hand—the safety

16

off—he looked out over the dimly lighted church, his vulturous blue eyes raking the boxlike confessionals, the wide main aisle and the two sections of pews.

There they were, the last two Soviet agents! They had reached the center of the church and, apparently by a prearranged plan, had gotten down in the pews, the man on one side of the aisle, the woman on the other.

Both Russians now stood up and looked toward Camellion, who signaled them to come forward with a wave of the Briansk. The man was first to leave the pew and start walking down the aisle toward the Death Merchant, a pistol in his hand. The woman followed.

"You got the Amerikanski agent? He is dead?" Alverian Voiny called out hoarsely, thinking Camellion was Alexi Kovasin.

Camellion did not reply. He couldn't. Although he spoke almost perfect idiomatic Russian, he had no idea how the voice of the man in the sacristy sounded.

Puzzled by the lack of a reply on Camellion's part, Alverian Voiny paused and strained his eyes to see "Kovasin" more clearly.

"Alexi, did you hear me?" A nervous edge to the voice.

The Death Merchant's hand tightened around the Briansk.

"He isn't Kovasin!" Sonya Torun screamed, her eyes growing round with instant fear. "Kovasin's trousers weren't that dark!"

The Death Merchant snapped up the Briansk, spot-aimed, and fired. There was a whispered *pop*. The solid nickel slug sped through the Gronskovitch silencer, struck Voiny in the chest and pitched him back like a store window mannequin. Voiny almost bounced when he hit the floor, landing on his back.

Camellion fired again. He missed. Sonya Torun had been too fast. Terrified, she had jumped sideways into a pew. One knee struck the kneeling bench while, with her free hand, she reached for the edge of the pew to break her fall. The Death Merchant fired before she had time to reorganize, before she could either raise herself up and fire at him or lower herself to the kneeling bench.

The machine pistol popped five times in rapid succession. Three of the nickel projectiles tore through the back of the pew and missed Sonya Torun. The fourth bullet struck her high in the right side of the head, tore through her skull and scrambled her brain. The fifth piece of nickel tore the back

17

of the pew in front of Sonya Torun, plowed into her right buttock, and came to rest against the ilium, the upper portion of the hip bone. The slug in Sonya Torun's head had killed her instantly. She lay there, wedged between the back of one pew and the seat section of another, one foot and ankle protruding into the aisle. Carefully the Death Merchant put a bullet into the foot. Part of the foot went flying. What was left on the ankle flopped back down to the floor and came to rest at a crooked angle.

Satisfied that the sow from the U.S.S.R. no longer existed as a personality and a bundle of memory banks, Camellion hurried back into the sacristy, shoved the corpse of the Russian from the door, put the Briansk into Kovasin's right hand and closed the stiffening fingers around the butt. The ridiculous trick would not work with even a third-rate police department in any part of the world. When a person dies, the fingers become rigid with a specific kind of contraction that, later, cannot be faked, should anyone place an object in the hand of the corpse and close the fingers around the object. Camellion was hoping that the police department in Paramaribo didn't have a trained medical examiner.

He pulled out the SIG automatic, switched off the safety, opened the outside door very slowly and stared out into the partial darkness. Seeing no one, he hurried outside and took stock of his surroundings. There was a one-story house 100 feet east of the church. *No doubt the priest's home.* Twenty feet east of the house was a solid wooden fence. Knuffelsgracht was to the south, Keizerstraat to the west. North of the church was a one-story darkened building. *A school, probably. What's the difference?*

Camellion ran to the fence, hand-vaulted over it and then got down, snuggling up to the wood. He looked up and down the alley, then to the west. Traffic was in one hell of a mess on Keizerstraat. Police cars, red roof lights flashing. A lot of smoke from the still burning Kawasaki. Half a dozen men carrying riot guns were moving slowly along the northern side of the church. Would they continue to look for him after they found the two Russian boars and the sow inside the church? There wasn't any way the Death Merchant could know.

And I'm not going to stick around to find out!

18

Chapter Three

A dedicated hypochondriac, Godfrey Gell unfastened the sleeve of the blood-pressure testing kit from his arm and folded the cloth. With almost loving care, he placed the aneroid sphygmomanometer in its zippered traveling case and put the case in the drawer of the desk.

"How was it?" asked Richard Camellion, who sat in front of the desk.

"Not bad. A hundred and twenty over eighty," Gell replied. Embarrassed because Camellion had walked into his office unannounced and had caught him pumping up the sleeve, Gell explained that while he didn't suffer from hypertension, "My father and mother had high blood pressure and I had a younger brother who had a stroke a year ago. He was only 41. Fell over in the shower and died within a few minutes." Gell leaned over the desk and lowered his voice. "And the next time you come to my office, give your name to Maria. I presume you did see her sitting behind her receptionist's desk? What did you tell her?"

Camellion unzipped a tobacco pouch he had taken from his coat. "I told her I was an old friend whom you hadn't seen in years and that I wanted to surprise you. I thought maybe the police might be waiting in here for me!"

"Or maybe the Russkies!" Gell said, his voice just above a whisper. He peered at the Death Merchant with a pinched, suspicious expression and watched Camellion take a few pumpkin seeds from the pouch and put them into his mouth. "If you're thinking that I had something to do with the Ivans tapping you in Watermolenstraat Park, forget it. I don't know how the other side did it, but I have a good idea."

"How did you know the KGB did try to hit me?"

Gell drew back, as if he couldn't believe what Camellion had just said.

"Oh, come off it, old boy. The whole town is talking about what happened last night. We have only one telly station in

Paramaribo, but this morning's news was filled with the riot in the park. Nine people died, not counting the four Russians. If they were Soviet nationals. You'd know more about that than I!"

"They were Russian," Camellion said simply, slumping down in the easy chair. "I never did suspect you of being in on the attempted hit. You didn't know I would be in disguise when I left the hotel. You couldn't even have suspected, since you didn't know about the makeup kit in the suitcase you gave me at the airport. If that case had been opened, I would have known it."

A curious look crept into Gell's gray eyes. "In disguise! Then my explanation doesn't fit!"

"Try me!"

"It's not a deep secret that I'm S.I.S.'s man here in Paramaribo, no secret at all." Gell sighed, pulled open a desk drawer, took out a pint of rum, and set the bottle on the desk. "The Soviet Union has an embassy here, and the KGB *Residentura* must know I'm S.I.S. The Surinam government knows but pretends it doesn't. Great Britain is a friendly power and does a lot of trade with Surinam. You know how those things are. It's the same in the United States, and the same kind of hypocrisy exists here in Surinam."

The Death Merchant nodded. "You have to be practical, Gell. Many things in life are not fair, as a President once said. Any moron knows that."

Having taken a few swallows from the bottle of rum, Gell wiped his mouth with a slim hand and gave Camellion an odd, undecided look.

"Are you sure you're an American and a member of 'the Company'? You don't sound like one!" The same peculiar quality was in his low voice.

Camellion awarded him a vulture's smile. "Which do you mean? I don't sound like an American—or a CIA man? Let me tell you something. Working for the CIA and being a member of the CIA are two different things. I work strictly for money. I'm not a member of the Central Intelligence Agency. But we're off the subject."

Gell agreed, with a contemplative stare. He was as tall as Camellion, with delicate features, a short, pug nose and fine blond-white hair worn long. Tinted rimless glasses hid his eyes. His gray linen suit needed pressing—the coat was hanging on the back of a chair—and his white shirt, unbuttoned to the waist, could have stood a good bleaching.

"It's like I was saying," Gell explained. "The Soviets know I'm the local S.I.S. man. When I heard the news this morning, I assumed the Ivans spotted us together at the airport, put two and two together, trailed you to the hotel and from then on kept an eye on you. You say you were in disguise when you left the hotel. Now I'm not sure how they tagged you. If you donned the disguise while in your room, there's only one answer. The KGB had a spot-man on your floor, on the room itself. All they did was tail whoever came out of the room. Do you know what branch of the KGB it was? I suppose that's a silly question."

Camellion didn't laugh as Gell had supposed he would. The Death Merchant merely said, "I can't be certain. The four were no doubt *Boyevaya Gruppa* emergency people sent in from Cuba. They were good. They had even anticipated the use of numerous kind of gases and had taken the antidotes. I'm talking about DP-3 stuff."

"I figured that's what you used while I was watching the news on the telly this morning," Gell said. "I have pipelines into the police, and they don't suspect the little to-do last night involves international intelligence. The four Russkies were using Costa Rican passports and Spanish names. The current thinking among local authorities is that they were communist revolutionaries. But the police know they were after you, that the four were trying to make a hit. The police don't know your name, but they're checking all the tourists. They'll be around to ask you questions."

"I watched the news, too, this morning. I hoped I could fool the police by putting a machine pistol in the hand of one Ivan. I can see now that was a waste of time."

"You're sure they were Russian?"

"They spoke hog-talk."

"Hog-talk?"

"They spoke Russian."

Gell hunched himself farther over the desk and put his hands on the top of his thighs. "Look, Camellion. I know about WINK-EYE-1. But I wasn't told why you came to Surinam. My contact in the British embassy said that you would fill in the gaps, if I asked you."

The S.I.S. agent looked expectantly at Camellion, who was looking around the room. The office wasn't the type used by corporation executives. Gell was behind a plain walnut-grain-finished desk. Six mist-green filing cabinets against one wall. A credenza; bottles of booze on top. A Naugahyde

21

black sofa. Three simulated-leather upholstered chairs. A small refrigerator in one corner. An old-fashioned floor safe. Two windows behind Gell, covered with Venetian blinds that needed dusting. On one wall was a large colored map of Surinam, showing the routes of Gell's Sightseeing Tours. The most expensive items in the office were the gold-henna wool rug and the large black recliner that Gell used as a swivel chair.

Camellion's head swung to Gell in question. "Tell me, is it safe to speak freely in here?" His voice was as direct as his eyes.

"This is a 'safe' room," Gell replied in his clipped, competent voice, but he no longer whispered. "Every morning I make a 100-percent sweep for any electronic surveillance monitors. I use a Dekkor RF detector and a full-spectrum receiver and analyzer. To be on the safe side, I turn on a 'white noise' generator—it's built into one wall—in case anyone has placed an electronic stethoscope transmitter outside the building."

Camellion smiled. "Why then were we whispering?"

Gell stared at Camellion almost sadly before he sighed, dropped his gaze, and answered in a normal tone of voice. "Habit! It's nothing but habit. I even talk in my sleep in a whisper. I believe you were about to tell me why you came to Surinam."

The Death Merchant zipped up the tobacco pouch, his expression thoughtful. "Two reasons. But first, I'd like to know if the local KGB ever permanently neutralized any S.I.S. agents here in Surinam. It will help me do an analysis on the probability of the KGB coming after me while I'm with you. My own thoughts are that the Russians will leave well enough alone. The go-around in the park last night has already created a big stink."

Gell pushed his glasses higher up on his nose and carefully chose his words. "A few years ago, one of our people stumbled onto something the Russkies were planning with the Cubans. We never did find out what it was. We did put together what happened to our man. The KGB grabbed him off the street, took him only God knows where and placed him in a tightly sealed room with a block of dry ice. The ice gave off carbon monoxide fumes, which killed him. Then the ice melted without a trace. We found him in an alley and were supposed to think he died of a heart attack. Don't worry. I'm convinced you're safe with me."

Gell could see the Death Merchant frown. For a moment he watched the man he considered to be some kind of Doctor Strangelove, a flicker of a smile on his lips.

"After we found Cecil, we neutralized two Russians," Gell explained. "It's too long a story to tell you how we did it. I'll just say for now that we used X rays to kill the military attache and the cultural attache. Both died within two weeks, of 'blood dyscrasia.' The Russians got the message."

"Not bad," mused Camellion. "Two for one, like the Israelis."

"Exactly, which leads to my point. We have an understanding with the hammer and sickle boys. They don't hit us, we don't hit them. On the other hand, WINK-EYE-ONE is important enough to make them break the agreement. You know how the Russians are."

"Up to a point, the actions of the KGB can be predicted, but there are those times when the Sword and the Shield will pull a surprise," Camellion said quietly. "For instance, the four who tried to make me a corpse last night."

"Three chessmen and a checker[4]," Gell intoned. He leaned back in his plush recliner and, with the bottle of rum in one hand, crossed his legs. "Well, it's possible she could have been a swallow[5]. The British intelligence officer grinned impishly. "I doubt it. She made it plain enough that she didn't want to screw you. She only wanted to kill you. Did you get a good look at the bitch?"

"Not up close. I did see enough of her to know she wasn't a swallow. She didn't have the looks or the figure. She was strictly a pig-farmer hit artist, and the Fu Manchu creep who tried to tickle my kidney with a shiv had to be a nash. I'm wondering how many more of the locals are working for the Soviets."

Gell couldn't reply, not with the bottle of rum tilted to his mouth.

After a moment, the Death Merchant said in a new tone, "I came to Surinam for two reasons. First, I wanted to size up the situation by getting a report from you. If the central

---

[4] *Chessmen:* an S.I.S. term for male KGB (or GRU) agents. *Checker* refers to a woman agent.

[5] *Swallow:* A Soviet female agent who uses sex as her main weapon.

23

government knows that WINK-EYE came down in the southwest part of this rinky-dink country, I assume you would have some information about it." His eyes probed Gell, who was capping the bottle.

"It's a dead end there, old boy." Gell half-smiled at Camellion. "Surinam is not a sophisticated nation. It's governed by blacks. Science and technology are nonexistent in this nation. I doubt if anyone in the Surinam government ever heard of the U.S.'s fabulous satellite. It didn't light up like a shooting star when it came down. There's no way anyone in Surinam could know. I don't even know myself! I mean regarding the crash. I guess the satellite came down like the capsules of the astronauts. At a certain height a parachute opened and the satellite came down like a feather?"

The Death Merchant nodded at Gell who, not giving him a chance to speak, continued by saying with exaggerated cheerfulness, "I'd wager my six weeks summer leave that your second reason for coming to Paramaribo is to find out if it's possible for us to organize an expedition, under cover of a tour, to get to the satellite. I'm right, aren't I?"

Camellion, rubbing the end of his chin, intentionally let a note of hope creep into his voice. "All things are possible if planned properly." He licked his lower lip, then added, "Within reason."

"You said that WINK-EYE came down in the southwest part of the country. Can you be more specific? Other U.S. 'spies in the sky'—and Soviet satellites as well—must have tracer beams on them. You Americans have the INTELSAT series and the AMSAT and COMSAT series. The Soviets must have a couple of hundred of their ORBITA and MOLNIYA babies in orbit."

"The U.S. National Security Agency has pinpointed the location within several miles," Camellion said. "We know and the Soviet Union knows that WINK-EYE is down somewhere close to the southern tip of the Wilhelmina Gebergte. We have got to get there first."

Gell frowned deeply, looked down at the desk and slowly shook his head from side to side. "Not with Gell's Sightseeing Tours you won't. The maximum distance of my route is Afobakka, a hundred and sixty miles into the interior. Worse, the area you mention, around the Wilhelmina Mountains, is the home of the Anacunna. Those damned red devils kill on sight anything that walks on two legs, except white men. They torture whites to death. It's said they roast them very

24

very slowly, but as far as is known, the Anacunna aren't cannibals."

"I gather you're saying that we can't get to the satellite from Paramaribo?" Camellion said with a slight laugh. He put his hands on back of his head and locked his fingers.

"You gather right," Gell answered without hesitation. "Even if the Surinam Department of the Interior granted permission to go that far into the interior, there's no bloody way we could disguise the expedition as a 'tour.' No way, laddie. Suppose we did get permission! Not a single one of the Surinamese who works for me would go into Anacunna country. It can't be done, Camellion."

Gell stared coldly at Camellion, as if expecting an angry retort. He seemed confused when Camellion looked past him and gazed through the window. Outside, in front of the hangar, mechanics were working on a U.S. surplus PV-2 Harpoon, a twin-engine cargo plane that had been developed by Lockheed during World War II. The airplane was painted a bright yellow. GELL SIGHTSEEING TOURS was painted in black letters on the side of the craft.

Camellion wanted to laugh. Ironic that Gell flew tourists in that ancient pile of nuts and bolts and yet was afraid to go into Anacunna territory. Nonetheless, the S.I.S. man was right. A search force operating from within Surinam was out of the question. Even before he had arrived in Surinam, the Death Merchant had known that such a scheme could not be executed. *The KGB knows it, too. And the KGB knows that we know it and that we know that THEY know it. The Russkies also have to know that we assume that they can't come in through either Guyana or French Guiana!*

"WINK-EYE must be tremendously important!" Gell broke the silence, his tone brittle, his smile looking like the remains of one he had given someone the previous day. "Why is that particular satellite so vital? I suppose you can't tell me because of security?"

"I can't tell you because I don't know," Camellion lied with a shrug. "The damned Russians know more about WINK-EYE than I do."

"All I can say is that you have one bloody problem!" Gell's tone clearly conveyed his doubt. He suddenly brightened and for a moment seemed to be holding his breath. "Guyana is your best chance," he said. "British Guiana became the independent nation of Guyana in 1966, but the London Overseas Department still has a tremendous amount of influence with the Georgetown government. Without British help the country would collapse overnight."

"It's out of my hands," Camellion said tiredly. "There was a rumor that an American expedition will be flown in from Venezuela." He leaned back and shut his eyes. For the first time, Gell had the impression that the tall American with the strange blue eyes was ready to accept defeat, his only defense a gloomy resignation to whatever might happen.

Godfrey Gell's eyes became hard, his mouth half-open in disbelief. "Venezuela! But that's ridiculous!" he exclaimed. "Why fly all the way across Guyana to reach Surinam when it can be done easied, by flying straight south in Surinam itself?"

"I agree," Camellion said. "I equate coming in from Venezuela with trying to take a bath while encased in a diving suit. However, the decision is not mine to make. I'm saying the hell with the whole business. Tomorrow I'm flying back to the United States."

"Venezuela! It's so damn bloody stupid!" Gell said angrily. "Why, goddamn it, we have a large and efficient network in Georgetown, a net that is part of the triangle that S.I.S. and the CIA use to monitor the Caribbean. Washington must be suffering from mental myopia. London is often just as stubborn. I should suppose that Moscow is as obstinate sometimes with its own agents."

"At least we know that WINK-EYE's crash nine days ago caught the KGB totally off guard in this section of the world."

"We do? How?"

"Because the KGB used a female expert from the Spetschasti, and expert KGB assassins are not common," explained the Death Merchant, slowly looking around the office. "By the way, any holes in your screens? Any kind of special ventilating system in this room?"

Gell stared in amazement at Camellion. He arched his thin eyebrows and his lips formed as though he might be getting ready to whistle. "The screens are new. And I don't think the Russians will drop poison gas into a nonexistent ventilating system!" He hesitated, then laughed. "Don't tell me that you're afraid of bugs?"

"I am, but not bugs of the *phylum arthropoda, class insecta!*" Camellion said. "I'm speaking of micro-electronic 'chip' mikes so small they can be carried on the backs of flies."

Gell's lower jaw almost dropped to his knees. "You have to be joking!" He could see plainly that Richard Camellion wasn't!

"I wish I were. I'm not. What might be called the ultimate bug is a micro-electronic circuit built on a chip of silicon—a 25-centimeter-diameter radio that can be fastened to the back of an ordinary housefly. It's really quite ingenious. Chip transmitters are pasted onto the backs of flies and the flies are sent into heavily guarded conference rooms by way of key-holes and ventilation systems. Before the flies are taken to the area, they are given sniffs of a certain kind of nerve gas which will kill them within a predetermined period of time. The idea is that the fly, or flies, will die within the target area; otherwise the buzzing of its wings would deafen the transmitter."

"I believe it," Gell said resignedly. "The Russians aren't as involved with gadgetry as the CIA, but the KGB often comes up with some weird devices. I recall the time a swallow tried to seduce one of our people in West Berlin. He was wise to what she trying to do and let himself be persuaded to shack up with her. What happened is still a joke in Whitehall. They were in bed, going through the preliminaries, getting ready for the main event. Our man bit into one of her nipples and discovered it was a fake. The entire nipple fell off. It was made of fine, flesh-colored rubber and contained a circular transmitter with a microphone that picked up sounds coming through the fine perforations in the rubber. Just think of it— a 'tit transmitter'! That only proves how stupid the KGB can be, sometimes. Or maybe Russian men don't suck on a teat when they make love?"

The Death Merchant smiled crookedly. "The nipple mike wasn't such a good idea. Because the fake nipple protruded a fraction of a centimeter above the genuine nipple, it was vital to equip the swallow with a pair to prevent her from appearing asymmetric. The KGB gave up the nipple mike after its scientists invented the transmitter pill, an aspirin-size radio that the whore swallowed before hopping into bed with the target. I had a CIA man tell me that when the swallow and the target were in bed and right in the middle of a 'navel engagement' the signals from the electronic pill sounded like a miniature sub-gun going off!"

Camellion got to his feet. "Where's your john?"

Still laughing, Gell also stood. Finally controlling himself, he replied, "On the other side of the reception room." Again

27

he laughed, a deep belly-roll of mirth. "The next thing you know, S.I.S. or the CIA or the KGB will come up with a transmitter that a woman can shove up her twat!"

"You're behind the times," Camellion said and smiled. "We have such a device. So have the Russians. The transmitter is about the size of a thumbnail and is fitted into the vagina like a coil contraceptive. You said on the other side of the reception room?"

"The door to you left."

"I'll find it." Camellion didn't want to ask the receptionist; he had always found it embarrassing to ask members of the opposite sex directions to a toilet.

As Camellion turned to go, Gell said, "When you get back, we'll have some lunch." He glanced toward the refrigerator. "I hope you like cold mutton. Actually, it's goat."

The Death Merchant left the office and went past Maria, the plump receptionist, who looked up from the book she was reading.

"The door to the left," she said, guessing where he wanted to go.

"Thank you," Camellion muttered without looking around at her.

He opened the door, stepped into the short hall, closed the door and started toward the toilet at the end of the eight-foot-long passage.

The explosion shook the entire building, the concussion so enormous that the hall door was torn from its upper hinge. The Death Merchant was thrown violently to the floor.

His ears ringing, his head pounding, Camellion staggered to his feet, rushed to the hall door, shoved it to one side and stepped into the wrecked reception room. Dozen of ceiling tiles had fallen. The desk of the receptionist and other furniture, scattered about at crazy angles, were covered with dust and broken chunks of plaster.

Maria lay sprawled out on her face to one side of the desk. The Death Merchant didn't know whether she was dead or unconscious.

The wall behind the receptionist's desk was wrecked. The explosion had blasted a large hole in its center, a jagged cavity ringed with chunks of plaster hanging on slats and wire reenforcements. The door and door frame were lying in the reception area, the side of the door that had been facing Gell's office pitted from various objects that had struck it.

28

Standing in the middle of the wreckage, Camellion turned as four men dressed in mechanics' coveralls rushed in through the outside door.

The four stared around them in disbelief.

"What happened?" one of the men asked, his voice grim.

"Call the police, and one of you take care of the receptionist," Camellion ordered. He then went through the mess into what had been Godfrey Gell's private office. The corpse of the man, minus his head, both arms, and his left leg, lay six feet from the opening. This section of the building had been totally wrecked by the terrific blast. Half of the north wall and half of the east wall had been obliterated by the bomb which, from the pungent odor of the fumes, had been composed of TNT.

The row of filing cabinets had been ripped apart into ragged sheets of the metal and burnt papers lay all over the area, including the ground beyond the ripped opening in the walls. Pieces of metal had slashed through the black Naugahyde sofa and the simulated leather chairs. Glass had been blown out of the window frames. The top of Gells' desk was cracked and his large black Recliner ripped to shreds, its stuffing and springs sticking out.

Of the refrigerator there was no trace, nothing except scattered pieces of metal on which were chunks of bloody flesh and cloth, ripped sections of white shirt, small patches of gray linen. The heavy compressor of the refrigerator lay toward the center of the wrecked room.

The Death Merchant stared stonyfaced at the northeast corner where the refrigerator had stood. Not only had the bomb demolished half of the north and east walls; it had also destroyed the ceiling in that part of the room. Camellion moved closer to the torn ceiling. Blue sky stared down at him—and an arm rested on a splintered ceiling brace!

The wheels of logic meshed smoothly in the Death Merchant's mind. *"When you come back, we'll have some lunch,"* *Gell had said.* The Death Merchant could never be positive. No one would ever know what really had happened. Yet the deduction had to lead to a conclusion: Gell had gone to the refrigerator and opened the door. The bomb must have been rigged to explode when the door was opened. *They planted it during the night.* Gell never knew it when he was torn apart by the blast!

The Death Merchant saw two of the mechanics come into

29

the room. He thought of leaving the area. No. The mechanics could identify him.

The third mechanic came into the room. "Maria is all right," he said to the other two. "She was only stunned. I told her to lie there and keep quiet until an ambulance arrives."

Maria can also put the ID on me. I'd better stick around!

He looked up again at the huge hole in the northeast corner of the room.

Score one for the KGB. But we'll get even!

Chapter Four

"Tell me your story again please, Mr. Camellion," said Zahar Soedardjo. Standing next to the Death Merchant, Soedardjo watched the two men from the ambulance place parts of Godfrey Gell's body into several rubberized canvas sacks. An ambulance had already left with Maria dePugh, the receptionist, who had become hysterical.

His hands behind his back, Camellion stood relaxed. To one side of him stood Zahar Soedardjo, chief of police of Paramaribo. On Richard's other side was Adam Msuya, chief of detectives. A mulatto who was almost as fat as a sumo wrestler. A white cop in a brown uniform stood behind the Death Merchant.

Camellion didn't protest that he had told the same story three times within the last fifteen minutes.

"As I have already told you, I was here visiting Mr. Gell," Richard said tonelessly, his face without expression. "Mr. Gell is an old friend. I first met him in London many years ago. We were about to have lunch. I left to go to the john. On the way, I heard the explosion, which knocked me to the floor. I got up, went into the reception room, found the receptionist on the floor, then came in here. You can see for yourself what I found."

"By 'john' you are referring to the toilet," Soedardjo said. He turned to Camellion, an expression of doubt on his face.

"It's an American slang term for toilet or restroom," Camellion replied automatically. "The word 'john' can also mean the customer of a prostitute. It can also be the name of an individual."

Adam Msuya frowned and regarded Camellion sternly. "This explosion and murder has nothing to do with a loose woman," he said severely in reasonably good English. "Mr. Gell was murdered by a bomb. Can you prove, Mr. Camellion, that it was not you who carried the explosive device into his office?"

The Death Merchant stared directly, deeply, into the eyes of Adam Msuya, who was suddenly afraid, suddenly conscious of a terror that was nameless.

"Am I under arrest?" Camellion quietly asked.

Zahar Soedardjo's smile was as counterfeit as the smile of an FBI agent who has been stationed in Las Vegas for five years.

"We don't arrest people until we are sure of their guilt," Soedardjo said oilily. "But I would advise you to answer. Cooperation will show your good will."

An Indonesian whose family had been in Surinam for 80 years, Soedardjo wore a red fez, had a large mole in the center of his chin, and possessed skin as smooth as a baby's. He appeared to be in his late forties.

Camellion said, "If I had carried the explosive into the office, I would have had to use a bag or carry a package of some sort."

"Yes, I would say that is correct," Soedardjo agreed. He no longer smiled. His eyes remained pinned on Camellion's ruggedly handsome face. "I would say at least 5 to 10 pounds of explosive was used."

"I would suggest that you have a talk with the receptionist when she's up to it," Camellion said. "She saw me go into Gell's office. She will tell you I wasn't carrying any package."

Chief Soedardjo did not speak. Adam Msuya removed his gray hat, wiped his half-kinky hair with a handkerchief and frowned at the Death Merchant. "The bomb exploded when you were going to the toilet?" he said. "You said you were thrown to the floor."

"I proceeded to get to my feet and then went back to the receptionist's office." Camellion nodded toward the four mechanics standing close by. "Ask them. They saw me."

Soedardjo asked, "Have you ever been an actor, Mr. Camellion?"

"I have a small ranch in Texas," Camellion said. *Ah-ha! They've found the stuff!*

"I asked if you had ever been an actor!"

"I wouldn't know an actor from a Hottentot!" Camellion laughed. "But what has this to do with Mr. Gell's murder?"

Adam Msuya took a step closer to the Death Merchant. To one side of his mind, he wondered about the strangeness of Camellion's eyes.

"Why did you come to Surinam?" he asked. "Our small nation is not exactly the Riviera."

"A vacation," Camellion said. "I chose Surinam because I had never been here before and because Bubbie was here."

"Bubbie?" Zahar Soedardjo asked.

"Mr. Gell's nickname in England," Camellion lied.

Camellion expected the next question, this one from Msuya. "Can you account for your moments last night?"

The Death Merchant continued to play it stupid. "What do my movements have to do with Mr. Gell's murder?"

Msuya's frown deepened. "Are you refusing to answer, to quarrel with us?"

"Not me! I hate a quarrel, because it interrupts a good argument."

Msuya seemed confused for a moment. It was Chief Soedardjo who smiled slightly and asked, "What did you do last night, Mr. Camellion?"

"Nothing that amounts to anything. I had dinner at the Surinam Torarica and walked around the city," Camellion said in an easy manner. "I was about to go into Watermolenstraat Park when I heard shots. Realizing there was trouble, I continued walking to the hotel. I stayed on Keizerstraat. But why do you ask?" *As if I didn't know why!*

"What time did you return to the hotel?" asked Soedardjo.

"What time did you eat lunch nine days ago?"

Soedardjo was puzzled. "I don't understand."

Camellion shrugged. "Only people who have something to hide, who need to establish an alibi, keep track of time. I don't know what time I returned to the hotel. Sometime around midnight, I think."

"You said you arrived in Paramaribo two days ago," Soedardjo said slowly. "Why did you wait until today to visit Mr. Gell?"

"I phoned him. He said he was busy. He told me to come today."

"Who took the call?"

"He did. I have no idea where his receptionist was at the time."

Adam Msuya's determination was unconcealed. A thin ridge of perspiration lined his upper lip. "And where were you going when you left here?" he asked, unrelentingly, his eyes holding on Camellion.

"I had planned to go to police headquarters," responded Camellion.

"Do you expect us to believe that?" Msuya's voice was pinched and gravelly.

33

"The truth cannot be changed," Camellion said defensively.

"But it can be twisted," Msuya countered.

"Why were you planning to go to police headquarters?" demanded Chief Soedardjo curiously. He finished lighting a long black cigar, dropped the match on the wreckage-strewn floor and blew smoke in Camellion's direction.

Camellion delivered his answer with a sting. "I was informed by Mr. Gell that the police were questioning tourists. You see, I wanted to cooperate."

For a long moment Chief of Police Soedardjo and Chief of Detectives Msuya studied the Death Merchant as if they weren't quite sure of what to make of him. The cop behind Camellion lit a cigarette and moved around to the side of Msuya.

Finally Chief Soedardjo said, "We did talk to numerous tourists this morning, those who arrived in Paramaribo within the last week. We did search your room at the hotel."

Camellion pretended not only surprise but indignation. *But you didn't find the makeup kit, or anything else!* "You searched my room!" he echoed, putting his hands on his hips. "But why? What did you expect to find? I'm not a criminal!"

"We searched the rooms of all the tourists," Soedardjo said in a mild tone of voice. "We had a very good reason. Eyewitnesses reported that a man with white hair and a white beard was responsible for the riot in the park last night. We know that the man, whoever he was, was in disguise. We have proof. A citizen found a white wig and a beard stuffed in a trash can."

The Death Merchant's expression remained very serious. *If you'd look in the bay you'd find a couple of SIGs and a bulletproof vest. The makeup kit is scattered all over the city!*

"How terrible! Why should anyone wear a disguise?" Camellion was the picture of naive innocence. "Tell me, isn't it possible that the person you are seeking might be a woman?"

"The assassin was a man," said Chief Soedardjo, his voice a continual challenge. "A woman could not have moved with such speed. Whoever the killer was, he was a professional. He was an expert and a crack shot."

Continuing his act of guiltlessness, Camellion gave Chief Soedardjo a missionary look of purity. "No doubt it was some murderous revolutionary. I certainly hope you catch the maniac, Chief. Law and order must prevail in any nation."

Camellion looked around at the wrecked office. "Tch, tch!

34

How terrible. Poor Bubbie!" He turned and looked inquiringly at Chief Soedardjo. "But I am confused. This killer in the park! Are you saying that in some way he was connected with Bubbie, with poor Mr. Gell?"

"It was the rumor that your friend, Mr. Gell, was a member of the British Secret Intelligence Service. Did you know that?" Soedardjo inquired in a low voice. His eyes were cold, suspicious, and probing.

The Death Merchant's expression of astonishment was perfect.

"Heaven forbid!" he exclaimed, putting a hand to his mouth. "How could such a rumor have gotten started? Why I've known Bubbie for years. And now you say he was some kind of spy." He sighed loudly. "But it's often difficult to separate truth from fiction, fact from rumor." *This South American banjo-butt doesn't believe a word I'm saying!*

"It requires two to speak the truth," Chief Soedardjo said evenly. "One to speak it and one to hear it."

"Truth is often a two-edged sword, its validity depending on who is wielding the blade," Camellion said. "I read that somewhere."

Adam Msuya's nostrils flared as his eyes raked up and down Camellion. There wasn't a single shred of evidence against the tall American and Msuya realized Camellion knew it. Score of Tourists couldn't prove where they had been the previous night. Neither Msuya nor Soedardjo believed the Death Merchant had planted the bomb that killed Godfrey Gell; the explosive device had probably been meant for both of them!

Chief Soedardjo tapped the middle of his cigar and looked at the uniformed police who were poking around the wrecked office. He moved six feet to the left, stooped down, and picked up a small black leather case, speaking to Camellion as he did so.

"It's a shame that your vacation must be terminated here in Surinam."

"I was planning to take a flight to Georgetown in a few days," Camellion said, wondering what was coming next. He watched Soedardjo open the leather case, take out the stethoscope, then the sphygmomanometer, and stare at them.

"A blood-pressure kit," Soedardjo commented. "If he had high blood pressure, it's cured now." He turned, looked at Camellion, and smiled like a salesman. "Mr. Camellion, at two-thirty this afternoon there is a flight leaving for Georgetown. You will be on that flight. You'll be escorted back to your hotel to pack. You will then be taken to the airport. Your passport will be given to you just before you board the plane."

Soedardjo reached into an inside coat pocket, pulled out Camellion's passport, which he had picked up at the desk of the Surinam Torarica, and handed the green book to Chief of Detectives Adam Msuya.

"Don't come back to Surinam," Soedardjo warned, staring straight at Camellion. "If you do you may never leave. We do not intend to let Paramaribo be turned into a battleground between the CIA, SIS, and the KGB. Do you understand me, Mr. Camellion?"

"It's your country, Chief," Camellion said with a smile.

He remained silent as a grim-faced Adam Msuya gripped him by the left arm, led him from the building, and marched him to a police car. He had other things on his mind, such as WINK-EYE-1.

The ultimate development in U.S. space technology, WINK-EYE-1 had been shot into space to perform a threefold mission: to monitor at close range the Soviet Union's ordinary satellites, to photograph the U.S.S.R's missile sites, and third—the most important of the three—to find and destroy two special satellites that Soviet scientists were using in experiments that 20 years ago would have been straight out of Buck Rogers.

One Soviet satellite used laser beams. Already American scientists had duplicated all the major effects of nuclear explosions under both laboratory and field conditions—with laser beams. These effects included generating shock waves, exploding wires, causing hypersonic winds, creating particle beams, and causing shock waves in liquids and solids as well as gases. American physicists had also used laser baems to duplicate high radiation damage.

The super-secret National Security Agency had evidence that Soviet scientists had made enormous scientific advancements with the destructive power of the laser. Lasers require less than 10^{-10} to 10^{-12} seconds (between one ten-billionth and one trillionth of a second) to vaporize steel or iron. It didn't require any imagination to realize what would happen if a laser beam hit an incoming missile. Equip a satellite with a broadbeam laser, lock the satellte over enemy territory, and the beam could knock out enemy missiles as they left the silos.

N.S.A. suspected the Soviet Union was experimenting with such a laser satellite. WINK-EYE-1 had to find and destroy that satellite.

People don't know it, Camellion thought, getting into the police car, *but the laser has just about made missiles obsolete.*

The second Russian satellite that WINK-EYE-1 had been programmed to destroy was a space lab devoted to experiments in plasma beams and microwaves.

Plasma, "the fourth state of matter," is too condensed a form of material to be called a gas. Ordinarily it occurs only in the center of a star, under tremendous pressure. But, using magnetic fields, plasma could be generated in a laboratory; potentially, it could be unleashed in a high-energy beam toward some military target—or an entire city. A major advantage over lasers is that plasma could be contained in a canister of some sort and dropped as a bomb. A plasma bomb the size of an orange could destroy a city the size of New York; there would be no radiation.

Microwaves? Just as deadly and just as quiet! Microwaves are radiation impulses in that portion of the electromagnetic spectrum lying between the far infrared and the conventional radio-frequency poriton—from 300,000 megacycles to 1,000 megacycles (1 mm to 30 cm in wavelength).

Microwaves literally fry the brain of a human being. If exposed to the right dosage, a person could be driven insane in a matter of hours.

The Soviet Union was experimenting with ways to utilize an orbiting satellite, or power station, that could not only beam intense microwave radiation to earth but spread it over a very wide area, the end of the beam striking the ground having a diameter as wide as 11.7 miles.

The Death Merchant sorted the neat files in his mind. Microwaves helped the KGB and the G.R.U. Microwaves also helped the CIA and N.S.A. fight the KGB and the G.R.U. The communications revolution of the past 10 years, which replaced many long-distance cables and telephone lines with microwave transmissions, enabled N.S.A. to work with great accuracy. Almost all long-distance transmissions of telephone or telegraph messages in the United States are now carried by high-frequency microwave radio signals. N.S.A. listening devices can be "tuned" to the microwave frequencies and scanned constantly.

Other new devices permitted the remote recording of ordinary conversations inside buildings from stations outside in mobile vans designed to look like delivery trucks. This new technique eliminated the need for planting hidden mikes or using other conventional "bugging" techniques; furthermore, the use of this technology was virtually impossible to detect.

There was a fly in the ointment of microwaves; the culprit was the Russian bear. The KGB has been, and was being, blatant in its use of electronic surveillance within the United States.

One of those rare individuals who had total recall, Camellion remembered what he had read in the September 8, 1975, issue of *Newsweek*:

". . . *The Russians have set up at least five listening posts across the country, including one at their embassy in Washington and others at Soviet offices in New York and San Francisco. Rooftop antennas enable them to intercept messages carried by microwave—including apparently long-distance telephone calls by U.S. officials.*"

That *Newsweek* didn't report was that the Russians had also buried automatic electronic devices on mountain tops and desert flatlands close to key American bases—including the SAC headquarters in Omaha, Nebraska. The buried units had pop-up antennas to record military communications. The recordings were transmitted to Soviet spy-in-the-sky satellites in orbit and then re-transmitted to the U.S.S.R.

That was another function of WINK-EYE-1—to intercept those messages from the hidden Soviet electronic devices and, by retracing them to their source, locate the buried monitors. Whether or not WINK-EYE-1 had performed that fuction was still a moot question because, while in orbit, WINK-EYE-1 had been programmed *not* to transmit to Cape Kennedy. By WINK-EYE's remaining silent, not a single message would be picked up by Soviet satellite or ground monitoring stations. Instead, all information was coded on tape, which was to be removed after WINK-EYE landed.

The liftoff had been perfect. WINK-EYE-1 had gone into orbit as planned. One hundred and seven times, at a height of 734 miles, it had crossed the length of the Soviet Union, each time its trajectory slightly different, each time its special Bivix camera presumably photographing every missile site possessed by the U.S.S.R.

Then the totally unexpected had happened: WINK-EYE had malfunctioned. Changing orbit, it had passed over the U.S. 84 times—no doubt photographing every U.S. missile site!

The officials of N.S.A., the CIA, and other U.S. security agencies became frantic! Every attempt to bring WINK-EYE-1 down in U.S. territory failed!

Oh, yes! WINK-EYE-1 had finally descended to earth—in southwestern Surinam! It was a foregone conclusion that if U.S. tracking satellites had traced WINK-EYE-1 to Surinam, so had Soviet tracking stations in space.

That afternoon, while relaxing on the plane that would take him to Georgetown, the capital of Guyana, the Death Merchant thought of the nuclear arsenals of the USA and the USSR. *Both of us have intercontinental ballistic missiles, intermediate-range ballistic missiles, medium-range ballistic missiles, short-range ballistic missiles, submarine-launched ballistic missiles, depressed-trajectory ballistic missles, fractonal-orbital bombardment systems, free-fall tactical bombs, free-fall strategic bombs, air-to-surface missiles, air-to-surface standoff missiles, air-to-air missiles—and it all adds up to an explosive power that equals the equivalent of 40 tons of TNT for every man, woman, and child on earth.*

This awesome array of kill-power placed the USA and the USSR in a strategic position felicitously known as Mutual Assured Destruction, ironically called MAD.

The Death Merchant had one consoling thought: while he was apprehensive, N.S.A. officials at Fort Meade, Maryland, must be frantic. They knew what Camellion knew: that the race was on, a contest between the USA and the USSR, to see which side would get to WINK-EYE-1 first, each side realizing that a single mistake might trigger World War III.

Damned odd, these human beings. They're not content with merely possessing the ultimate weapons of destruction. Sooner or later, morbid curiosity will drive man to see how they work. . . .

Chapter Five

Called "The Land of Six Peoples," Guyana is a unique country in that it is the only English-speaking democracy in South America. Becoming independent in 1966, Guyana (an Amerindian word meaning "land of many waters") remains in the British Commonwealth. It was a founder of CARIFTA, the Caribbean Free Trade Association.

There wasn't anything uncustomary about the colonial building which housed the American embassy in Georgetown, the coastal capital of Guyana. However, one room in the basement of the embassy was extremely unusual: it was a "Mother Room," with lead-lined walls. Even odder was the huge acrylic dome in the center of the Mother Room. In the trade this was known as the "Fishbowl." Between the Fishbowl and the four walls of the Mother Room were six white-sound generators, a Dekkor jamming transmitter, and a Dekkor spectrum analyzer.

Everything inside the Fishbowl was made of plastic, the six chairs and the table, everything but Richard Camellion and the four men sitting with him at the table. Only the three ashtrays were made of glass; they were superfluous, since no one was permitted to smoke in the Fishbowl.

"There's one thing we can be positive of," Wyatt Keydrove said. "The Soviets will utilize their entire espionage apparatus in Cuba to get to WINK-EYE before we do. They have to get the tapes or spend billions of rubles moving their missile sites; and they've got to know what WINK-EYE might have learned about their two experimental space stations."

"The Russians would even get a consolation prize—the location of our own missile silos," said Oliver Lippkor, the second N.S.A. officer. "That crazy damned satellite must have photographed every ICBM location we have—the U.S., Alaska, Canada, everywhere!"

Holding the rank of colonel in the U.S. Air Force, Lippkor was a muscular, heavy-jowled man with curly black hair and darting black eyes. Within N.S.A., he was considered an authority on Soviet espionage in the Caribbean region.

Roy Bolinger, the CIA station chief at the embassy, nodded slowly in agreement. "We can burn our calendars," he said. "The Russians have. All we can do is go into Surinam and find WINK-EYE. Camellion's plan is the most logical."

"The government of Guyana will not interfere in any way," Kenneth Sedgwick, the British S.I.S. agent said enthusiastically. "Prime Minister Burnham gave his word to our ambassadors this morning."

"My God! I trust they didn't tell him about WINK-EYE?" Keydrove exclaimed, staring at the British intelligence agent, who was a stocky, handsome man of medium height.

"We have proof that two members of Burnham's cabinet are nashi," Bolinger said mechanically. "There are dozens of KGB agents in Georgetown."

Kenneth Sedgwick continued in a patient voice, although he nervously rubbed his hands together. "Mr. Simmons, the U.S. Ambassador, and Mr. Wilmorton, the British Ambassador, only told the Prime Minister that a grave situation, involving world peace, was developed, and that it is vital that an expedition be allowed to use Guyana air and ground space in our strike into Surinam." The S.I.S. agent's eyes moved to Bolinger. "Suppose they had told the Prime Minister about WINK-EYE? The Russians know the satellite is flat on its ass in Surinam, and the KGB isn't stupid. The logical route for us is to go south through Guyana, then cut east into Surinam. A moron could deduce what we're going to do. To think we can fool the commies is to fool ourselves!"

"We do have one advantage, in that the nearest Soviet base is in Cuba," Roy Bolinger commented. A short man, not heavily built, he weighed only 142 pounds. In his late thirties, he had a long face, a sharp, thin nose, and a crooked thumb on his right hand. An odd-looking bird, he had brown hair that was so thick he looked top-heavy. But in spite of his appearance, Bolinger possessed a natural-born talent for complicated intrigue.

"And so are we—eighteen hundred miles away, if we use Marines from Guantanamo," grunted Wyatt Keydrove, who held the rank of colonel in the U.S. Army. "The moment any Marines pull out of Gitmo, the KGB will know about it. I'm telling all of you, we must be extremely cautious."

41

The Death Merchant turned his full attention to Keydrove. "The hell with the Russians. We must be realistic and face up to the fact that we're going to have to battle it out with the Russians and maybe with the Cubans as well in southwest Surinam. The only way we won't meet them is if we get unlucky and the pig farmers get to WINK-EYE before we do. The U.S.I.B.[6] has given us the green light to do anything necessary to get to WINK-EYE. We have no problem in that respect."

Camellion's eyes, focused squarely on Keydrove, were faintly accusing, his voice irritated. "You were the N.I.O.[7] who analyzed the overall situation and recommended to N.S.A.'s N.I.P.E.[8] that the most pragmatic method of obtaining the tapes was a direct strike into Surinam. Now you talk about caution! Why are you having second thoughts at this stage of the game?"

"I agree with you, Camellion," Roy Boliger said bluntly. "The sooner we strike, the sooner we'll get the tapes."

Colonel Keydrove folded his hands on the table and looked calmly at Richard Camellion, as if he were attempting to produce an instant psychiatric profile of the man he considered to be not only an intruder but also a ruthless, amoral mercenary.

"Mr. Camellion, I don't think you're in any position to evaluate my evaulations." Keydrove's voice was haughty, almost supercilious. "N.S.A. does more than eavesdrop on Soviet space vehicles, and I am positive there are certain features about WINK-EYE you are not aware of. For those reasons I must be cautious."

"Pish and tosh!" sighed Camellion, who then proceeded to talk with a mechine-gun delivery: "I'm fully aware that N.S.A. methods are marvels of modern electronic technology. Information is collected by monitoring stations which include U.S. spy ships, surveillance planes, earth satellites, and ground-based listening stations." The Death Merchant's grin

---

6 U.S.I.B.: United States Intelligence Board.

7 N.I.O.: National Intelligence Officer. An analytical officer whose function is to prepare estimates on a regional operation. Such an officer is appointed by N.S.C., the National Security Council.

8 N.I.P.E.: National Intelligence Programs Evaluation.

was devilishly sly. "N.S.A. also monitors thousands of telephone circuits, cable lines, and microwave transmissions, to say nothing of high-speed radiotypewriters, computer data of international corporations, and even intercepted diplomatic pouches."

"Any monitoring that NSA does is done for the good of the nation," Wyatt Keydrove snapped. "For example, in recent years N.S.A. has begun targeting all communications relating to drug smuggling from Latin America. N.S.A. has also been producing economic intelligence in the form of reports monitoring the international grain market—all for the good of the American economy."

Lippkor blinked, looking bewildered. Roy Boliger, the CIA man, smiled. The fact that he was a Company man automatically put him in competition with the two N.S.A. agents. Kenneth Sedgwick, the British intelligence agent, kept his eyes on the table—better to say nothing and not get involved in any kind of disagreement between the American agents.

"Goddamn it, Camellion! Whose side are you on?" Keydrove finally burst out, glaring furiously at Camellion.

"Suppose you go to hell," Camellion said with a chuckle, leaning back in his chair. "Or suppose I report to P.F.I.A.B.[9] that the two of you wasted a lot of time on ridiculous nonessentials, like making idiots of yourselves by trying to lean on me. Better yet, why don't I tell you why you're really worried: because WINK-EYE was programmed, among other things, to monitor one of the Soviet space stations that is thought to be directing a certain kind of microwave beam that can influence the behavior of people." Camellion grinned. "How do you like them apples?"

They didn't! Keydrove's pale skin turned the color of chalk.

Oliver Lippkor's mouth opened slightly in shock and stayed that way.

Rubbing his hands slowly together, Boliger gave Camellion a strange but admiring look. "I didn't realize that you had been briefed on our 'Mind War' with the Ruskies!"

Kenneth Sedgewick said, "We've been in a psychic arms race with the commie chaps for the last seven years. S.I.S. has known for quite some time that Soviet scientists have

---

[9] P.F.I.A.R.: The President's Foreign Intelligence Advisory Board.

been experimenting with ways and means to telepathically influence the behavior of other, alter their emotions or health, or even kill them by directing a kind of psychic double-whammy at them." His eyes sought out Boliger's. "We worked with your people on the N.B.I.T. study."

Boliger nodded. "That was the *Novel Biophysical Information Transfer Mechanisms* study, based on the premise that the decade-old microwave signals beamed against the U.S. and the British embassies in Moscow might have an operational experiment behavior modification, using 'psychotronic' methods, that is, involving psychic powers amplified by special devices. We never did learn anything definite. One theory is that the Russians hope to mislead the West into believing that they are far ahead in parapsychology research so that we will either waste scientific resources trying to find out what they are up to, or do productive research which they can then tap into because of our more open system of scientific reporting."

"There is evidence of other Soviet tests," said Camellion in a constricted undertone. "Tests that include sending to the percipient the anxiety associated with suffocation and the sensation of a dizzying blow to the head. The real gut issue, as far as Western intelligence is concerned, is whether the Soviets have perfected some means by which detrimental effects of subliminal prception can be targeted against U.S. or Allied personnel in nuclear missile silos. Such a subliminal message could be carried by television signals, telepathic means, or by some kind of microwave arrangement."

"Perhaps beamed from one of the Russian space Sputniks your American WINK-EYE was to investigate," said Sedgwick in a low, serious voice.

"That was the general idea," Camellion said.

"NASA's Goddard Space Center has been picking up strange signals from one Russian satellite for weeks," Bolinger said. "Trouble is, the signals can't be deciphered."

Wyatt Keydrove coughed slightly. "I suggest we get down to the business at hand," he said acidly, his look averting the Death Merchant's. Then he looked at Camellion. "A strike is the only way, but I feel if we can plot the Russians' probable course of action, we might be able to avoid personal contact with them." He blinked rapidly at the Death Merchant. "If that's satisfactory with 'Captain Midnight' here?"

Camellion ignored the sarcasm. "You have the floor. Tell

us how you think the Russkies will attempt to get at WINK-EYE." He smiled pleasantly at Keydrove and Lippkor.

Lippkor said in a matter-of-fact voice, "Shortly before you arrived in Georgetown, we received word from D.C. that a Tupolev-144 left Moscow about ten A.M., Moscow time, this morning. A probable-course plot indicates the plane's headed for Havana. Arrival time about six A.M. tomorrow morning."

The Death Merchant reflected for a moment. Called the "Charger" by NATO, the Tupolev-144 held a secure place in history as the world's first supersonic airliner.

"What's your point? Are you suggesting that the Russians are flying in special troops to Cuba?"

"We don't know. We are cretain that a Charger has never before landed in Havana," Keydrove said lightly. He folded his arms across his chest, leaned back, and cleared his throat. "The Russians can't send a force through Brazil, Venezuela, or French Guiana. None of those nations would permit it. Anyhow, the Ruskies don't have the time. They have to fly in; they have to fly over one of the Guianas, and a Tupolev Charger would be the logical plane of choice. A Charger can carry up to 140 troops and can reach a maximum altitude of 62,000 feet."

"That makes good sense," the Death Merchant said, pushing the tiredness from his voice. His shoulder muscles ached and his head was heavy with fatigue. "The Charger could fly straight south over French Guiana, then cut due west across Surinam to the southwest edge of the Wilhelmina Mountains. The plane could fly low and the Red troops could parachute down. Who could stop them? The air defenses of Surinam and French Guiana are nil."

"It would still be a terrible risk for the Soviet Union to take," Roy Boliger said, uncertainty in his voice. "Not only would the actual drop be very dangerous, but just think of the international repercussions if the situation got out of hand. I say, it would make the Cuban missile crisis seem insignificant in comparison."

"The USSR must make the attempt," the Death Merchant said. "The Soviets are in the same fix we're in. We both have a tiger by the tail and neither one of us can afford to let go. The side that does, loses."

"Yes, that's true. But how would the Russian special force get out of Surinam?" Sedgwick raised his eyebrows in doubt. "A Charger can't land in the jungle. No transport can. A big

45

bird would require a level clearing the size of a large airport. We're missing something."

"The only way they could do it would be to use an air-lift operation," Lippkor said firmly. "The Soviet Union has half a dozen big Ilyushin IL-86s, or Starlifts, based at Havana. They're equipped for ground-to-air snatch work. As big as a Starlift is, it can slow to 150 m.p.h. and not stall."

"Yeah, and with new sky-hook methods, the Ivans could grab and lift 10 men at a time. I hear they're pretty good at such techniques."

Colonel Keydrove put his bony hands palms down on the table. Fairly tall and in his early fifties, he looked anemic, possessed hollow-set eyes and had a tooth missing in the upper left front of his mouth.

"We'll have to fly our boys in from Guantanamo," he said forlornly. "I'll use the embassy shortwave to get the move in motion. If we assume that the Russian Charger lands in Havana at six o'clock tomorrow morning, we can further calculate they'll head south as quickly as possible, right after refueling."

"Right off we have bad trouble!" Lippkor grumbled. He looked around at everyone sitting at the table. "Our boys won't get here until tomorrow afternoon. Well, by God, we can use the same sky-hook technique. With a Globemaster we—"

"Hold it!" interrupted Roy Bolinger, holding up his hands. "We should have told you earlier, but the way the conversation was going . . ." He let his voice drift off and gave the Death Merchant a quick glance. "As you know, I met Camellion at the Georgetown airport. As soon as we got to the embassy—"

Camellion cut in. "I had Bolinger contact Fort Meade right after we got here. Thirty specialists from the CIA's Double-Zero Department and a couple of space scientists are flying to us right now. They should arrive about ten tonight. We can be airborne in the two helicopters by midnight, two A.M. at the latest."

Lippkor turned to an angry Keydrove, disgust plain on his heavy, broad face. "I knew the CIA's Office of Operations would have to get in on the act!" He swung his gaze back to Camellion and Bolinger. "I must admit, if anyone can get the job done, the Double-Zero specialists can."

"Why weren't Lippkor and I consulted on the matter?" demanded Keydrove, although his voice, lacking any kind of challenge, was not angry. Earlier he had detected an unfathomable quality in Richard Camellion which had warned him that he was in the presence of a very unusual individual, almost as if this man named Camellion were a member of some alien species.

"Colonel, haven't you been informed of the command override?" Bolinger seemed as surprised as Oliver Lippkor was sullen.

"There was the time factor," the Death Merchant said, loosening his tie. "Roy and I were here at the embassy four hours before you and Lippkor returned from the estate outside of town."

Keydrove looked from Camellion to Boliger, slight alarm on his thin face. "What the hell are you talking about? What command override?"

Bolinger nodded toward the Death Merchant. "J.I.C.[10] has placed Camellion here in complete charge of the entire operation. Didn't your superiors in N.S.A. notify you and Lippkor?"

"Camellion, we owe you an apology," Lippkor said with some effort. "We thought you were trying to run the whole show without authorization."

"Whitehall notified S.I.S. in Georgetown several days ago," Sedgwick said innocently. He smiled at Camellion. "Unless you're not 'Eagle-One!' "

" 'Eagle-One, Minus Nest Three, Rock Haven Seven,' " Camellion said. "Satisfied?"

Wyatt Keydrove couldn't conceal his embarrassment. "There's been a goof-up somewhere." He finally managed to face Camellion. "Neither Ollie nor I were notified. Yes, I apologize. You're in charge. But I can't help but be curious. You're not an official agent of any department, yet the J.I.C. has placed you in full command!" He went on recklessly. "It's none of my business, but such a procedure is unprecedented. Frankly, just who in hell are you?"

Camellion, who was opening a coughdrop-size box, frowned slightly at Keydrove and Lippkor, both of whom were staring expectantly at him.

"Let's say I'm a man who's lucky, who has a way of getting a job done, and the J.I.C. knows it. That's all there is to it."

---

[10] Joint Intelligence Committee of the Joint Chiefs of Staff.

He reached into the box and took out a chunky drop of *Grandma's Honey Horehound*, placed it in his mouth and held out the box to the others at the table. No one seemed to notice.

Closely watching Camellion, it was Oliver Lippkor who said positively, "You're the Death Merchant!"

At mention of the dreaded title, Bolinger and Sedgwick's eyes widened with intense curiosity. Keydrove inhaled loudly, unable to conceal his amazement. However, Lippkor didn't get the reaction he had expected from Camellion. There was not the slightest flicker of tension in Camellion. There had not beem the barest hint that his true identity had been discovered, if he were the infamous 'Death Merchant.'

"I've heard rumors about such a man," Camellion said in a bored manner. "Personally I've consigned him to the same category as Santa Claus and the Easter Bunny." He smiled at Bolinger. "More likely he's a myth dreamed up by the CIA. But let's get down to business."

"I would suppose that the Double-Zero specialists will bring all the necessary equipment?" There was a new tone of respect in Keydrove's voice. He peered at the Death Merchant. "There isn't anything to do but wait until they land. Everything is set at Werk-en-Rust. There are two British Tomcat helicopters waiting. They're similar to our CH-46A Chinooks and can do the job easily. Range is not a problem, either. The round trip, from Georgetown to the WINK-EYE area, is roughly six hundred miles. After the Tomcats drop us off, they can return to Guyana and wait across the border, fly back in and pick us by radio signal. If they can't land, we can use rope ladders."

"What is Werk-en-Rust? It sounds like Dutch for 'Work and Rest,'" said Camellion. Sucking on the piece of horehound in his mouth, he looked at Keydrove, waiting for an explanation.

"That's good guessing," Keydrove said. "It's the name of the estate where the two helicopters are. It's really a cocoa and coffee plantation seven miles east of town."

The N.S.A. officer went on to explain why plantations had such unusual names. During the eighteenth century, Guyana changed hands a number of times. Sometimes the Dutch controlled the country, other times the French or the British. Finally, by the end of the century the British were the largest racial group. The many names of the plantations recalled the switchback course of politics, privateering, and human suffer-

48

ing. Fear Not, Two Friends, Endeavour, were British. Vreed-en-Hoop (Peace and Hope) Werk-en-Rust (Work and Rest), Meer Zorg (My Sorrow) were Dutch; Chateau Margot, La Bonne Intention and Mon Repos, French.

"I guess you noticed the preponderance of blacks when you passed through Georgetown," Sedgwick said, taking over the conversation. "They're descended from slaves. When slavery was abolished in 1834, the plantation owners, finding they were without a work force, began to import labor. The East Indians, from India, proved to be the most resilient and suitable for agricultural work. Today they form the largest racial group."

"We and the S.I.S. have a combined operation out at Work and Rest," Bolinger said. "Together we operate a radar station and a Sat-Track microwave setup. That's one reason why we can be so positive about where WINK-EYE came down." He took a pack of L&M Long Lights from his shirt pocket and toyed with the cigarettes. "We'll know the moment the Russians get within range of our radar. If the UFO is at extremely high altitude, we can assume it's the Charger. The radar station can use a scrambler and UHF us the data. That might give us a slight edge."

"It definitely will," agreed Sedgwick, "but only if we get there ahead of the Russians."

Colonel Lippkor looked thoughtful. "When you get right down to it, we don't have any hard evidence that the Soviets will make a try for WINK-EYE. We might not have any trouble at all, except maybe with the—what's the name of that tribe of Indians?"

"The Anacunna," supplied Bolinger. "They're not a problem. If they attack, we'll blow them into little pieces."

"The Russian force will be there," Camellion said, a positive quality in his voice. "The KGB didn't try to whack me out in Paramaribo just for the fun of it. And why do you think a bomb was planted in Godfrey's office? I think the big bang was supposed to get both of us."

"Plus the fact that the Russians are scared stiff of the neutron bomb," interjected Bolinger. "They figure it demonstrates a major American technological breakthrough that puts us a big jump ahead in sophisticated weapons systems."

"The Soviets will do their best to get to WINK-EYE," Keydrove said. "Hell, it wouldn't surprise me if the damned commies made an attempt to lift the entire satellite from the jungle floor. It wouldn't be too difficult, and the Ruskies are

49

noted for their *chutzpah* when their backs are up against the wall."

The Death Merchant studied Keydrove. *He's no dummy. His high cheekbones denote intelligence! The forehead is low, but the broad furrows show cynicism. Straight lines at the corners of the mouth. He has an unhappy, dissatisfied nature. Good. He'll be a good man when the going gets rocky.*

Camellion said, "Another thing we must understand is that we can't be certain which route the Russians will take. I don't suppose that it really makes any difference. Either they'll be ahead of us or they won't. There is a slim chance that the KGB in Surinam has reported by now that we might be using Venezuela as a jumping-off point. If they go for the story, the lie might have some bearing on their own actions."

Four pairs of eyes jumped questioningly to the Death Merchant.

"I wasn't satisfied with Godfrey Gell's security setup in his office. Just in case he missed a bug, I told him that plan was to use Venezuela. So who knows what the KGB might believe?"

"Gell's secretary was working for the East German *Staats-Sicherheits-Dienst*, the S.S.D.," Sedgwick said calmly, scratching behind his right ear. "Gell didn't know it, and we didn't tell him about her. He was shacking up with her, and we didn't want to risk his blowing the show. We were piping false information to her through him. Instead, the damned KGB loused up the works by blowing Gell all over his office. I guess the joke's on the SSD, too."

Bolinger put the L&Ms back into his pocket. "She was a lousy agent. You were wise to her. She wasn't worth a damn to the East Germans."

"We won't be worth a damn either if we don't get out of this bubble chamber," Camellion said. He pushed back his chair, stood up, and leaned over the table. "The only thing we can do for the moment is go out to the plantation and wait until the double-zero unit arrives at the airport." His eyes raked the four men. "There's the matter of transportation from the airport. Any suggestions?"

Roy Bolinger pushed his chair to the table. "We can send in trucks from Work and Rest to meet them. By the way, don't forget the package I brought you from the States." He smiled slyly at Camellion. "Special weapons?"

Camellion smiled right back. "A change of socks."

Putting on his jacket, Lippkor gave Camellion a serious look.

"Once the plane lands at Georgetown airport and our men get off, the local KGB will guess what's going on. Have you considered that?"

The local airport is the only space large enough to accommodate the transport," Camellion said. "The plane will land and taxi to the end of the field. It will be 'sanitized' and without markings, and the double-zero boys will be in civilian clothes. We might fool the local yokels, but not any Russian agents. Time is so short it doesn't really make any difference."

One by one, going through the narrow door, the five men left the Fishbowl. "I have to stop by the British embassy before I go to the plantation," Sedgwick said as they walked up the wooden stairs.

"We'll drop you off and wait," Bolinger suggested. "I suppose all you have to do is report in to your station chief."

"And get his official permission to go with you into Surinam," explained the S.I.S. agent.

Almost to the top of the stairs, Colonel Keydrové nudged Camellion's elbow. "Lippkor and I will remain here at the embassy until it's time for the transport to land. We want to keep monitoring radio transmissions from the Soviet embassy. It's only a block away. We've broken two of their codes, but they might know it. They could be playing the old radio game with us."

"We can't transmit from our embassy to the plantation, even on UHF," Lippkor said in annoyance. "Sometimes the commie sons of bitches jam us. Then again, we're not certain what their own cryptologists have done with our codes. We've put out a number of decoys but the Russkies haven't taken the bait."

The five men left the basement and entered the ground floor of the U.S. embassy, the Death Merchant thinking about the large radar station at Belem in Brazil. *Time enough to disiuss the Brazilians after we get to the plantation. Maybe within a few days it won't matter. Maybe within three or four days the entire world will be radioactive. . . .*

Outside, twilight was deepening into nightfall.

There would be a full moon.

Chapter Six

The Buick Opel moved east over the wide, hard dirt road, the beams of its headlights casting a yellow-white glow on palm trees and tropical flowers and plants as Kenneth Sedgwick took the car around a curve now and then.

Every so often the Buick passed a house built close to the road, a wooden house painted white, its carefully designed shutters a brilliant green. Each house rested on six-foot stilts. Even though the sea was safely at bay, Georgetown could still be flooded when heavy rains coincided with high seas—a reminder that Georgetown had once been known as the capital of "Mudland," named for the swamps around it and the brown, alluvium-laden sea water.

Occasionally, Camellion, Bolinger, and Sedgwick could see, through a break in the trees and tangled growth, moonlight glinting on patches of water and on Guyanese Victoria Regia water lilies, the world's largest aquatic plant, one of its fronds so large it could support a small child. Deeper in the swamp lurked another rarity: manatees, those gentle seacows, who were first, so it is said, mistaken for mermaids. Overhead, the quiet sky was spotted with blobs of powder-puff clouds.

There was a long stretch of road ahead and Sedgwick's foot pressed down harder on the gas pedal. The Buick speeded up.

"It was a good idea picking up weapons at the embassy," he said, directing his words at Camellion who was in the rear seat, "although I don't think such precautions are necessary. The KGB knows that we British still have a lot of influence in Guyana. If they tried anything cute in this area, it would be like an atheist cursing out loud at a Christmas mass being celebrated by the Pope."

"You might be right, but I think that being pessimistic will keep you alive longer," Roy Bolinger said. "Like Camellion said, who knows what the KGB might do? The Soviets are desperate and they don't have one ace from the whole damn deck."

Very cautious around firearms, he checked the safety of the fully loaded British Welgun, to make sure that the submachine gun would not go off accidentally.

In the back seat, Camellion sat toward the right, looking out the window. For the first time in days he felt comfortable and safe. Underneath his sports jacket, he wore a specially designed shoulder holster under each armpit, each spring holster filled with a Custom Model 200/International Auto Mag Pistol. Each stainless steel autoloader was fitted with a 4½-inch Mag-Na-Ported barrel rifled for a .44 Magnum cartridge. Next to Camellion on the seat was a metal case containing the rest of the Lee E. Jurras weapons system—almost all of it. There were four 10½-inch barrel extensions, two of .41 Caliber, two of .357 caliber. There was another AMP with a 6½-inch barrel (.357), a steel shoulder stock, and an M8-2X Leupold scope, plus boxes of ammo of various calibers.

Both hands on the wheel, the wind blowing through his hair, Sedgwick said half in jest, "Our governments should give us a bonus for operations like the one coming up, especially the way the cost of living has gone up. Last month the cost of living went up a Guyana dollar for a fifth. The way things are going, I'm going to end up with a Korean orphan supporting me! Of course, you pickle factory boys[11] are paid more than we in the S.I.S."

"Not as much as you might think," joked Bolinger, glancing sideways at Sedgwick. "My monthly check is so small my next-door neighbor cashes it—and he's on welfare!"

The Death Merchant, who was not in the mood for banter, ended it by breaking into the conversation. "Can you trust the men who will drive the trucks to the airport?"

"They're East Indians," Sedgwick said. "We can depend on them, not only because we pay them well. They despise communism, considering it just another form of slavery, which it is."

Bolinger half-turned to Camellion, a crooked, cynical smile on his thin lips. "I'm curious, Camellion. Are you always so cautious?"

---

[11] It has never been made clear why British Intelligence sometimes refers to the CIA as "the Pickle Factory."

"No. Most of the time I'm paranoid. It's the only way to keep two steps ahead of Big Daddy Death. Take a tip from me, Old Rattle Bones is always around, always waiting."

"I suppose that's one way to look at it," Bolinger philosophized. "Oh maybe it's just that God works in mysterious ways."

"I guess He does. I suppose that's why I'm confused most of the time."

A short distance ahead, the road curved gently up an incline. Sedgwick slowed the Buick and started to ease around the long curve. At the end of the curve was a wooden bridge, with 12 × 12-inch rosewood beams laid end to end at the edges on each side. Built to withstand the weight of heavy trucks, the bridge was built over a small stream and, from bank to bank, stretched about 30 feet.

The Buick was going around the final length of the curve, the end of the bridge only 30 feet away, when the headlights raked some of the trees on the opposite side of the stream. The twin beams, moving from right to left, briefly outlined a man who quickly dropped down. Nonetheless, he didn't escape the keen eyes of Sedgwick and Bolinger. However, the Death Merchant did not see the man because Bolinger obstructed his forward view.

"It's either an ambush or else they've mined the bridge," gritted Sedgwick. He leaned forward over the wheel and began to slow the car.

"What did you see?" Camellion was all business.

"The headlights picked up a man on the other side," Bolinger said, staring through the windshield. "He was carrying either a rifle or a machine gun."

"Stop at the edge of the bridge, then back up and put on speed," Camellion ordered Sedgwick. "They'd be fools not to have men on both sides of the bridge."

"I can hardly back up without stopping, now, can I?" Sedgwick responded. "I've been in situations like this before."

The British S.I.S. officer braked the Buick at the end of the bridge, quickly shifted to reverse, then pushed down on the gas pedal and warned, his eyes glued to the rear-view mirror, "Brace yourselves! I'm going to head for the side of the road where we can ditch."

The car shot backward, Sedgwick turning the wheel, keeping his eyes riveted on the mirror, and gradually increasing speed.

"Are you going to stop to our left or our right?" Camellion asked.

"To the left! Beside that clump of *pinua* bushes."

"In that case, pass me your Welgun, Bolinger. I'll cover the two of you when you get out. From your side you won't be able to fire to the left."

A shot rang out while Bolinger was passing the Welgun across the back of the seat, and a bullet hole appeared in the glass of the door next to Bolinger. The slug missed Bolinger and Sedgwick and zipped through the open window to the left of the British agent.

Sedgwick bent lower over the wheel, as low as he could get and still see the rear-view mirror. Bolinger scooted down in the seat so his head was below the edge of the windshield and even with the dashboard. "Damn it! That was close!" he muttered, and pulled a Smith & Wesson 9-millimeter pistol from a shoulder holster.

In the back, the Death Merchant edged himself down between the seats and waited. No point in wasting ammunition. Better to save cartridges until Sedgwick stopped the car.

More shots—pistol shots—rang out from the trees to the right of the road. A slug cut through the windshield, burned across the space where Bolinger's head would ordinarily have been, and smacked the glass of the rear door to Camellion's left.

Moments later, a cursing Sedgwick turned the wheel sharply to the left. Bouncing and jerking, the Buick tore off the road and shot sideways. "Communist-loving bastards!" snarled Sedgwick and jammed on the brakes. Its tires churning grass and weeds, the car skidded to a stop, its back bumper only a foot from the trunk of a palm tree.

"Go in low under my fire," yelled Camellion at the same time that Sedgwick pushed down on the handle of the door next to the driver's position. The Death Merchant reared up, opened the door to his left, and raked the trees and shrubbery with a blast of Welgun fire, the hail of 9-millimeter slugs popping off bark and chopping apart leaves. Sedgwick and Bolinger practically fell from the Buick and, on their hands and knees, crawled quickly to a thick clump of *ceibo* bushes that had spread out and twisted around palm trees, like tendrils of a cancer. Once Sedgwick and Bolinger reached the bushes, the Death Merchant tossed the machine gun to Bolinger.

"Cover me!" shouted Camellion.

Camellion grabbed the handle of the metal case, pulled one of the Auto Mags, and started moving through the open door. No sooner had he reached the ground than gunfire exploded from the right side of the road, the furious racket of a submachine gun—*It sounds like a Beretta!*—and the more piercing crack of a pistol. More shots rang out from the left, farther up. Then the roaring of the Welgun as Bolinger sent slugs at whoever was firing at them from behind.

The Buick Opel shuddered. Glass dissolved. There was the sound of deep thuds, enemy slugs tearing into the metal of the car. Within seconds the car was riddled. A bang as the right front tire exploded. The car listed slightly. Another projectile, having punched its way through the right rear door, hit the metal case of the Jurras weapons system and ricocheted with a loud whine. Several more narrowly missed the Death Merchant's head, although he never heard their passing.

Branches tearing at his clothes, Richard crawled into the *ceibo* bushes, pulled the case after him and whispered to Sedgwick and Bolinger, both of whom were lying belly-flat, "Have you spotted anyone?"

"One gunflash," hissed Sedgwick. "Behind and fifty feet up."

Then, much to the surprise of the three men, they heard the crack of several pistols 100 or so feet to the south—one, two, three, four shots; but not a single bullet came within yards of Richard and the two intelligence agents with him.

"They've lost us," Sedgwick whispered, with a hint of satisfaction in his voice. "They're shooting blind, trying to draw our fire to get a fix on us."

"Yeah, but they're all around us," Bolinger said angrily. "We're pinned down. We can move west but not very far. The swamp's there, and it's full of quicksand."

For several moments there was complete silence. Moonlight filtered down through the palms and tangled vines and tree flowers, speckling the ground with scattered patches of soft light that constantly shifted as the breeze moved the palm fronds.

More slugs, coming from all directions, ripped into the leaves and vines around the three men. None came close. There were more loud ricochets as lead bounced from tough parts of the Buick. Other projectiles chewed into softer parts of the Buick, which already resembled a giant piece of blue-painted Swiss cheese.

"The attackers from across the road aren't sure that we're out of the car," Camellion said. "We must move farther back. If and when the gas tank explodes, we'll be splashed with burning wreckage."

Dragging the heavy metal case, Richard began belly-crawling, squirming his way west through the undergrowth. Bolinger and Sedgwick inched after him, pushing on the metal case from behind. Camellion stopped when he had judged the distance to be about 40 feet and whispered, "You two take care of the shooters toward the bridge. I'll go after the ones to the south and across the road." He glanced at the small Walther P-38K in Sedgwick's hand. "Is that the best you have?"

"It's better than a slingshot," Sedgwick muttered, then added, "and I'm a very good shot."

"I have two more magazines for the Welgun," Bolinger said. "We'll make out all right. Just worry about yourself, Death Merchant."

With both Auto Mags in his hands, the Death Merchant began to crawl south, pausing every now and then to listen. He could detect faint movement from ahead, the rustles of leaves and the parting of bushes as the enemy crawled in his direction.

Once more the Beretta across the road began snarling. Camellion dropped flat but kept watching his front and each flank. *The damn fool! He's behind the times. He's still firing at the car!*

What eventually had to happen happened. Slugs found the gas tank; there was a loud explosion, a bright but brief flash of fire and smoke, and the Buick blew apart, flaming wreckage flying up and sideways and briefly illuminating a large area with an eerie, shimmering glow. The smell of burning rubber and cloth, of flame-seared metal, and the stink of scorched grass and weeds.

Camellion had only experience to count on; that's all he needed. Judging from the sounds ahead, the gunmen—*More than two?*—were 50 to 60 feet away. If only he had grenades. *And if my great aunt had wheels instead of feet, I could roll her down the highway!*

Hearing gunfire behind him, including the roaring of the Welgun, he snaked to the right and headed for a large clump of tall elephant grass not far from a fairly large *gumusmum* tree whose thick leafy branches offered dark cover from the

57

bright moon. Richard paused to listen intently, but heard nothing but firing behind him. Six feet from the clump of grass, he held one Auto Mag a foot and a half from the ground and fired twice, straight ahead, the two blasts ringing throughout the jungle and the surrounding swamps.

The echoes were still getting off to a good start as Camellion jackknifed himself into the tall tangle of grass. He hoped that the killers ahead had seen the flashes from the muzzle of the AMP; even more he hoped that his ears would not fail him.

The Death Merchant got his wish. Both Wu Wen-ch'eng, a Chinese, and Basappa Charkaran, a Hindustani, had seen the two bright flashes.

"We have him!" Charkaran said in English. He reared up and fired off four quick shots from his big Astra revolver, the flat-nosed .357 Magnum slugs streaking into the grass only feet from Camellion, who forced himself to wait. More cautious than Charkaran, Wen-ch'eng got to one knee and snapped off two rounds with his Arminius revolver, the two .38 projectiles popping into the grass even closer to Camellion than Charkaran's had. Both men then dropped flat and waited.

The Death Merchant's ears were as good as ever and his sense of pinpoint direction had not deserted him. He was now willing to bet his life that he could slam slugs into the enemy position close by.

He looked to the right. The *gumusmum* tree was only eight feet away. He again judged the distance, fixing the position in his mind. *Do it!* He raised one Auto Mag and in six seconds spaced out six shots, each .44 bullet six to seven inches horizontal to its predecessor, all six projectiles not more than eight inches from the ground. Camellion then crawled for the protection of the *gumusmum* tree and snuggled down flat behind its trunk. Other than the sweet scent of tropical flowers, he could smell swamp water.

Basappa Charkaran and Wu Wen-ch'eng saw the first two flashes from the muzzle of the AMP. Then, before either man could hug the ground, one .44 projectile pancaked into Wu Wen-ch'eng's forehead and blew off the top of his head.

A horrified Charkaran, splattered with blood and tiny bits of gray brain and white bone, tried to bury himself in the ground. The third .44 bullet came within an inch of the back of his head; the fourth, fifth, and sixth slugs also missed.

Trembling, wanting to gag from the bloody mess thrown

on him, Charkaran wondered what to do. He wasn't the only one. Richard Camellion was also waiting. The difference was that the Death Merchant knew what to do.

Roy Bolinger and Kenneth Sedgewick were having better luck than the Death Merchant, principally because they had a scatter-gun. As Camellion belly-wriggled south, Bolinger and Sedgwick crawled north. Prepared to use the old shoot-and-lure technique, they kept eight feet apart and paused every so often to listen, to get a fix on the enemy ahead. And when they stopped, the enemy stopped. Finally, when the two intelligence agents calculated that to move in closer would lower their chances of staying alive, Bolinger whispered to Sedgwick, "Now's as good a time as any. Give them three shots."

While Bolinger readied the Welgun, Sedgewick fired three rapid shots with his P-38K, placing the slugs several feet apart. Quickly then, he squirmed from his position and crawled behind the trunk of a palm tree.

Nothing happened! The enemy was not falling for the trick.

Their brains aren't out to lunch! Bolinger thought in disgust. He put his mind in gear and tried to remember where he had last heard movement up front. It couldn't be more than 40 feet. He looked to his right, sized up the *ceibo* bushes and the bamboo, and made up his mind. Why not? How else could he find out?

The CIA agent reared up, raised the Welgun and chopped the bushes ahead with a full magazine of 9-millimeter slugs, moving the roaring machine gun slightly up and down and widely from side to side.

Vadim Myskivlov and Lew "Chip" Hardy, on their hands and knees, were trying to crawl closer when Bolinger opened fire with the British chatterbox. With bullets poking holes in the humid air all around them, the two men desperately tried to flatten themselves, Myskivlov cursing furiously in Russian.

Twenty-seven projectiles only made a lot of vegetation unhappy! But two full-metal-jacketed bullets bored into Myskivlov. One went through his right cheek at an angle, tore through the left side of his throat, and waved a bloody goodbye through the back of his neck. The second slug slammed into the biceps of his left arm. As dead as Joe Stalin, the GRU major flopped to the moist ground, blood pouring from his slack mouth and pumping out the back of his neck.

The third bullet struck Chip Hardy, the renegade American, who was wanted for murder in Chicago, fraud in Florida, and bank robbery in California. As luck would have it, the bullet went through his open mouth at a sharp angle, broke off three left molars and departed through his cheek. Although not serious, the wound was very painful. With blood pouring all over him, Hardy was convinced that half of his face had been shot away. In panic, he let the .38 Rossi revolver slip from his fingers and stumbled to his feet, turned around, and started to retreat, crashing through the vines and bushes.

In the meanwhile, Bolinger had squirmed to a new position and was shoving a fully loaded magazine into the Welgun. However, Sedgwick, who was still behind the palm tree, heard Hardy crashing through the forest, making more noise than a drunken bull in a bell shop!

Sedgwick raised his P-38K and fired at the noise ahead, spacing out the last four rounds in the Walther automatic. Two millimeters missed. A third hit Hardy in the small of the back and skidded to a halt in his spleen. The fourth piece of lead banged him between the shoulder blades and finished kicking him forward.

Hardy did not have time for remembrance. All his life he had been unable to control a situation. Now all control was gone; he had been invaded by Death and the conquest was ultra-swift. His consciousness falling into an endless hole, Hardy dropped to the ground and lay still, his left arm extended straight up—his hand caught in a spider web of tangled vines.

His Welgun reloaded, Bolinger crawled over to Sedgwick, who was shoving a new clip into his Walther.

"Come on, let's get closer to the road," urged Bolinger. "We can watch the other side and see the bridge."

Richard Camellion was rapidly losing patience, but not to the extent that his instinct for self-preservation had vanished. He was almost certain he had whacked out one of the men ahead; for all he knew, maybe both.

Let's find out! He thrust an Auto Mag around the side of the palm tree and pulled the trigger twice, firing in the direction of the enemy ahead. Instantly he pulled back behind the tree and waited.

I hope the next trick works!

Immediately, Basappa Charkaran answered Camellion's fire with two rounds from his Astra revolver, neither .357 Magnum projectile even coming close to the palm tree protecting the Death Merchant. To Charkaran's astonishment, he was rewarded with a loud, high-pitched cry of agony.

Charkaran held his breath, straining to hear, every nerve taut, constricted. Had one of his slugs really found flesh and blood? Or was it a trap? He fired two more rounds in the direction of the yell, then jerked back and hurriedly thrust cartridges into the cylinder of the big Astra. Still uncertain, he decided to wait.

Bolinger and Sedgwick had worked themselves as close to the road as possible when they heard the high-pitched scream to the south.

"I say, you don't think that was Camellion, do you?" Sedgwick whispered hoarsely. "No, he's too good. He could wear boxing gloves and put a Swiss watch together."

Bolinger studied the road only 50 feet to the east. Parts of the Buick were still burning, the flickering flames throwing dancing shadows over the trees and bushes. A hundred and fifty feet to the north was the wooden bridge, strangely quiet in the moonlight, then dark and almost invisible as a piece of cloud closed over the yellow face of the moon. Nevertheless, Bolinger could still detect the outline of a figure that came out of the bushes on the other side of the stream. Carrying either an automatic rifle or a machine gun, the man started to run across the bridge.

Kenneth Sedgwick also had seen the figure. "We can't let that much fire-power get on this side of the bridge," he whispered. "The machine gun on the other side of the road is all we can handle."

"He's almost to the center of the bridge," Bolinger said. "That's close enough."

He raised the Welgun, sighted on the running figure, and squeezed the trigger, trying for a 10-round burst. The Welgun roared.

The man on the bridge acted as if he had run into an invisible wall! He jerked back, then to the left, then to the right, all the time jumping up and down, as though he were barefooted and dancing on carpet tacks. With seven 9-millimeter slugs in his body, he fell over the side of the bridge and splashed into the water 10 feet below. There was a lot of shrill whistling from manatees, already disturbed by the racket of gunfire.

The Beretta chatterbox from across the road once more started screaming, this time slugs coming dangerously close to Bolinger and Sedgwick as they desperately scrambled to new positions. As suddenly as the Beretta had begun firing, it stopped, the triggerman not wanting to reveal his position.

Bolinger and Sedgwick kept down, Bolinger watching the bridge, Sedgwick keeping an eye on the darkness across the road. His P-38K wasn't much good at a distance, but he would be able to pop the machine gunner if the enemy got brave and tried to charge.

Bolinger and Sedgwick heard the engine before they actually saw the vehicle. Its headlights off, a station wagon leaped forward from a side road that was hidden by a mass of trees and shrubbery, to the right of Bolinger and Sedgwick, on the opposite side of the bridge.

"Well, well! More company's come to call," smirked Bolinger.

"I say, old bean, maybe it's their tea time!" Sedgwick grinned.

The driver of the station wagon turned to the south and headed for the bridge just as the length of cloud left the moon and soft white moonlight once more illuminated the area.

At 40 miles an hour the station wagon—a Brazilian Ford—started across the bridge, the driver slowly increasing speed.

"He can't be charging us, he doesn't know where we are," whispered Bolinger. "There's only one answer. Whoever is driving intends to pick up the others on the road across from us. He knows the hit has failed and figures that the only thing to do now is to get the hell out." He patted the warm barrel of the Welgun. "The son of a bitch will never make it."

Just then they heard six loud *whooommmms* in rapid succession, perhaps 100 feet to the south.

"Camellion and those weird Auto Mags of his!" Sedgwick grinned evilly. "I told you they couldn't kill that Yankee. I tell you, Bolinger, that chap gives me the creeps."

Some minutes earlier, Basappa Charkaran had arrived at the conclusion that he had indeed killed one of the enemy and that it would be safe for him to move ahead. Slowly, pulling himself along on his elbows, he began to inch toward the dark area where he had heard the cry of pain. He didn't know it, but all he was doing was telegraphing his general position to the Death Merchant.

Camellion listened carefully for half a minute, then leaned out from behind the tree and, using both Auto Mags, sent six slugs toward the very slight snapping of twigs and rustling of leaves and branches.

Charkaran was in good health one moment and handless the next! A .44 bullet had struck his left wrist and had blown away his hand. He screamed from pain and fear, forgot the extreme danger he was in, and got to his knees. A second later he was dead and falling backward, a gaping hole in his chest and practically headless! A .44 bullet struck him in the chest; another .44 hit him just above the nose and exploded his skull.

Satisfied that he was no longer in any immediate danger, Camellion reloaded both Auto Mags, all the while listening to the engine of the station wagon. The way the engine was roaring, he knew the vehicle contained enemies and that it was coming from the opposite side of the bridge. Keeping as low as possible, he moved east through the brush and lay down belly-flat when he came to a spot that afforded him a full view of the length of wide road, as well as the junglelike mass of trees and entanglement on the other side of the road.

No sooner had he stretched out on the damp ground than the station wagon, having raced across the bridge, came tearing down the road, headed south, the man next to the driver spraying the west side of the area with short bursts of machine-gun fire. Camellion hugged the ground, but he looked up when he heard the screech of brakes. The driver had brought the station wagon to a stop 100 feet northeast of Camellion. All the while the music box continued to play its deadly symphony, the rain of lead chopping through leaves and vines. There wasn't anything Bolinger and Sedgwick could do but hug the ground and hope that none of the projectiles found them.

The Death Merchant stood up and moved to the side of a tree. Grim-faced, he realized now why none of the slugs were coming in his general direction: *The moron with the machine gun doesn't know I'm here. He thinks the three of us are still together. That's it! The station wagon has stopped to pick up the man with the Beretta. They're giving it up as a bad deal that didn't go down!*

63

Camellion next received a slight surprise when he saw not one but two men come out of the thicket on the opposite side of the road, one man carrying what appeared to be a Beretta 9-millimeter Model 12 sub-gun. Keeping the station wagon between them and the west side of the area, the two men hurried for the car.

The Death Merchant raised both Auto Mags and began firing, snap-aiming at the machine gunner in the car and at the man with the Beretta, who was between the station wagon and the east side of the road.

A .44 AMP slug crashed through the windshield, hit the man with the machine gun in the left shoulder, tore off his arm, and almost pitched it into the rear seat. Another .44 Bullet hit him in the left temple and popped open his head with all the power of a missile tearing through a wall constructed of tissue paper.

A .44 bullet hit the man with the Beretta in the left hip and kicked him in front of the other man. The AMPs continued to roar, sounding like baby grenades. The man who had dropped the Beretta caught a bullet in the side before he even hit the ground. The other man was pitched back toward the east side, his right leg half-blown off and rib bones protruding from the hole a .44 slug had put into his rib-cage.

By now Roy Bolinger had jumped up and was triggering the Welgun so its slugs were punching holes in the station wagon. The windows dissolved and so did the head of the driver, not only from two 9-millimeter Welgun projectiles, but also from a .44 Magnum slug that popped him in the face.

Copper-sheathed lead found the gas tank and, with a loud roar and a flash of fire and smoke, the station wagon blew apart, flaming metal flying like enormous piecse of shrapnel. The four corpses began to burn. Cartridges exploded. A rear wheel, flung 50 feet in the air, came down and, with part of its tire burning, crashed through the trees to land only 20 feet from where Bolinger and Sedgwick were standing.

Then there was only silence, marred only by the sound of flames consuming the combustible parts of the wreckage and by the sweet stink of human flesh being roasted . . . seasoned by the odor of burning rubber and cloth and plastic and leather.

"We've done a lot of 'wet work' tonight," Sedgwick muttered. "I hope we're as lucky when we get to Surinam."

Bolinger lowered the hot Welgun. "I think they're all dead. I'm going to take a chance. Drop the second I yell."

Sedgwick nodded and Bolinger yelled, "CAMELLION?"

Leading the way cross-country, Sedgwick went first. Camellion was behind him, his hands at the bottom corners of the metal case. Supporting the other end of the case, Bolinger followed. Every few hundred feet, the three men stopped to rest for several minutes.

The Death Merchant looked up at the moon. The clouds seemed to be thickening. "Are you sure that Work and Rest is only a few miles from where the ambush fell flat?" he asked Bolinger and Sedgwick.

"I'm positive," Bolinger said. He sat next to Camellion on the metal case. "We can't be more than a half-mile from the plantation. Before long the guards will challenge us. As soon as we reach the plantation, we'll phone the embassies and let our people know we're safe. Since the phones are tapped, that will be a good spit in the face of the KGB."

The Death Merchant's eyes raked the darkness ahead. "We'll have to have the bridge checked out," he said. "I think they planned to blow us to kingdom come once we reached the center of the span. There are probably two or three packs of plastic explosive underneath the center."

"I don't think so," Bolinger said. "I think they were going to riddle us once we reached the bridge, maybe wait until we got to the center. I think they were all so dumb that when they were born the doctors took one look and slapped their mothers."

Camellion's head shook a denial. "They were smart enough to be in position ahead of us, but to do that didn't take a lot of intelligence. Soviet agents were watching our embassies and, since they know about Work and Rest, it was ordinary deduction for them to assume we would come this way. Half a moron can put together a simple squad hit."

"What happened tonight proves that the Russians are desperate," Bolinger said, "or the KGB would never have attempted violence in an area where we have all the strength. It's the KGB's sheer gall that makes its agents so dangerous. They're very good, the best-trained in the world."

Sitting on one end of the metal case, Sedgwick turned all the way around and looked at Camellion. "I say, you were wrong about the P-38K. I got one of those chaps back there

65

at a jolly good distance. I should suppose the hollow points I used helped a lot."

Camellion gave the S.I.S. operative a pathetic smile. "Don't ever put your faith in hollow points when you're using pistol bullets. The working velocities of pistols—or, more correctly, autoloaders—are not adequate to give reliable expansion. A better solution is to pick a bigger caliber and use a bullet that has more power and force and punches a hole all the way through."

Unexpectedly a red light blinked three times several hundred feet ahead. There was a pause, then two more rapid blinks.

"It's our people from the plantation." Sedgwick stood up and rubbed his hands together. "They've come after us."

Chapter Seven

"Already a full hour late," Col. Valarian Agyants said bitterly. "The center will expect a detailed report on the reason for such inefficiency."

"It is not the pilot's fault, we know that," Col. Pavel Tisbal commented. "He had to land in East Germany because of engine trouble. It is the mechanics in Moskva who will have to answer a lot of questions."

The two KGB officers glanced at their superior, Gen. Yuri Chekalov, head of the KGB in Cuba. Chekalov stood by one of the windows of his office on the 16th floor of the National Institute for Agrarian Reform. Remaining silent, Chekalov could see that the *Plaza de la Revolucion* was almost devoid of traffic—and not just because the hour was only 7:00 A.M. Petrol was rationed and only highly placed Cubans and their Russian "advisers" had automobiles.

For a few minutes General Chekalov watched Russian and East German-make cars crawling along. His eyes moved to the gigantic sign on the side of the National Arts building, which stood to one side of the plaza: *"Viva El Partido. Unido De La Revolucion Socialists."* Chekalov frowned slightly. The Cubans . . . yes, like stupid *kolkhozniki*[12] they had to be told what to do day and night, twenty-four hours of each day. Why, the Cubans could not even manufacture a decent grade of toilet paper. What was important was that this backward island was close to the *glavni vrag*[13], only a medium missile away from the United States.

A pudgy man who looked like a friendly grandfather, Chekalov turned from the window and walked across the

---

[12] *Kolkhozniki*: Russian peasants who live and work on a collective farm.

[13] *Glavni vrag*: the main enemy.

67

room, limping slightly. Doctors had managed to save the leg, but the German shrapnel had done its work well. Thirty-six years later he was still limping.

Chekalov glanced at the dozen telephones on his huge desk, then sat down in a padded chair close to his desk. He crossed his legs, careful of the creases in the trousers of his neat gray suit.

Col. Pavel Tisbal and Col. Valarian Agyants shifted nervously in the straight back chairs in which they were sitting. They too wore civilian clothes. Both waited impatiently for General Chekalov to speak.

"Gentleman, General Andropov can't blame us for the delay of the plane," he finally said. "But we had better be prepared to explain why our agents in the Special Department failed, not only twice in Paramaribo but once in Georgetown." His gray eyes sought out an uncomfortable Colonel Agyants, a sandy-haired, intense-eyed man built like a wedge—broad, powerful shoulders, the torso tapering to a narrow waist. Agyants was chief of all the agents in the *Mokryye Dela*[14] *Spetschasti*, which was responsible for all assassinations in the Caribbean area and South America. Col. Tisbal's *Mokryye Dela* department embraced Central America and Mexico.

"The assignment of your agents was to kill the American," General Chekalov said, his voice a cold warning to Agyants, his tone a signal of his readiness to reject any answer which might fail to suit him. "They didn't succeed in the park. The bomb killed the British agent but didn't even scratch the American. The intended ambush outside of Georgetown was an even worse disaster. The local trash who assisted are of no consequence, but the deaths of our own people are a different matter. Tomekko and Myskivlov, as well as the ones the American killed in Paramaribo, were all highly trained. The First Chief Directorate had a lot of time and training invested in them, except Myskivlov, who had only been lent to us by the *Geh Eh Ru*. Worse, Sonya Torun is—or rather, she was—a niece of Major Bassoff, who is one of Andropov's

---

[14] *Mokryye Dela*: Russian for "wet affairs." Translated into English the term means "dirty affairs." A KGB euphemism for assassination.

aides. We're going to have double trouble. My real worry is the *Geh Eh Ru*[15]."

"Yes, Major General Burdiukov will demand a full investigation when he reads the report," Colonel Tisbal said glumly. Tisbal had not been directly involved in the Paramaribo and Georgetown operations, but he was a high official in the KGB *Otdel*[16] in Havana. Any chastisement from Moskva that might be directed at General Chekalov and Colonel Agyants would eventually rub off on him. He scratched one side of his ruddy face and glanced aprehensively at Agyants.

"I sent the best agents in Cuba to those areas of operation," insisted Agyants in a firm voice. "In turn, they chose the best of the local *Nashi*. General Andropov himself could not have done better, nor could Major General Burdiukov."

"Naturally. But you're missing the point," General Chekalov said agreeably. "The responsibility for the success or failure of the missions rests with you, Colonel Agyants. And if you are *my* responsibility." A man with a philosophical nature, Yuri Chekalov laughed, a low, amused laugh. "Colonel, we are in the same identical position, or to use an American expression, 'the same vessel.' Either we decide on the same reasons for failure or else be demoted together."

Thinking of how to reply, Agyants shifted his eyes, one small corner of his mind wondering why General Chekalov preferred such a plain office. The walls were a dull green, the furnishings heavy and well-worn. The only feature that indicated the office belonged to a high-ranking officer was the thick carpet on the floor. The most conspicuous item in the room was the large safe with triple combination dials. Of

[15] *Geh Eh Ru*: This is *the Glavnoye Razvedyvatelnoye Upravleniye,* or 'G.R.U.' the Chief Intelligence Directorate of the Soviet Military Staff, the fourth department of the General Staff of the Red Army. The G.R.U. was built up by Leon Trotsky with the help of—oddly enough—Capt. George Hill of British Military Intelligence. There is bitter rivalry between the KGB and the G.R.U.; but, unlike the KGB, which is widely known in the Soviet Union, the G.R.U.—in Russian the initials would be pronounced *Geh Eh Ru*—is not known to the average Soviet citizen. The organization is never officially mentioned, since, officially, it does not exist.

[16] *Otdel*: It can mean either "section" or "group."

course there were standard photographs of Leonid I. Brezhnev, the first secretary of the Party (the KGB called him "The Boss") and of Yuri Vladimirovich Andropov, the scholarly-looking chief of the KGB (who was called "The Spider").

The only hint of personal luxury in the office was the 8-inch high by 10-inch long Clydesdale horse resting magnificently on one corner of the desk. Made of solid brass, the horse had been given to General Chekalov by an agent stationed in the United States who knew the General was an avid collector of brass figurines.

Colonel Tisbal interrupted Agyants' thoughts by saying, "Do you suppose there is some way we could place the blame on the D.G.I.?" When he saw Chekalov frown in disapproval, he answered his own question. "No, I don't suppose there is."

"It was a waste of time and effort to even suggest it!" Chekalov's manner was more than stern, his tone bordered on open hostility. His shaggy brows arched and he glared at Tisbal, who was of medium height and build and wore his dark hair in a crew-cut. "The Cuban intelligence service would never be involved in anything as sensitive as an operation connected with the American satellite. To even try to implicate the D.G.I. would be a masterpiece of stupidity, particularly since we control the D.G.I. through our advisers."

"I only made a suggestion," mumbled Tisbal. He stretched out his legs and looked away from General Chekalov. An ugly man with a beaklike nose and a wide mouth that was perpetually sullen, he could, however, smile engagingly when he wanted to.

"A suggestion of that nature to the home office would only tighten a noose around your neck," warned Chekalov more calmly.

Col. Valarian Agyants got to his feet and started across the room. "There isn't any explanation we can give the center," he said and sat down heavily in a larger chair. He turned toward a curious General Chekalov. "We can't wave a wand and turn failure into success. I feel we should be perfectly frank with Moskva. Any attempt to rationalize what has happened, any kind of apologetic stance, will sound like that which we are trying to avoid—an excuse."

General Chekalov nodded slowly, a thoughtful expression on his full face.

"There isn't a department in the intelligence service of any nation that can claim a constant 100 percent success,"

Agyants proceeded to say. "I sent to Surinam and to Guyana the best agents who were available to me. I—"

"We sent," intoned Chekalov solemnly.

"Very well. We sent the best, and the best failed us. Call it fate, call it an act of God. But we can't change facts."

"Call it anything but an act of God!" Chekalov said with a bitter smile. "We can be sure that is one explanation that the center would never accept!"

In spite of the seriousness of the situation, Tisbal and Agyants both laughed. Then, taking a pack of Vittorias from his coat, Colonel Tisbal became serious.

"The truth is that bad luck has plagued us all the way back to Moskva," he said. "The Tupolev is more than an hour late at this moment. The last radio report was that the craft wouldn't arrive until seven-thirty, if not later. By the time it lands, refuels, flies to Surinam, and gets into position for the drop, the British and the Americans will have reached their precious WINK-EYE-1." He sighed heavily. "If that should happen, we'll all be lucky if we're not reassigned to the Arctic Circle!"

General Chekalov studied Colonel Agyants. "You are sure? There can be no mistake regarding the time the enemy force in Guyana lifted off?"

"I wish there were," said Agyants. "But the reports we received from our embassy in Georgetown was definite. The American force landed at the Georgetown airport at eleven-fifteen last night. At two forty-five this morning two helicopters left the plantation named Work and Rest and headed south. Presumably, the helicopters will fly straight south until they are parallel to the Wilhelmina Mountains, then fly east into Surinam."

"There is no way to close the time gap," General Chekalov said harshly. He folded his hands and began to rock his knuckles back and forth. "No way humanly possibly unless—" He turned quickly and stared at his two department chiefs. "Helicopters! What type?"

"British Vickers LM-V-14s," Agyants answered instantly, his eyes puzzled. "They are troop-carrying craft, commonly called Tomcats, similar to our Mikhail Mil 4s. The Tomcat is slightly larger."

Colonel Tisbal took the Italian cigarette from his mouth. He was also at a loss to understand his boss's reasoning. "But, General, the enemy force is in such close proximity to Surinam that it can easily use helicopters to get to the satellite.

Even if the helicopters can't land, the American zero-zero experts can descend by means of rope ladders. From all our reports, what very little we have, the Americans are very good. We all know how innovative they are!"

"They can drop to the satellite, extract the tapes and other coded data and be gone before our men even get there!" said Colonel Agyants, looking oddly at General Chekalov.

"Under ordinary circumstances, yes," Chekalov said smugly. "But I am inclined to think that this Camellion, this American leading the strike, is much too cautious to make a direct drop over the site of the satellite."

"The use of helicopters doesn't prove that either way," Agyants said.

"A drop directly over the satellite would be the shortest route and the most direct approach," offered Tisbal, more confused than ever. "I think Camellion would be foolish not to go straight in."

"He would, if it weren't for the Brazilians!" corrected Chekalov, smiling slightly. "We know that he is an extremely prudent individual. Or do you think he is so foolish as to have forgotten the large radar installation at Belem? He knows that Belem picked up WINK-EYE when it came down." General Chekalov shook a finger at Colonel Tisbal. "Camellion, clever man that he is, will act accordingly. He will not drop directly over the satellite. He will drop some distance from the area and creep up on it. He will not risk falling into any trap."

"The Brazilians wouldn't dare try to get to the satellite," Agyants said slowly. "To cross into Surinam? No, they wouldn't risk the international implications."

Colonel Tisbal stated his opinion. "The governments of Brazil has been at odds with Washington for months. It would be quite a coup for them if they could obtain WINK-EYE and use it as a weapon of blackmail." He leaned over and crushed out his cigarette in an ashtray close to his chair.

General Chekalov looked in disgust at Tisbal. "Colonel, it's a pity that when God made you a moron, He didn't give you the face to go with it! The government of Brazil doesn't want any serious trouble with the United States. The Brazilians dislike Yankees, but they hate and despise the Soviet Union. That damn fool Castro saw to that years ago, he and that dreamy, would-be savior, Che Guevara. Idealists never seem to realize that saviors always turn out to be men."

Reddening, Colonel Tisbal inhaled deeply, a flush of anger

72

crossing his battered face. Very quickly he recovered his composure and listened to Agyants, who was saying, "General, then it is your opinion that the Brazilians will always side with the U.S. against us?"

"Of course." Chekalov spread his hands. "The United States is the only real power on this side of the globe. If the Brazillians want the Satellite, it's only because they want to turn it over to the Americans."

"This time factor," Tisbal said, "I gather you feel that if the Americans have to trek through the Surinam jungle, our people might still have time to effect an airdrop over WINK-EYE?"

"It's a very slim chance," answered Chekalov, his tone amiable. "But the possibility is there. It exists. We have—"

He swung his head toward his desk as one of the telephones rang. Very fast for a corpulent man he was on his feet and the phone was in his hand, the receiver against his ear.

Tisbal and Agyants stared expectantly at him.

"Good, good!" the General spoke into the mouthpiece. He paused. "And the fuel trucks?" Another short pause. "Excellent. Double check your security. We shall arrive in time. We'll use the helicopter on the roof."

Tisbal and Agyants smiled at each other; the call had to be from Cienfuegos Field, the military airport outside of Havana.

Chekalov returned the phone to its cradle, turned to his two underlings, who were now standing, and took a pair of sunglasses from the handkerchief pocket of his coat.

"The jet will land at eight o'clock," he said. "Major Lyalin radioed personally from the plane."

"Major Lyalin?" inquired Colonel Tisbal, pausing in his lightning of another cigarette. "I think I have heard of him."

"Major Viktor Lyalin. He will lead our force."

"I have heard of him," Agyants said. "They call him the Hammer." A satisfied smile flowed over his face; he checked to make sure his pistol was secure in its belt holster underneath his coat. "Perhaps there is a very good chance that we'll get our hands on the American satellite. We'll know in a few days."

Putting on his dark glasses, it was General Chekalov's turn to smile. "Yes, Colonel, we'll know in a few days, if not sooner. But you shall have advance notice."

Agyants stared at the General.

73

"Your department comprises the Caribbean and South America. On that basis, I am sending you along with Major Lyalin and his force. I'm sure that the Center will be pleased with your enthusiasm, with your volunteering."

On their way to the roof, where the helicopter was parked, the three men spoke little, for which Colonel Agyants was grateful. Worried and disgusted, he recalled an expression the Americans were fond of using: *caught between the devil and the deep blue sea.*

Now he was in that position. *I'm caught between a board of inquiry, a possible demotion, and the deep, green jungles of Surinam! Damn Chekalov!*

Chapter Eight

Richard Camellion didn't break the news to the men until the two Tomcat helicopters were loaded with equipment and the entire force had been assembled for the general briefing. Then he told them the expedition was not going to fly directly to the sattelite, but that the two helicopters would land—or the men would climb down a rope ladder— ". . . ten miles from WINK-EYE's location. The space-ball's within half a mile of the CL-coordinates worked out by N.S.A.'s land and space tracking stations." Richard paused and looked calmly at the puzzled faces before him. "I'll tell you why we're not going to take a direct route. It would be too much of a risk. Doing it my way will enable us to reconnoiter the region."

The reaction he had expected from Rudolf Graff did not materialize. The leader of the CIA Zero-Zero contingent only stuck out his Matterhorn of a chin, put his huge hands on his hips and grinned at Camellion. The rest of the men seemed relieved.

"I take back everything I was thinking about you, Camellion," Graff said in his deep voice. "We were given strict orders to follow you into hell if necessary, but none of us were going to go in blind." He cracked another big smile from ear to ear. "Hell, yes! We're going to get along just fine."

"You've got the right idea about a recon," said Anthony Flecher, who was second in command of the Zero-Zero force. He stood next to Graff, his thumbs hooked in the slit pockets of his tiger suit. "If the commies got there first, it would be like the commie mother-friggers of booby-trap WINK-EYE."

Graff's big black eyes bored into the Death Merchant. "You've had some experience in this kind of fruitcake business?"

"Some. I've been in fire-fights all over the world. Even on Mount Ararat, believe it or not."

"I believe it! Unless you tell me you found Noah's Ark."

75

Graff became serious, the lines tightening in his deeply-tanned face. "How about torrid climates?"

The Death Merchant felt like laughing. *Brother, if you only knew a tenth of it!*

"Mexico, Cuba, Brazil, Egypt, India, North Africa—should I continue?"

"No need to. You've paid your dues." Graff repeated in an odd voice, as if remembering bloody and murderous days from the past. "And so have we . . ."

Camellion congratulated himself. He had been right in his earlier analysis of Graff. *He doesn't tiptoe through the tulips. He roars in at full steam. He's a pragmatic realist who knows the score. Good!*

"Let's go get the satellite and maybe prevent World War III," Camellion offered.

Standing close by, Kenneth Sedgwick said quietly, "Or start it!"

Graff scowled and looked at Sedgwick the way Hitler might have glared at a war resister demonstrating against toy pistols! "A final war might do the human race some good!" Graff sneered. "It sure as hell would be more exciting than watching a fly try to frig a flea!"

The Death Merchant walked toward the nearest Tomcat.

Dawn was a brand-new baby when the two British LM-V-14 helicopters, their turboshaft engines making a tornado of noise, came straight down through the towering trees of the rain forest and settled heavily in the large clearing. The pilots, two S.I.S. agents from Georgetown, turned off the engines and the huge rotor blades stopped revolving. In the rear of each Tomcat was a clamshell hatch. The instant the blades stopped turning, each large hatch opened like a giant mouth and the men came down the short ramps. Armed with Colt M1 heavy assault rifles, 10 Zero-Zero members took up positions around the uneven clearing; others began to unload supplies that would be carried to an adobe hut hidden by trees, a very short distance north of the open space.

The expedition was still in Guyana. The helicopters had landed 180 miles south of Georgetown. This touchdown was only the first leg of the journey, this landing at an outpost used by S.I.S. for the smuggling of certain items into Surinam, the border of which was only 17.3 miles to the east. WINK-EYE-1 lay 118 miles to the southeast.

Camellion stood to one side, watching the unloading. The

cartons and boxes were for the two British secret intelligence agents stationed at the hut. There was extra supplies for the four pilots—two extra pilots in case two became ill—who would return to the clearing after they dropped off the members of the expedition 18 miles from the satellite's coordinates.

Once again the Death Merchant computed the reality of the situation. Including Graff and Flecher, the Zero Zero force numbered 27 men. Then there were Bolinger, Sedgwick, and Colonel Lippkor. And seven other men. Four were East Indians, Guyanese nationals who worked for S.I.S. They would act as porters, carrying the extra ammo, the spare grenades and the light machine gun.

Two were aerospace scientists: Calvin Leitch, Ph-D., was a tall, thin, bespectacled man who seldom spoke and who was constantly referring to a pocket calculator and making notes in a large leather-bound notebook. Dr. Foster Bangold was in his middle forties, 10 years Leitch's junior. A nervous-mannered, chain-smoking egghead, Bangold gave the impression that he was waiting for something terrible to happen.

William Henderson, the CIA firearms expert, was the seventh man. Mild-looking and quiet, Henderson was the burly outdoor type, his features rugged, his skin weathered by sun, wind, and rain. Almost totally bald, he had a thick, untrimmed mustache and a week's growth of beard. Camellion wondered if he ran around in The Company's Research and Development Division looking like a bum.

The previous evening, Roy Bolinger had mentioned to Camellion that Henderson was going to field test a new, rapid-firing submachine gun that weighed only eleven pounds. The East Indians would carry the ammunition for the mystery weapon, but Henderson kept the machine gun in a closed, black plastic case. He never let the case out of his sight. Back at Work and Rest, he had even taken it into the toilet with him.

I'm the thirty-eighth man, thought Camellion. *Thirty-eight against—how many?*

He watched the East Indians and members of the Zero-Zero force carry boxes across the north end of the clearing and hurry into the jungle, one of the S.I.S. agents from the station-hut leading the way. The four helicopter pilots tagged along, the two who would actually pilot the Tomcats stopping at the edge of the forest. The second S.I.S. station-hut spook and Kenneth Sedgwick stood in front of one 'copter, talking

77

in subdued tones. Colonel Lippkor, the two scientists, and William Henderson were engaged in conversation with Tony Flecher, who was waving a hand toward the jungle and explaining the type of terrain they could expect to encounter in Surinam. Roy Bolinger and Rudolf Graff were near Camellion, discussing the Anacunna savages.

All the Zero-Zero fighters wore tiger-stripe-camouflage combat coveralls, high Moc-Toc field boots and bush hats. The other men were dressed in conventional Ranger coveralls, with more familiar shade patterns of brown and green camouflage.

The heels of his hands on the tops of the flap holsters buckled around his waist, the Death Merchant thought of something else that Bolinger had told him the previous afternoon: *I have a tip that the DDCI[17] is going to ask you to go to Japan—if you're still alive.*

Japan? Why?

Something to do with the Rengo Sekigun, the Japanese terrorist organization!

The United Red Army! Camellion had said. *Japanese Communist fanatics who mix murder with crackpotism and Bushido!*

The Death Merchant now thought: *But first there's the small matter of an American satellite in Surinam. . . .* The entire business, the two helicopters, the men standing around talking in the clearing surrounded by tall, broad-leafed evergreen trees, some of which were over 100 feet tall—*Right out of the National Geographic! All we need are a few Indian women nursing pigs!*

. Camellion's gaze settled on Bolinger and Graff, the corners of his mouth moving upward in a slight smile. The two men were a Mutt and Jeff pair, the 6-foot-5 Graff as huge as Bolinger was small. Another thing was that Graff was more peculiar-looking than Bolinger. A small head on a big body made Graff appear to have been assembled from mixed-up blueprints. His head appeared even smaller, because he wore his hair in a very short crew-cut. *He reminds me of a gigantic owl!* With his large dark eyes, the Zero-Zero commander had eyebrows that, growing dark and black and straight, curved downward, like half-parentheses, as if to outline the somber, watchful orbs. His thin mouth was a little crooked,

---

[17] DDCI: Deputy Director of the Central Intelligence Agency.

slanting down to the left. In contrast, his chin resembled a square-set Rock of Gibraltar.

During the flight to the clearing, Graff and Camellion had traded tales of their experiences in various parts of the world. Graff turned out to be a rare breed in another respect: he was a war-lover, a man who lived only to fight, to duel with danger, to enjoy the excitement generated with by the unknown. In 1966 he had given up his studies at a seminary and put his dream of becoming a missionary behind him to enlist in the U.S. Army and go to Vietnam.

"Don't ask me why I did it," he had explained to an interested Camellion. "In another four months I would have graduated and gone to Africa with five other ministers. What I saw in Vietnam convinced me that I had done the right thing by quitting the ministry. 'Saving souls' is more ridiculous than asking an elephant to pass the peanuts. Hell, I don't have to tell you that it all amounts to nothing more than a slick commercialism geared to bring in the bucks. It only proves that people are as gullible as they were years ago, when you expected them to be stupid. I mean, compared to what we know today."

"I should suppose people are intelligent in accordance with the superstitions of their time," Camellion had mused.

"That's right. Hell, way back in colonial days, outraged clergymen attacked Ben Franklin for inventing the lightning rod. They argued that the use of the 'Franklin Rods' challenged the Scriptures and the will of God. They said that when a bolt of lightning struck, it was divine punishment. They changed their minds when lightning smashed into a church where gunpowder was stored. The explosion killed eighty-two people. We presume it was 'divine punishment' and that all the good people shot straight up to heaven . . . their souls, that is."

Roy Bolinger and Rudolf Graff walked over to Camellion. Graff dropped his cigarette on the ground and crushed it with the toe of his boot. Without glancing at Camellion, he reached into his hip pocket and pulled out a map.

Bolinger was enthusiastic. "We've been discussing a new route," he said to Camellion. "It's a route that will save time and give us more protection against the Anacunna."

Camellion got down to look at the map Graff was spreading on the ground. Graff, on both knees, took a ballpoint pen from one breast pocket of his tiger suit and, with the point retracted, tapped a square in which a red X was drawn.

"Last night we decided on this spot, which is slightly more than eighteen miles southeast of the satellite," Graff said. "We agreed on that position because the immediate area is all savanna. The Tomcats can land. We won't have to go down a rope ladder and we can see the total area for an estimated radius of a mile."

"Affirmative," said Camellion. "The danger is the forest that begins several miles ahead. A lot of savages could hide in there and we can't go around it." He leaned over the map and tapped a red circle with the end of a finger. "Somewhere within this half mile area lies WINK-EYE. Our—"

"Tell us something we don't know!" growled Graff impatiently. He closed his mouth when he saw that Camellion had every intention of continuing. Graff noticed Colonel Lippkor and Dr. Leitch coming toward them.

"Our original plan was either to land or drop down ten miles from the satellite. We extended the route after looking at a more up-to-date map and discovering the postage-stamp-size savanna. But now you both feel that we should head straight for the foothills. I would suppose about here." He tapped a spot on the map and looked steadily at Graff, and Bolinger. "Tell me I'm wrong!"

"By landing in the foothills of the mountains we could avoid the forest and, possibly, any contact with the savages," insisted Graff, his olive-black eyes as hard as his voice. "Better yet, we'd shorten the distance to WINK-EYE by ten to twelve miles—and I'm talking about walking distance. Now you tell me I'm not right!"

As assertive as Graff, Bolinger added quickly, "We can't afford to ignore the Russian schedule. We must assume the Soviets are going to drop within half a mile to a mile of WINK-EYE and that they'll use a Charger to come into Surinam. It's the only strategy the Russians can use that makes sense." He nodded to Colonel Lippkor and Dr. Leitch, acknowledging their presence, then looked apprehensively at the Death Merchant, who gave him a frosty smile and said coldly:

"Helicopters make a lot of racket. They can be heard for five miles or more. To land in the mountains would be just as dangerous as to come down on the grassland. On the plain we have to go through the forest and risk the Anacunna. In the mountains, unless we could find a small valley

80

or plateau, we'd have to hover and have the men descend on rope ladders. We could be caught cold turkey in an ambush. Think about it. Weigh the odds."

"My God! We're changing the route again?" queried Lippkor.

"That's the general idea, if the 'Boss' agrees," muttered Graff. "If we drop closer to the satellite, we'll save lives and time."

"Or get us all killed!" Lippkor said sharply, his full face growing dyspeptic with alarm. He stared first at Graff. Next, he gave Camellion a long, searching look. Both men made him think of happy alligators getting ready to snap their jaws on innocent victims.

Graff grinned up at the N.S.A. agent. "Oh, come now, Colonel. You can't expect to chop down a bee-tree without expecting a few stings. It's all part of the game."

Lippkor shook his head decisively. "Don't get cute with me, Graff. What you're suggesting is that we go after a bee-tree with no netting and very dull axes. There is never a reason for being either suicidal or foolhardy. My advice is to leave bad enough alone."

Camellion got to his feet and turned to Lippkor, who was running his fingers through his curly black hair.

"Under ordinary circumstances you'd be correct, Colonel," Richard said patiently. "But in this instance, Graff and Bolinger are correct. If we come down on the plain, we're in danger. If we descend in the mountains, we'll still be halfway to hell."

"But in the foothills we'll be ten to twelve miles closer to the space station!" Graff's deep voice darted in with the force of a two-edged dagger. He stood up and folded the map, looking grimly at the Death Merchant.

"Or ten to twelve miles less marching!" pointed out an eager Roy Bolinger. "We can save more than a day—and maybe the satellite."

Dr. Leitch's voice was tight. "Won't it take longer going through the mountains?"

"We'll not be in the mountains, only on the lower slopes," Bolinger said. "We'll only have to cross knolls and a lot of rock-ribbed humps and the like. There'll be some hilly areas, but nothing that requires climbing equipment or any special skill."

Camellion said simply, "We'll take the mountain route. Colonel Lippkor, please contact Colonel Keydrove on one of the helicopter radios and advise him of our new approach to the satellite."

"Use Code Fourteen-Y-Little B," Bolinger said. "The KGB monitoring stations will grab the message, but we'll be in the mountains and back home again before they decipher it."

Colonel Lippkor, his wide face forlorn, shook his head in defeat. *Trying to reason with Camellion—or that kill-crazy Graff!—was as silly as trying to throw a lasso over a moth!*

"Very well, if that's how it's to be," the N.S.A. agent said. "But Wyatt is going to think we've all become screwballs!"

He looked for a long moment at Camellion and Graff and took a deep breath before turning and going into one of the Tomcats.

Without a word, Dr. Leitch walked off and joined Dr. Bangold, who was in some kind of deep discussion with William Henderson.

Graff scratched the end of his nose. "I get the feeling that Colonel Lippkor was insulting both of us!" he joked, nudging Camellion with an elbow. "Can't say that I'm going to bite my nails over it."

With a slight smile, Camellion focused his attention on Roy Bolinger. "Roy, tell the pilots about our new course. With their maps it shouldn't take them more than ten minutes to plot a new course. Wait! Tell Sedgwick first and let him tell the pilots. They're all S.I.S.; they're his boys."

"Right." Bolinger moved off toward Sedgwick, who was still talking with the S.I.S. agent from the station hut.

The Death Merchant said to Graff, "Are you positive that your men are ready to deplane the moment we get there, whether we walk out or have to crawl down a rope ladder?"

Graff chuckled deep in his throat and grinned, his lips going back over his teeth like a wolf's. "Have you ever stopped to think about words. Why is it people '*de*-plane,' but never '*de*-train,' '*de*-bus,' or '*de*-boat?'"

Camellion surveyed the Zero-Zero chief's face, thinking that he liked Rudolf "Preacher" Graff. The man had that rare quality of basic honesty, hypocrisy being as alien to him as truth was to the communists.

"Good buddy, your men?" Camellion repeated.

"You had damn well better believe we're ready!" Graff spoke harshly, yet he wasn't angry. "All their equipment was sorted and ready before we lifted off from the plantation. Each man has his assigned place on one of the Tomcats. His equipment is next to him. All he has to do slip on his pack, grab his colt M1 and jump." He paused in reflection. "We're both lucky in one respect. We don't have to deal with Colonel Keydrove. Our gears wouldn't have meshed with his. He's all army."

"Old oaks can't bend with the wind," Camellion said. "They can only break."

"See ya." Graff turned and strode over to Tony Flecher, who was checking the East Indians and the Zero-Zero men who had returned from the S.I.S. hut in the jungle.

Camellion's thoughts were one big smile. His reverse psychology had been a success, although for a time he had been afraid that neither Graff nor Bolinger would suggest a new route to WINK-EYE-1. Either way was very dangerous—*But it was they who suggested the change, not I. They can't hold me responsible.*

But the main reason why Camellion, by planting the idea the day before, had subtly maneuvered Graff and Bolinger into thinking that the change of route had been their original idea was that the word would spread among the men that they had talked him into it; the men would interpret this as a signal that Camellion was a reasonable man. As a result, the group's confidence would be increased.

Resentment always reared its ugly head during a kill-strike. It was a normal reaction on the part of the men, a human reaction. You remove men from familiar surroundings. You control their movements and put them at the mercy of cause and effect. You increase their apprehensions and expectations. For a short time you control their lives and they resent it.

The first helicopter lifted into the humid air, its two engines making a terrific noise, the enormous downdraft scattering dust, twigs and leaves in the clearing, creating a cloud as the pilot of the second Tomcat prepared his craft for the climb into the sky.

Very soon the two choppers, parallel to each other, were flying east at 6,500 feet.

One hundred and six miles to go!

Chapter Nine

Close to the end of a long journey! Below was a mantle of dark green, an immense ocean whose green waves undulated in the breeze. Although the two helicopters were at a height of several thousand feet, the canopy of the Surinam *hylaea*, the rain forest, appeared to be one vast sea of treetops, majestic and overpowering. It was a world of its own, an opulence of forest life that evolved through the seasonless workings of a warm, wet climate, that shaped its various creations imperceptibly through eons of geologic time. In the extreme tropics there is no winter or spring, only perpetual mid-summer. The uniformly high mean temperature varies within a range of only about 5 degrees between January and July and hovers about 80 degrees the year around. During the seasons of rain, wild avalanches of water recurrently descend in thunderous cloudbursts that may disgorge 30 inches of water in as many days. In such periods the forest roof drips almost continually, even under cloudless skies. Beneath it the atmosphere is charged with moisture and the forest corridors lie dank and sweltering. By day the canopy of treetops retards evaporation; by night, like a giant greenhouse, it imprisons the heat of the day. This "greenhouse effect" makes plant life proliferate with incredible luxuriance. New leaves compete riotously to fill each sunlit chink in the tangled roof.

But this was not the rainy season.

To the north were the jagged blue-gray *Wilhelmina Gebergte*. The mountains weren't much to look at and never excited the imaginations of climbers. The highest peak was only 4,200 feet.

Gradually, as the two helicopters flew southeast, the *hylaea* began to thin. The pilots of the two copters kept watching the compasses and glancing at a map every now and then, making sure of the coordinates. Very quickly the two big whirlybirds drew closer to the lower slopes of the Wilhelmina Mountains. The foothills stood half-naked, the forest sparse in those places where the mountains started to lift their broad shoulders into the cooler realms of mist, the green roof disappeared and there were only ferns of various sizes and stunted trees decorated with moss. The terrain became more rocky, tiny plateaus of open sand or rock or grassland occasionally popping into view. In other places large hills covered with slag and slate glistened in the sunlight.

The men inside the two helicopters stared through the windows at the ground rushing by. The 'copters had dropped to 800 feet, and there wasn't anything below that looked friendly.

In the Death Merchant's Tomcat, the pilot had just ended a conversation with the man at the controls of the other helicopter; now the pilot reported over the intercom system: "We're only twenty-six miles northwest of the W-E-ONE location. Shortly we'll swing to the new six-zero-three course."

"I'm going up front and make sure," Camellion said to Bolinger and to Graff. "Make sure all the men are ready to"— he smiled at Graff who was looking at him—"get off the bird."

"Five minutes firing time?" Graff asked. "Five minutes should be the minimum. Fact is, I already told Tony to use a five-minute blast with the twin thirties in his bird. Hope you don't mind."

"I don't. But you're lucky you didn't tell him to take six minutes."

Camellion began stumbling toward the cockpit, steadying himself by holding onto the center guide wire. Once inside the cockpit, he glanced at the pilot, who looked as young as a college freshman, sat down in the copilot's seat, slipped on the headset microphone, switched on the radio, and contacted the pilot of the other Tomcat.

"This is Iceberg-Seven," the Death Merchant said. "Come in Polar-Cap-Four."

"Polar-Cap-Four." The voice came through the headset. "What's up—other than us?"

"As previously instructed, do not go beyond the six-mile limit. I repeat: do not take your iceberg closer than six miles to the North Pole location. Watch our floe. We'll take the lead. Whatever we do first, you follow up second. Acknowledge. Over."

"Acknowledged, old dear. Over."

"Out."

The Death Merchant switched off the radio, removed the headset and its attached mike, and turned to the pilot.

Harold Arlington didn't speak until he had completed the swing to the new course and checked the compass.

"I got it all," he said. "It's all up to us."

"Any questions?"

"Yes. We're not to get any closer than six miles to the American satellite. But where do I take her down? I assume you want to get in as close as possible to the six-mile radius?"

"Start looking for a place to set down as soon as I leave the cockpit," Camellion ordered. "If you can't land within six to eight miles of the W-E-ONE coordinates, go the full distance and find a spot on the six-mile line. We'll use the rope ladders and the drop-cargo line."

On returning to the cargo section, Camellion saw that two of the Zero-Zero force were attaching Vickers machine guns to the mount of the gun port to his left. As soon as the twin Vickers were secured on the swivel rod, the two men pulled cable lines from reels on the wall and snap-linked the cables to the back of the safety belts they wore. While Olin Maxton fastened boxes of ammunition to the rod of the mount, Wayne Loos opened the gun port by unlatching the sliding door and pulling it to one side. Loos then moved around to Maxton and opened the cover of a Vickers machine gun, preparatory to inserting the cartridge belt with the first round in the slot of the feed tray. Maxton loaded the other Vickers. When the belts were in place, the covers closed, and the machine guns ready to fire, Maxton pushed the guns into position, so both barrels protruded through the opening of the large, square gun port.

Below, the ground rushed by with incredible speed. It was as if the landscape were moving and the helicopter suspended in space. And still Arlington continued to drop lower toward the ground.

Tension mounted. There was little talking. Hanging onto the guide wire, Camellion stood near the center of the chopper. He caught Bolinger's eye. Bolinger took the L&M cigarette from his mouth, smiled, pointed downward and made a finger motion across his throat. But does he mean us or the enemy? The slightly-built CIA agent made Camellion think of a *Sheruth Modiin*[18] agent he knew. Richard always thought of

_____

[18] *Sheruth Modiin*: the Military Intelligence Department of Israel —not to be confused with *Hamosad*, the worldwide Israel intelligence service.

Moshe Brosh as a kind of Jewish leprechaun—a short, slight creature with a comical beard and a huge mustache. Only Roy Bolinger never wore an embroidered red and green prayer shawl.

Camellion felt sorry for Humin Shartam and Ram Fakharuddin. Terrified, the two East Indians sat rigid, so stiff that the vertebrae of their spines could have been welded together. In contrast, William Henderson, the weapons expert, didn't appear the least bit concerned. A cool customer, he wasn't even looking out the window. Instead, he sat with his back to the rounded wall, his expression that of a bored passenger in some city's subway system.

The large helicopter was now flying at an altitude of only 250 feet. The other helicopter, at the same height, was 300 feet to starboard.

The Death Merchant glanced at his wristwatch. *I don't think we're going to be able to land. Damn it, we're going to have to use the rope ladders.*

Finally Harold Arlington's voice came over the intercom. "Attention, chaps. We're nine miles from the W-E-ONE coordinates, or three miles from the limit. There isn't any place that looks safe enough for a set-down. I'm going to the limit line and find a spot to hover. You chaps will have to use the bloody ladder."

The Death Merchant began to move toward his seat position in the chopper. Rudolf Graff picked up his field pack and called out as he slipped an arm through one of the straps, "Get ready, men."

The 12 Zero-Zero members were as precise as a group of well-trained dancers. In unison, they got into fighting shape, slipping on their backs and gathering equipment.

The Death Merchant prepared his own gear. He put on a cotton game bag that had two large pockets in front. Each pocket was filled with spare magazines for the Auto Mag pistols. Over his left shoulder went the wide strap of a shotgunner's shoulder bag, the bag resting on his left hip. The bag contained a dozen fragmentation grenades. Over his other shoulder went the strap of a sportman's carry-all shoulder bag made of tough cotton duck. He checked items on the belt supporting the two AMPs in their leather holsters—a canteen, a VHF/FM radiotelephone in its case. He picked up the bag containing spare magazines for the Colt heavy assault rifle and fastened the bag rings to the snap-links in his belt, just behind the carry-all bag. Finally, he slipped into the teardrop rucksack and buckled the straps over his chest. He was ready—either to kill or to die. . . .

Graff had been occupying himself with Humin Shartam and Ram Fakhruddin, making sure that the two East Indians had strapped on their Browning autoloaders and briefing them on descent procedure.

"Don't look down or up when you climb down the ladder," he instructed. "Keep your eyes toward the horizon; keep looking at a level angle. The ladder will sway but don't worry about it. Two men on the ground will be holding the end. Just look toward the horizon and you'll be safe enough."

The two East Indians nodded, and Graff turned to Camellion, who was close by. "Any special ideas on the drop?"

"The usual procedure," Camellion said. "Men first, equipment second. Unless you know of a safer method." He took the radiotelephone from his belt.

"I wish I did but I don't. I—"

"*Attention*." Arlington's voice came over the intercom. "*Prepare for the descent. Brace yourselves*."

There was a change in the sound of the blades as Arlington changed the pitch and the cyclic rate. The helicopter began to drop. The Death Merchant looked through a window and saw that the other helicopter was also dropping.

"*This is it, chaps. The end of the line. We're at sixty feet and I can't go lower*."

The Death Merchant pressed the button of the channel that was on the same frequency as the intercom system, then switched on the radio-telephone.

"Arlington, don't leave the controls," Camellion spoke into the tiny mouthpiece. "It's all right to put the bird on automatic pilot, but don't leave the controls, just in case. Over."

"Affirmative. When all of you are on the ground, give me the 'Go' signal. Anything else?"

"No. Have a good trip back. Out."

Camellion switched off the RT and shoved it back in the case on his belt. "Let's see what we've got," he said to Graff and to Bolinger, who had walked over.

The three men moved to the gun port and looked out. As far as they could see were high, irregular hills covered with wind-cut bushes. There was some ground and grass, but mostly there were only *hammadas*, arid stretches of bare rock, naked and exposed to the sun.

"It doesn't look like vactionland," Bolinger muttered grimly.

"I don't think it has the *Good Housekeeping* Seal of Approval either," commented Graff, rubbing his rock-size chin.

"But there's not a sign of our Russian or Indian friends." Camellion shrugged. "For that matter, not a single Brazilian. Let's get on with it. The longer we hang in the sky, the more danger we're in."

The clamshell doors were opened manually, one of the Zero-Zero force turning the wheel as other Zero-Zero boys prepared the ladder, which was coiled around a drum bolted to the floor. The "rope" ladder was not made of rope, although the rungs were of wood, each rung 31″ long and 6″ wide: The "rope" was three steel cables, two at each end of the rungs and one in the center.

The drum latch was pushed down. Two Zero-Zero men pulled out the end of the ladder, carried it to the open clamshell hatch and dropped the short length over the bottom ramp. A man turned on the drum motor and the drum began to revolve.

As the end of the ladder dropped closer to the ground, other men attached boxes of equipment to the cargo cable that had been pulled out from the cargo drum and lay stretched the length of the compartment.

"The ladder's touching ground," called out Hubert Boston, one of the Zero-Zero fighters. "Shut off the drum."

The Death Merchant slung the Colt M1 over one shoulder. "I'll go down first." Coolly he looked from man to man. "I want two men to go with me."

"We'll both go," Graff said, his tone insistent.

"No. You're too important to risk." Camellion was firm. "If I catch a bullet, if we've walked into a bad situation, you'll have to take command, you're the only one suited for the job."

"You're right," conceded Graff. There was no trace of pride in his voice. He had spoken only the simple truth.

"I'll go with you, Camellion," volunteered Terry Lemmons, raising his Colt M1.

"Me, too," offered Virgil Mild.

All of a sudden the Vickers machine guns from the other helicopter began roaring. Men from the chopper had begun climbing down the ladder and the gunner had opened fire, raking the area beyond the landing site with streams of .30 caliber slugs. If any enemy were around, he had better keep down.

"Molly, Mary, and Moses! Fletcher's beaten us to it," growled Graff. Yet there was a pleased look on his triangular owl's face. "Better get your butt on the ladder, Camellion."

The Death Merchant and Mild and Lemmons moved toward the clamshell doors. Graff turned to Olin Maxton who was anxiously fingering the handles of the twin Vickers. "OK, Olin. Do your target practice."

Maxton pressed the thumb-plates and the Vickers came alive. Cartridges began exploding at the rate of 550 rounds per minute.

Halfway to the ground, the Death Merchant looked down and saw that Tony Flecher and two other Zero-Zero members had already reached the ground and that two of the men were steadying the ladder for the other men who were coming down. Tony Flecher and his group were only 150 feet away.

The Death Merchant increased his pace, the ladder swaying back and forth, not only from his own efforts but from the movements of Wild and Lemmons above him and the downward draft generated by the big blades of the hovering helicopter.

Faces stared down from the door of the craft. All the time, the four Vickers machine guns fired short but steady bursts into the surrounding area, the long-nosed slugs striking rocks in the distance and creating a storm of ricochets.

Camellion's feet touched hard rock and he was off the ladder. Another minute more and Mild and Lemmons were on the hard gray rock. Each man held the side of the ladder as Camellion, the Colt M1 in his hands, studied the area. Getting to WINK-EYE wouldn't be a picnic.

The entire operation didn't take more than 10 minutes. The men hurried down the two rope ladders and immediately scrambled into firing positions. They dropped into hollowed-out depressions or got down behind rocks known as "dikes"—long ridges of once-molten rock, disgorged as lava from eruptive fissures in the sides of vanished volcanoes and now hardened.

The equipment to be lowered was scanty, since each man carried his cold rations in the pack on his back. The cargo that existed was in the helicopter that had carried Camellion—spare ammunition, the case of cartridges for William Henderson's "mystery" weapon, the AMP case, two Sonde

90

shortwave radios, a box of instruments for Leitch and Bangold, and 125 pounds of a form of plastic nitroglycerin known as Composition-Y, commonly called "Comp-Y."

This weight was more than enough because, in theory, the cartons would have to be carried by the East Indians, although it was understood that everyone would pitch in and help, or a fast pace could not be maintained.

As soon as the cargo was on the long slope of the big hill, Rudolf Graff and Hershel O'Connor switched the controls of the two drums and the hatch to Harold Arlington, after which they came down the ladder. Once they were on the ground, Camellion contacted Arlington by radiotelephone and gave him an All Clear. Taking over in the cockpit, the pilot pressed several buttons; the drums began to rewind the cargo line and the steel cable ladder.

The other chopper waited, its pilot having already rewound his drums and closed the hatch.

The cable and ladder disappeared within the maw of the hatch. Two lights began blinking on the control panel in the cockpit. Harold Arlington pressed two buttons and slowly the double doors of the hatch started to close. The two "shells" drew together; then the "clamshell" was tight. An amber light glowed on the instrument panel, the signal that the hatch was secured. *Good. Time now to get the hell out of Surinam! Back to Guyana!*

Pilot contacted pilot. The roar of the turboshaft engines became louder and louder. The rotor blades spun faster and faster. Like two enormous dragonflies the camouflaged helicopters—neither bore a single identifying marking—rose into the sky and soon were gone. But Camellion and the other members of Knit One, Pearl Two did not feel deserted; they were too busy preparing for their trek to WINK-EYE-1. The sooner they found the sophisticated space station and yanked out the coded tapes, the quicker they could call the S.I.S. jungle base in Guyana on one of the Sonders and have the helicopters pick them up.

Tony Flecher, who seemed to operate independently of Graff, quietly gave orders. Some Zero-Zero men began to assist the East Indians with assembling the aluminum litter on which the boxes would be carried. Other Zero-Zeros posted themselves at strategic positions around the wide, fairly open area. They snuggled behind dikes or got down beside slabs of wind-carved igneous rock protruding upward at crooked angles. The sky was an ocean of pure Holland blue, the sun pure torture.

Flecher asigned four Zero-Zeros to Drs. Leitch and Bangold as the two space scientists checked their instruments. Two more Zero-Zeros went over to Bill Henderson, who was sitting on a rock, calmly smoking a cigar. He frowned and waved them away. They smiled and sat down beside him.

The Death Merchant, Bolinger, Graff, and Colonel Lippkor, as well as Sedgwick, consulted a large colored map spread out on the ground to one side of a large conical rock that shielded them from the sun. Roy Bolinger charted the course, based on the coordinates of the location of WINK-EYE-1. Consulting a course protractor and working with parallel rules, he soon found their position and estimated the distance to the satellite. At length, Bolinger put down the hard-bearing compass and placed the point of his pencil on the map, at the place where he had drawn an encircled dot and marked it FIX.

"This is our present position," he said, glancing at the perspiring faces around him. He moved the pencil an inch. "This is the location of WINK-EYE. Bear in mind that the satellite position is within half a mile to a mile of error and is based on the coordinates given us by N.S.A. N.S.A. could be wrong."

"It's possible but not very likely," Colonel Lippkor said studiously. "The main ground station at Pasadena, California, confirmed the complete declination, the latitude and longitude, and the altitude when W-E-ONE started to in-orbit. The azimuth, everything."

"But we must consider the possibility of error," insisted Bolinger.

"Yes, I know what you mean," Lippkor said. "The possibility does exist. It would be unrealistic to ignore it."

"You're both right and wrong," Camellion said. He continued to look at the map. "I think we must assume that the space station is where it's supposed to be. It's all we have as a starting foundation; otherwise, we wouldn't be able to chart a route." He looked up from the map at Roy Bolinger. "I see that is what you have done."

"First I found our present position," Bolinger said without any lightness. "Then I used the satellite coordinates and proceeded accordingly. It's basic navigation."

"And I can't even do decimals!" Kenneth Sedgwick said sadly.

"How far away are we?" Graff looked at Bolinger and asked.

"I estimate that we are five-point-two miles from the estimated satellite position. That distance includes the possible half-mile to mile error on all sides. This means that if the satellite is where it is supposed to be, we are then slightly less than five miles from the target."

"Still quite a distance on this kind of terrain," Sedgwick said.

"You said it," Bolinger agreed. "As you see by the map, there's nothing between us and the satellite but rocky hills. We'll have cover but so will any enemy."

"If trouble comes, we don't want a Mexican standoff," Graff said.

"There are a few sandy areas and some scrub, but not any jungle, except in the immediate vicinity of WINK-EYE," Bolinger went on. "WINK-EYE is lying at the edge of the rain forest—or rather, just within the forest." He paused. "Let's face it: We're going to have to have a lot of luck."

He looked up, waiting for remarks from the others who were studying the map on which Bolinger had marked the course—a dashed red line—from their present position to the space station. At the satellite site was a triangle around a dot. It was marked RDF RAD FIX. RDF meant that the location had been fixed from a radio detection finder. RAD meant fix-position by means of radar. In this case, both the RDF and the RAD coordinate schemes had been fixed by orbital tracking satellites, plus beam-wave bounce that had been picked up by the National Aeronautics and Space Administration's station at Pasadena; the tracking facilities at Cape Kennedy and at Cape Canaveral had also "seen" WINK-EYE-1 go down.

Someone had to ask the question, and Graff did. "Suppose the satellite isn't there? Suppose it's not where it's supposed to be?" The small head turned to Camellion, a cold expression on the small face. "Then what do we do? We sure can't go running around the jungle yelling 'Hey, Satellite! Where are you? Here, boy! Here, boy!' "

Sedgwick and Bolinger laughed.

"I hardly think we'd get a reply," Colonel Lippkor mused, smiling.

"It's not a bit funny," Graff snapped. "You might think it's a joke, but you won't be laughing if the apples start falling

93

upward toward the tree! And don't forget the Anacunna. Their favorite torture is skinning the victim alive."

"The idea of becoming a lampshade in some savage's jungle hut is not very appealing!" Sedgwick said thoughtfully.

The Death Merchant spoke. "I'm counting on Leitch and Bangold to find WINK-EYE, once we're close enough for them to use their instruments."

"One of their gadgets is called an Alphaometer," Bolinger said. "It's supposed to pick up some kind of wave signal from WINK-EYE.

"You mean if whatever is sending out the signal in the satellite is still in operation," Graff said in disgust.

"You're a pessimist, my American friend," Sedgwick said wryly.

"I'm a realist, my British colleague!"

Camellion reared up slightly and called out, "Dr. Bangold, Dr. Leitch. Please come over here."

The two aerospace scientists, followed by the four Zero-Zeros, walked over to the Death Merchant and his group. Camellion and the other men got to their feet.

"We have the route to the satellite plotted," Camellion told the scientists. "But we need to know more about the satellite and the tracking process the two of you will use."

"Basically, there are two types of communications satellites," replied Dr. Leitch. He removed his dark glasses. "There are passive reflectors and active repeaters. The reflectors simply bounce waves back to earth, but the active repeaters are much more sophisticated. They can store a message indefinitely, or send it back to earth repeatedly and to different stations at the same time."

"Which type is WINK-EYE?" asked Bolinger curiously.

"Neither type, hence the designation of the numeral 'One' to WINK-EYE," explained Leitch. He pulled a handkerchief from his pocket. "You see, W-E-ONE is very special. There is no other satellite like it. Excuse me a moment." He began wiping his thin, tired-looking face.

"WINK-EYE had three prime duties," Dr. Bangold said, taking up the explanation. "Monitoring the Soviet Union's domestic satellites was the least of these duties. The second most important directive was for WINK-EYE to photograph the entire Soviet Union for hidden missile installations. Up to four months ago, we knew every single ICBM the Soviets had. We could pinpoint every silo. We had this information

94

due to our tracking satellites. This information was kept up-to-date and turned over to NORAD."

"The American North American Air Defense Command," Sedgwick said.

"Yes, that is correct. NORAD knows the location of every Soviet ICBM. Or rather, it did. The Soviet Union had begun building new silos we can't locate by conventional means. That is why WINK-EYE was built. We can't tell how WINK-EYE was to accomplish the mission, whether by photography or by other means. We weren't made privy to that information." He took a pack of cigarettes and a Bic lighter from a shoulder bag.

Dr. Leitch put away the crumpled handkerchief and said, almost in a whisper, "WINK-EYE's third function was the most important of the three. WINK-EYE was to lock in on two Soviet satellites that were experimental stations. One station was experimenting with laser beams and microwaves. To give you an idea of how far Soviet scientists have progressed, we are almost positive that it was microwave particles, beamed from that Soviet satellite, that caused the blackout in New York City last summer. For the sake of security, the public was told that lightning was responsible!"

Leitch put on his dark glasses and glanced up at the sky. "I'm not used to this kind of sun."

The Death Merchant get down on his heels by the side of the large rock. The rest of the men did the same, including Calvin Leitch and Foster Bangold, Leitch saying, "The second Soviet station was connected with experiments in plasma —and by plasma, I am not referring to the fluid portion of the blood that is minus the red and white blood cells. I shan't bore you with the technical details. Let me say that plasma can be called another state of matter. Compared to plasma, the H-bomb is a toy!"

Colonel Lippkor's sharp black eyes darted around the group. Even the four Zero-Zero men were hanging onto every word. "It was WINK-EYE's job to laser-beam the two Soviet stations out of existence," Lippkor declared, hurrying the conversation along.

"You're right, Colonel," Bangold said, as nervous-mannered as ever. "WINK-EYE was programmed to destroy both Russian satellites, but not until it had absorbed the signals, the information impulses that the two satellites were transmitting to Soviet stations on earth. After its data banks were full, WINK-EYE would then destroy the two Soviet stations. But it didn't happen. The two Soviet stations are still there, orbiting at 24,000 miles."

Dr. Leitch said, "In fact, we don't even know if WINK-EYE stole any data from the two Russian stations. To fool the Russians, there weren't any transmissions from WINK-EYE. Everything was recorded on its tapes. The only thing we do know is that WINK-EYE went over the United States eighty-four times and, presumably, photographed all our missile installations, although we can't be positive. We won't know until we find the tapes and get them back to the States to be read."

Bangold, who was quick to notice the mannerisms of people around him, saw that a puzzled Camellion was waiting for a chance to speak.

"You have a question, Mr. Camellion?"

"I was under the impression that WINK-EYE was a geosynchronous satellite. Yet part of its job was—"

"What does that mean?" Graff boldly interrupted, peering demandingly at the Death Merchant.

Glancing at Graff in annoyance, Richard quickly explained. "Geosynchronous is the term used for satellites that keep pace with the rotation of the earth. Such satellites are also referred to as being geostationary."

"Very well put, Mr. Camellion," Dr. Leitch said, his tone complimentary. He smiled at the other men, his thin lips stretching back over big white teeth. "You see, many satellites are in low orbit, a little over a hundred miles up. Eventually they come down and burn up because they are not outside the earth's gravitational pull. The more permanent satellites are balanced with gravity twenty-two-thousand-three-hundred miles, or higher, above us. They are constantly moving in larger orbits, some of them at speeds of five to six miles per second. But WINK-EYE was not a geosynchronous satellite."

Dr. Bangold looked at Camellion. "What were you going to ask a moment ago?"

"Was WINK-EYE ever at the same orbit as the two Russian satellites?" Richard asked. Moving his body, he sat down yoga-style, legs tucked underneath him.

"The two Russian stations were ten miles apart, but parallel to each other," Bangold said in a patient voice. "WINK-EYE was in the center, but thirty miles lower."

"What's your problem?" asked Dr. Leitch, frowning slightly when he saw Bangold light another cigarette from the previous butt.

Camellion said, "WINK-EYE was scheduled to photograph missile bases in the USSR. A Bivix high-resolution infrared observation system is very good; yet beyond five hundred miles it isn't worth a damn. Was WINK-EYE first supposed to do its job on the two Russian satellites and then come down to photograph the Soviet missile sites, or what was the procedure? The only possible answer is that WINK-EYE was a miniature spaceship that could go up and down like a yo-yo!"

For a long moment the two scientists studied the Death Merchant.

"Mr. Camellion, you are very knowledgeable about space science," Bangold said, a baffled expression on his pale face. "And you have guessed correctly. WINK-EYE was a space vessel in the true sense, one that could go in any direction under our control."

"At least N.S.A. thought it had total control," Bolinger said.

Dr. Bangold cleared his throat and blew smoke through his nose. "We think the trouble developed in the guidance system," he said sadly. "The computer brain defied our commands. Based on WINK-EYE's erratic behavior, one could say metaphorically that the brain suffered a nervous breakdown." He thought for a second, then grunted. "Or went completely psychotic, since it photographed our own silos."

"And then committed suicide by going down in the jungle!" said Dr. Leitch. "Our only chance now is to find WINK-EYE and retrieve the magnetic tapes. How close are we?"

"Less than six miles," the Death Merchant answered. "Tell us about your tracking instruments."

"One instrument only for tracking," Doctor Leitch informed him. "An Alphaometer—a spinoff development from the Lyman Alpha spectrometer. It was developed—the Alphaometer—by *Discus*[19]."

"WINK-EYE has an Alphaspectro-generator that gives out a continuous signal," Dr. Bangold said. "To help us locate the station after it came down, in case something went wrong."

[19] *Discus*: Pentagon jargon for D.S.C.S.—Defense Satellite Communications System.

"The signal has a strength of twenty-thousand billionths of a watt at 6.38 gigahertz—enough to work with."

The Death Merchant rubbed the tips of his fingers across his forehead. "Let's see, frequency has to be considered along with power. A gigahertz is one billion hertz—I think!"

"I don't even know what a hertz is!" quipped Sedgwick. He put a hand on the butt of the Colt Python buckled around his waist; he wore another CP .357 Mag in a hos<u></u>lter on his chest.

Colonel Lippkor gave a low chuckle. "Hertz is a car rental agency," he said mischievously. "But in this case hertz is the basic measure of frequency with which an electromagnetic wave completes a full cycle from its positive to its negative pole and back again. There's more to it than that, but I don't know enough to explain it."

"Nor do I," admitted Camellion, surprised at Colonel Lippkor's humor.

"It's very simple," said Dr. Leitch. "If your transmission propagates waves at the rate of one hertz, that means each wave completes one cycle per second. The signal is said to have a frequency of one hertz."

Partial understanding showed on the faces of Graff and Bolinger. Camellion and Lippkor listened attentively.

"That sounds like low frequency," Camellion said.

"Very low frequency," nodded Dr. Bangold. "Most radio signals are electromagnetic waves at frequencies between five-hundred kilohertz and thirty million megahertz."

Dr. Leitch said, "The signal from WINK-EYE is being sent out with almost no power, but with waves at frequencies up to six billion, three-hundred and ninety-million hertz—or that many completed wave cycles each second."

"These signals can be picked up with the Alphaometer," said Dr. Bangold. "The closer we get to the satellite, the stronger the signals become. But we must be within four-thousand feet of the space station before we can begin picking up the signals."

Dr. Bangold looked around him, as if listening. Camellion wished the scientist wouldn't always look so damned scared to death.

"Let's hit the road!" Camellion said and stood up. The other men got to their feet and adjusted the straps across their shoulders and chest.

"I'll make a final check with Tony," Graff said, "then we'll get moving." He moved off toward Anthony Flecher, who was talking to the Zero-Zero men, who carried CGL-4 grenade launchers on their Colt heavy assault rifles.

Doctor Leitch consulted a pocket watch. "It's only seven-fifteen and I'm burning up," he said. "I can't understand why the temperature is already so high." He glanced at Camellion, who was studying the area to the east.

"I suppose it's because there is no shade," muttered Leitch.

"The rocks lose their heat very quickly at night," Colonel Lippkor said, "but heat up just as quickly the minute the sun comes out. And rocks reflect heat. That's what we're feeling."

"No breeze and not a cloud in the sky," Sedgwick said with a grimace. "We're going to do a lot of sweating before we reach WINK-EYE."

Turning, Camellion looked toward the west. The hills, bare except for scattered bushes and clumps of tough ginno grass, looked as inviting as a wolverine protecting its young.

The Death Merchant blinked rapidly and stared again through the sunglasses. For a moment he had thought he had caught a very brief flash several hundred feet away, the kind of glitter that results when sunrays strike a polished surface, such as a mirror.

NO! I was not mistaken!

Again he saw a quick, fleeting brightness, an instant of shining.

And this time he saw the face above the glint!

"Everybody down!" he shouted at the top of his voice.

He was throwing himself to the rocks when the stillness of the morning was shattered by gunfire!

Chapter Ten

As soon as the Tupolev-144—the Soviet *"Concordskii"*—was airborne and Cienfuegos Field was only a five-minute memory, a brooding Col. Valarian Agyants saw Maj. Viktor Lyalin coming down the long aisle toward the tiny lounge in the rear of the supersonic airliner.

The two men had met only an hour ago and, for a number of resons, Agyants had taken an instant dislike to Lyalin, who was in the Sixth Direction of the Fifth Chief Directorate of the KGB. It was the sole function of the Sixth Direction to suppress nationalism among the 100-odd ethnic minorities in the Soviet Union and among the satellite nations of Europe.

It seared Colonel Agyants' personal and professional pride that he was being forced to take orders not only from a lower-ranking officer but from a younger man as well. A younger man who was good-looking and had the body of an athlete. While Agyants was all chest and shoulders, Viktor Lyalin was well proportioned, his muscles evenly distributed.

There was that damned left hand of his, an artificial hand! Envious by nature, Agyants hated any man who could sneer at a physical disability and turn defeat into victory.

Worse, Lyalin was a sadist.

On the way to Cienfuegos Field, General Chekalov had told Agyants and Colonel Tisbal why he was confident that Major Lyalin would accomplish his mission in Surinam: because of his "efficiency" and *kvas patriotism*. Chekalov had then mentioned how Major Lyalin and his unit during the invasion of Czechoslovakia had machined-gunned Czechs at the mere appearance of what Lyalin considered "Fascist activity." Efficiency? Patriotism? Crap! It was brutality, pure and simple. Why else did they call Lyalin the Hammer? And General Chekalov, that wily old bastard, knew it.

"It was in Vietnam that Major Lyalin lost his hand," Chekalov had said. "He was serving as an advisor to our North Vietnam comrades. An American machine-gun bullet

100

blew his hand off. He was flown back to Moskva and eventually was fitted with a prosthesis, an artificial hand. He was only a captain then."

General Chekalov and Colonel Tisbal! *They're not fooling me!* At least Agyants was positive about Chekalov. Right now the General was sorting ways and means to protect himself; he had influential friends in the party *apparatchiki! If the tapes aren't recovered from the American satellite, I'll be blamed. I'm certain of it.*

Rage seethed within Agyants. How had he come to this— seated in the ass-end of a *Concordskii* and dressed in the camouflaged battle fatigues of an ordinary soldier, he, a colonel in the assassination department? *Because of bad luck!* he told himself philosophically. Because his best agents had failed in Surinam and in Guyana. They had been the best. The failure couldn't have been due to sloppiness on their part. *Chort vozmi!*[20] Who was this Richard Camellion?

Colonel Agyants concealed his feelings and smiled as Major Lyalin sat down in a plush leather chair trimmed in chrome, placed a nylon stuff bag on the floor between his legs, and began rummaging through it was his right hand. Colonel Agyants watched him, a smile pasted on his mouth. After a minute or so, Lyalin pulled a bottle from the bag and Colonel Agyants saw that it was Kinzmarauli, a rare and hearty red wine from Lyalin's native Georgia.

Lyalin smirked at Agyants' amazement, leaned closer to him and whispered with mock cautiousness, "You see, Colonel? There are always ways to get the best, if one knows how."

You arrogant swine! That was another reason why Agyants loathed the younger man—his familiarity! As if they were close friends!

"Yes, yes. That is true," Agyants said suavely and leaned back in the chair, enjoying the softness of the cushions.

Major Lyalin stood up, handed the tall green bottle of wine to Colonel Agyants, and said in a normal tone of voice, "I'll get glasses from the bar."

He swayed, put out his arms and steadied himself as a stiff air current rocked the aircraft. The sleek, needle-like airplane, in high-speed configuration, its nose and visor raised,

---

[20] *Chort vozmi*: "Devil take it"—the approximate Russian equivalent of "Damn."

101

the nose-planes retracted, was still gaining altitude. The pilot would level off at 62,000 feet, then increased the power of the four turbofans until the maximum cruising speed of Mach 2.35 (1,550 mph) was reached.

Lyalin went across the small lounge, walked behind the bar, and slid back a glass door. He reached in with his right hand and took a wine-glass from the rack. He moved his left arm, bending it at the elbow, and the hook that was his left hand snapped open. He placed the stem of the glass between the two "fingers," moved the arm again, and the hook closed. Lyalin removed another glass from the rack, shoved the door into place, walked back across the lounge, sat down, turned to Agyants, and held out his arms, extending the glasses.

"Go ahead, Colonel," he said, chuckling at Agyants' discomfort. "Take the glass from the hook the way you would from an ordinary hand. You will be able to pull it free. Then hand me the bottle."

Agyants pulled the glass from the hook, took the other glass from the Major's right hand, and handed him the bottle. Agyants watched in fascination as Lyalin used the hook prosthesis to pull the deep cork from the bottle.

"Hold the glasses, Colonel."

Agyants held out the glasses, marvelling at the dexterity with which the Major poured the wine, at how he used the hook in conjunction with his right hand. In some strange way, Agyants was just as spellbound with the hand as he was with the hook. The long fingers moved with all the subtleness of tentacles, each digit seeming to have a mind and will of its own.

Colonel Agyants took a sip of wine—*delicious!*—and listened politely as Major Lyalin said, very seriously, "Colonel, do not be embarrassed by my hook; there's no need to be. I realize that most people are intrigued at the sight of a man with a hook at the end of his wirst." An amused smile formed on his lips. "At home, I often wear a metal mechanical hand covered by a skin-colored rubber glove. Strictly for looks. The hook is the most commonly used device. It's more effective, although it repels people."

"Our Soviet scientists are very good," commented Agyants with false sympathy. "The day will come when they develop an artificial hand that functions as well as a regular hand."

Major Lyalin nodded approvingly. "Scientists all over the world have been working for years on such a device. They've been trying to utilize electrical energy as the source of hand control. The theory is that electrodes can be built into the artificial part and activated by the patient's own muscle contractions. The electric current generated by these muscle contractions is then be amplified by batteries. Such myoelectrical devices are in existence, but they're crude and not too effective. I prefer the hook and—hold my glass a moment."

The Major handed Agyants the glass, bent down, and reached into the stuff bag. He moved his hand around for several moments and pulled out a foot-long case which he placed on the arm of the chair. He opened the black case by pressing the catch on one side.

"And these!" Major Lyalin smiled in anticipation at the surprise he expected from the Colonel.

In the lid of the case a larger hook snuggled in a cut-out compartment. In the bottom of the case were two stainless steel knives, the end of each fitted with bolt threads. One knife was double-edged and 7 inches long. The second blade, 10 inches long, was shaped like a pyramid, with the top edge toward the apex.

Colonel Agyants stared at the two knives. He could see that they were as sharp as a brand-new safety razor.

"I often use one of the blades in the field," Lyalin said happily. "All I do is detach the hook from the arm-harness and screw in one of the blades. I'm looking forward to using the blades on the enemy, once we're in Surinam."

He closed the knife case and shoved it back into the bag.

"I doubt if we find a single American in Surinam," said Agyants sagely, handing a wine glass to the Major. "The time factor is against us. I'm convinced we're wasting our time."

Major Lyalin, his eyes narrowing, took a sip of wine, swallowing noisily. He could scarcely disagree with Agyants in regard to the loss of time.

A hundred miles from Havana one of the turbofans had again malfunctioned. The *Concordskii* had not been able to land until 8:45 A.M. Work on the turbofan and refueling had consumed another 80 minutes. The aircraft hadn't taken off until after 10 o'clock! There would be another delay when the craft reached Surinam and the pilot maneuvered the plane into a position that would permit Lyalin, Agyants, and the 90 men of the Sixth Direction force to parachute to the ground.

That was another worry for Colonel Agyants. He had never parachuted from an airplane. But there was more to it! A *Concordskii* was not designed as a drop carrier. It was a question of lift and balance, a matter of wing surface and engine thrust. When a Tupolev-144 was several hundred feet from the ground, it was meant to come down, to effect a full landing, albeit there wasn't any aerodynamical reason why a *Concordskii* couldn't skim in low and then grab for altitude. But it would be a dangerous tactic, even under the best of conditions. A faulty turbofan weighted the balance toward a stall; should the airliner stall at only a few hundred feet, a crash would inevitably follow.

Major Lyalin gave Agyants his most enchanting smile.

"Colonel, didn't one of our regular agents, working at the S.I.S. plantation, radio a report that the man named Camellion is leading the American force?"

"He did, at one o'clock this morning. Richard Camellion is the boss of the enemy expedition." Agyants wondered along what lines the major might be reasoning.

"This Camellion, he is the same man your agents failed to eliminate. Is that not so?"

"*Da.* The same man."

"Good!" Major Lyalin declared. "Camellion is not *malenky chelovek* in his thinking! He is not a little man in his planning. As cautious as he is, he and his men will advance on the satellite with great care. Oh, no! He won't drop close to the location. They'll approach the space station from the perimeter."

Agyants breathed deeply. "It's a gamble then. You are counting on us getting to the satellite while Camellion and his men are still on the march. That's cutting it close, maybe too close. We don't know that he's not going to make a straight drop."

"I don't think so," said Lyalin nonchalantly.

"There is another possibility. The Americans could be waiting for us," said Agyants sourly. "We outnumber them more than two to one, but they could still kill a lot of us while we were floating down on our chutes." He paused, added, "Naturally we must do our duty," and took several swallows from the wide-brimmed glass.

Major Lyalin hunched a shoulder. "It's a chance we must take. We will do our best. The Center cannot expect more. But, Colonel"—he swung his head very quickly toward Agyants—"there is something very important I want to discuss with you."

Instantly on guard, Agyanst said "Yes?" very carefully.

Leaning closer, Lyalin became confidential. "Colonel, you

know how it is at home. The black market feeds on a lot of things—American rock records, stereo sets, watches, transistors, foreign clothes—you know what I mean. It's all part of the *blat*[21]."

Colonel Agyants kept his momentary astonishment concealed. The nerve of the man! He is either dangerously reckless or has powerful friends in very high places.

"So?"

"Certain kinds of American magazines are very valuable on the black market," declared Lyalin, his voice husky. "I was wondering, Colonel. Since you have agents going back and forth between Cuba and the U.S., would it be possible for you to obtain *Playboy* and *Penthouse* magazines?"

---

[21] *Blat*: The American equivalent is "greasing the palm." Technically *blat* does not involve money, it's giving a favor in return for a favor. In Russian, this is *ty mne i ya tebe,* or you for me and me for you." We would say, "I'll scratch your back and you scratch mine."

Chapter Eleven

The first bursts of rifle and submachine gun fire killed instantly Dr. Bangold and four of the Zero-Zero men. The five men had been a few seconds too slow in dropping behind rocks.

"Oh, my God!" mumbled Dr. Leitch, his voice skating on hysteria. The scientist lay flat, next to Richard Camellion, his face on the rock, his hands on the back of his head.

Conscious of his own heartbeat, Camellion looked around. Six feet to his right the bloody corpse of Dr. Bangold lay crumpled on its side. Hugging the ground on the other side of Camellion were Lippkor, Bolinger, Sedgwick, and Dr. Leitch.

"By God, the damned Russians didn't waste any time!" Bolinger said with bitter resentment. He pushed the barrel of his M1 between two rocks and angled for a firing position.

"Hold your fire!" Camellion said sharply. "Don't shoot until you have a target. We don't have any ammunition to waste."

There was another short burst of fire from the larger rocks ahead to the west, then an eerie silence.

"They're trying to draw us out," Colonel Lippkor whispered. "They have us pinned down, but good—a Mexican standoff all right!"

The Death Merchant looked across the corpse of Bangold and saw Rudolf Graff, Tony Flecher, and some of the Zero-Zero boys huddled behind part of a jagged dike. More Zero-Zeros protected the flank, using for cover the weirdly shaped igneous slabs that jutted upward from the floor of the slope. For the time being, everyone was safe. *For all the good it does us. We're on a slope, a long incline that's covered with small hills and patches of big rocks. The enemy is behind the hills, in the rocks above us. We couldn't be in a worse position.*

Once more Camellion looked to his right. The four East Indians, each clutching a Colt heavy assault rifle, were also behind the dike of rock. Close to them, sitting with his back to the rock, was Bill Henderson, calmly smoking a cigarette. A scoped .30 M1D snipers' rifle lay across his lap. *A cool customer, that bird.*

Richard was relieved to see that the boxes of ammo and other equipment were close to the East Indians. The cartons were bulletproof, but not against high-velocity slugs repeatedly striking the same spot.

An angry-faced Graff glared at Camellion across the open space, then took the radiotelephone from his belt.

Camellion turned on his own set.

"We're pinned down but good." The big man's savage voice was tinny as it came through the RT. "I told the men not to fire and waste ammo. I have some ideas, but I want to hear yours first."

"We sit tight and worry them," Camellion said. "When they get nervous enough, I think they will either charge or try to outflank us. I'm counting on both."

"Good thinking. That's all they can do, unless they've got a lot of patience and decide to wait us out."

"They won't have that kind of patience. They haven't reached WINK-EYE or they wouldn't be risking a battle with us. They're racing against time just as we are. When they charge, have your men with the grenade launchers go to work. I'll use the grenades and the firing as a cover. I'll go to the left and try to get above them."

"You're nuts!" Graff's heavy voice was a warning. "They'll blow you all over the hillside! Why not have several of the men over here go with you? They could take half a dozen TEA grenades and roast the sons of bitches. I guess you know they're not Russkies. At least they're not using Russian weapons."

"Don't send any men across that open space." Camellion was firm. "They'd never make it. We'll do it my way." He switched off the RT, shoved it into its case, turned to the men beside him, and explained what he was going to do.

"I'll go with you, if you want," offered Colonel Lippkor. "Two would have a better chance."

"I don't want," said Camellion frankly. "There's not enough cover for two men, and two men would get in each other's way."

He removed his rucksack and other equipment, everything but the shotgun bag and the game-bag vest.

"I don't want any of you getting trigger-gippy. Don't fire a

107

single round until the enemy charges and our first grenade goes off," Camellion said. He began to crawl on his hands and knees to the left, keeping close to the rocks. In some places the rocks were so low that, although he snaked by them on his belly, they were barely above his head. Nonetheless, within the next 15 minutes he managed to wriggle upward, at a left angled slant, 100 feet. He stopped when he reached the four Zero-Zero men who had been assigned to watch over Dr. Bangold and Dr. Leitch. He quickly told them what he had in mind and said, "Cover me when I make a run for it."

"You're going up there alone?" Jose Meridias looked like a young Pancho Villa. "Why, that ridge is a good two hundred feet from here!"

Enemy guns replied for the Death Merchant. From a few hundred feet to the west—but only 100 feet from the position of Camellion and the four Zero-Zero men—automatic weapons snarled in hatred, sending a rain of deadly projectiles at the American force below. Scores of ricochets screamed. Rock chips became as thick as hail. From high up, to the west, a light machine gun began firing short, methodical bursts, raking the lower rocks from left to right, then from right to left. When the slugs of the light machine gun weren't striking the rocks, rifle and submachine gun bullets were. Camellion's men could only keep down and do a lot of hoping.

The Death Merchant switched on his RT and contacted Rudolf Graff.

"Listen, Rudy. The enemy doesn't know that I and four Zero guys are here. Not a single bullet has come our way."

"I was wondering where those four were!"

"None of you can look out or you might get your heads blown off. I can see from up here. If and when the enemy charges, I'll tell you when to fire the grenades. You have the launchers loaded?"

"And waiting. We'll fire the first spread at thirty yards and five yards apart. I'll keep the RT open." He gave a little laugh. "Let me know if you get killed and can't spot for us."

"I'll send you a wire on the hot line from hell." Holding the RT unit in one hand, Camellion snuggled closer to a table-size rock, leaned around to one side, and stared through the intermingling branches of a thorn bush. First two, then three, four, and more men began creeping from behind rocks and dashing forward, running from rock to rock toward the

108

Americans on the incline below; all the time, the light machine gun and other automatic weapons gave them cover fire.

The enemy wore green and brown patterned fatigues, but the shape of their headgear and the arrangement of the cross-straps over their backs and chests were clearly Brazilian. Their weapons were Brazilian army and police issue— Pinero ARs, P-77 submachine guns, and P-AV4 carbines. And no doubt .45 Largo Llama autoloaders in their holsters.

"Those poor dumb bastards," whispered Hubert Boston. "They're walking right into it!"

The Death Merchant waited. When the first wave of Brazilians was 95 to 90 feet from the dike, Camellion held the radiotelephone close to his mouth and said, "Now!"

A few seconds later the first four grenades sailed over the dike and exploded among the first line of Brazilian soldiers. There were several screams of agony. Arms and legs were torn off. A few decapitated heads shot skyward. Bodies were pitched into the air and, amid a shower of dust and broken rocks, crashed back to earth and lay still. The Brazilians not killed or wounded either turned and attempted to retreat, or else flung themselves down in a frantic effort to find safety in the rocks.

There was no safety. The CGL-4 launcher was chambered for the 40-millimeter grenade, and the four Zero-Zero operators reloaded and fired with great speed and expertise. The next four grenades exploded on an average of 40 yards from the dike and 10 yards apart. More Brazilians were butchered, watering the rocks with their blood and bits of flesh and cloth.

"How are we doing?" Graff's voice jumped from the RT.

"You've killed at least a dozen and wounded twice as many," the Death Merchant reported. "The rest are either in retreat or making like postage stamps on the ground. Give them another four-round salvo and I'll move out."

Ten seconds later the next four grenades exploded, the thundering roars echoing throughout the hills. Camellion pulled the two Auto Mags, and thumbed off each safety lever. He jumped up and began to weave and dodge to the southwest, keeping as low a profile as possible. At times he stumbled and almost fell in his rush to reach the next chain of rocks that offered cover.

The moment he was clear of their guns, the four Zero-Zeros cut loose with their Colt ARs, concentrating their fire on the enemy light machine gun. Two of the Zero-Zeros then began raking the entire area. Scores of 7.62-millimeter bullets stabbed into the rocks. The light machine gun and a dozen other weapons stopped firing as the surprised Brazilians, ducking for cover, took stock of this new development.

The leader of the Brazilian expedition, Lt. Col. Eugene Ormenente, didn't know what to do. His plan to wipe out the *Rusos—Rusos* or *Americanos! It made no difference!*—had blown up in his face. If only he had listened to Capitan Darselas! Now it was too late. They were too far away from the *Rusos* to use grenades.

The momentary lull in the enemy firing offered Graff and the rest of the Zero-Zero men their opportunity. They opened fire with their Colt M1s, peppering the Brazilian positions with hundreds of 7.62-millimeter projectiles.

The Brazilians had spotted Camellion. In desperation, half a dozen Halcon commandos slid down from the top of the long ridge and moved south to head him off. Other Halcons, risking enemy fire from below, did their best to cut the single figure apart with rifle and submachine gun fire.

Ba-zinnggggggg! Ba-zinnnggggg! Ba-zinnnggggg! The screech of ricochets screamed at the Death Merchant, the vacuum-suck of a 9-millimeter bullet only half an inch from his right ear. Hot metal bored a double hole through his right pants leg, at the knee, going in one side of the cloth and coming out the other side. Several more bullets came within inches of his chest. In desperation, he leaped forward and dived to one side of a group of small boulders the size of washtubs. Enemy slugs burned the air all around him. Bullets zinged off the rocks, howling in failure to reach him. There was a 10-foot rock dike to the south; so fast did Camellion crawl for its protection that he seemed almost to be swimming, his arms and legs flailing before and behind.

He reached the side of the dike. It was tilted toward him at such an angle that he had the wild, fleeting thought that it might topple over. Richard did some superfast analysis. Ahead was an open, pie-shaped area. Beyond it was a kind of V-shaped trench that angled up to another ridge 30 feet above and 50 feet back from the high crooked crinkle the Brazilians were occupying.

Camellion crawled to the end of the dike, looked around the edge, and saw six Brazilian commandos coming down through the V-shaped trench. Several of them saw him, yelled a warning, jerked to one side, and raised their Pinero-77 submachine guns. A third and a fourth commando reached for grenades hanging from cross-straps. The last two Brazilians threw themselves flat behind rocks.

Camellion pulled the triggers of the two Auto Mags, the stainless steel weapons roaring with the volume of small cannons. A .44 Magnum slug cut into the midsection of one of the Brazilians as he tried to get his machine gun into action. The impact doubled him over and pitched him back into another man who was trying to pull the pin from a grenade. The second Brazilian with a sub-gun didn't utter a sound when a .44 blew a cup-size hole in his chest and switched off his life. He dropped the Pinero chatterbox and pitched to one side, a look of complete shock on his dead face.

The Death Merchant fired two more times. His third slug slammed into the left shoulder of the man who had been trying to pull the pin from the grenade. The man screamed, spun around, dropped the grenade, and fell forward on his face, his arm hanging by only a few ropes of muscle, blood sprting from the left axillary artery. The remainder of his life could be measured in seconds.

Just as the fourth man frantically tossed the grenade, Camellion's fourth .44 bullet struck him high in the right leg, knocking him down.

Camellion, catching only a glimpse of the grenade in midair, jerked to the side of the dike, opened his mouth, and yelled to lessen the pressure which would have to come from the concussion.

I'll have to be damned lucky!

He was! The commando had not had the time to aim the grenade or to pitch a hard throw. The grenade fell short and exploded 10 feet in front of the dike. The front and top of the dike deflected the shrapnel, but the roar continued to resound in Camellion's head as he pulled two grenades from the shotgun shell bag, pulled the pin of the first one, and threw it over the dike with all his might. He tossed the second grenade on the echoes of the first explosion. After the blast and the *ping-ping-ping* of shrapnel against the rock, he dared a look around the end of the dike. The first grenade hadn't done any damage. Neither had the second. However, it had landed closer to the trench-passage and shattered the nerve of the two Halcon commandoes who had escaped Camellion's first slugs. Now they were trying to retreat, to scramble back up the trench and wait for the Death Merchant from one side at the top.

111

Camellion fired the Auto Mag in his left hand, the big autoloader roaring. He watched the bullet smash one man in the small of the back and slam him against the man in front who did his best to keep his balance. He was still trying when the Death Merchant fired again and the .44 slug struck the man in the left hip, tore all the way through his body, exploded his right hip, and went on its violent way.

For a moment, crouched exulantly against the side of the dike, Camellion listened to the Colt M1s of his people answering the weapons of the enemy. He didn't take time to shove new clips into the half-empty AMPs. He jumped to his feet, ran around the end of the rock, and sprinted forward, leaping first one way and then another, as though the soles of his boots were filled with springs. Bullets zipped across his path, both in front and in back of him. The slugs thinned out as he neared the end of the trench, panting heavily from the exertion. Not only had Graff and the other men set up a rapid cover fire, but intervening rocks between Camellion and the Brazilians made it increasingly difficult for the enemy to get a clear shot at him. Yet Capitan Darselas had guessed his intention and was now trying to cut him off. Several other Brazilians, with more nerve than common sense, had attempted to climb to the next ridge 30 feet above. Both men had been riddled with slugs from below.

Camellion reached the lower end of the V-like passage and began leaping over bodies in an effort to reach the opposite opening and claw his way up to the next ridge. He had to step on the last two corpses, which blocked the passage. Ten feet later he came to the end of the slanting ditch, got down by the right side and stared at the tiny horizontal ravine—*It's only a big ditch!*—into which the V-passage opened. Beyond the ravine was the grade that twisted upward to the area he would use to get to the higher ridge. The ravine was only 20 feet wide.

But a bullet needs less than half an inch. And who might be coming to call from the right-hand side?

Camellion took out another grenade, pulled the pin, and flipped the grenade in a curving arc to his right. He stood on the balls of his feet and waited, taking in lungfuls of air thick with gunpowder fumes. The instant the big blast faded, Richard charged across the opening and headed straight for the grade. In a hurry, he didn't glance to left or right. If he had looked to the right, he would have seen that the grenade had not killed anyone. It had exploded far ahead of Captain

Juan Darselas and the three men with him, showering them with shrapnel but not wounding anyone seriously. By the time the four Brazilians realized they were still alive, Camellion had reached the opposite side of the ravine and was clawing his way among the rocks, determined to reach the large rock 25 feet away. Down in the enormous ditch, Captain Darselas ran toward the grade, the three Halcon regulars stumbling after him. Darselas, angry at having been tricked like a third-rate amateur, had only one goal: to kill the man who had thrown the grenade. Darselas closed in on the grenade-blast site at the same time that the Death Merchant wriggled down behind the dome-shape rock at the top of the grade. Wise in the cute little tricks of Daddy Death, Camellion had no intention of moving up another 10 feet and hippity-hopping north. No indeed! Not until he was positive that his rear and flanks were clear. He could see that both sides were safe: If anyone were coming after him, he or they would have to take the same route that he had just taken. Since the incline was thick with rubble, it would be impossible for anyone to approach from below without his hearing them, even above the gunfire.

The Death Merchant waited. Five minutes would be ample.

Below, Captain Darselas took the chance: He stuck his head around the side of a monumentlike rock and stared up the grade. The men in back of him glanced fearfully at each other, one of them daubing at his bloody left eyebrow with a handkerchief. A half-inch lower and the piece of shrapnel would have blinded him.

Juan Darselas weighed the odds and decided that the lone enemy had to be hurrying to a position where he could lob grenades down on the Brazilian forces below. What else could he be doing?

Darselas turned and motioned to the three men. "Come, if we hurry we can still stop him," he said.

In the lead, a P-77 submachine gun in his hands, he started up the sharp grade, stones rolling noisily under his feet. The three men followed.

Camellion heard the four Brazilians approaching, the sound of tumbling rubblestone signaling the progress of the commandos to him. He waited until the men were halfway up the incline, then pitched a grenade over the domed rock.

Captain Darselas saw the small, dark object tumbling toward him out of the sky and yelled *"Granada!"*

"Grenade" was the last word he said in his 37 years of life.

113

There was a tremendous flash of fire and an enormous crashing. All reality ended for Darselas and he became a nothing in the cosmic stream of time. The explosion blew off his left arm, obliterated his face, riddled him with shrapnel, and tossed him and two other men 10 feet into the air. Darselas and another man were dead, but the third body moved slightly after it came back down. A moan slipped through the bloody lips.

The fourth Brazilian—10 feet behind the other commandos—had been knocked to the ground by the explosion and stung in numerous places with shrapnel. Otherwise, he was unharmed. Stunned, deafened by the explosion, he was trying to get to his feet when he looked up and saw the face staring down at him from the top of the grade. There were shiny, strange-looking *pistolas* in the hands of the man who owned the face. One of the muzzles flashed a tongue of flame. The commando felt an instant of agony in his chest. Dead, he fell sideways into eternity.

Camellion looked down at the passage, which resembled an untidy slaughter house. The large side rocks and rubblestone were blood-splattered and peppered with tiny bits of flesh and bloody clothing. An arm was lodged between two rocks. A hand, the fingers half-closed, lay on the rubblestones a few feet from the man who had lost it.

The commando who was not quite dead moved slightly and moaned again. He managed to raise his left arm.

"May your path be strewn with golden carpet tacks!" murmured Camellion. The AMP in his right hand roared. The body below stopped moving. The arm fell to the rocks. The moaning ceased.

The Death Merchant turned, dug his heels into the rocks, and stomped his way another 10 feet up the slope. He was soon at the area that would permit him to move north. He didn't waste any time counting loose gravel. Knees bent and stooped so low his head was parallel with his waist, he hurried north for 250 feet, then turned and crawled another 45 feet up a slope cut with crooked water channels.

Ten feet from the top, he lay flat and snaked to the edge. Four feet from the edge, he removed his hunter's bush hat, thought of a poem titled "Stranger in a Strange Land," crawled the rest of the way, and carefully looked down. Some 30 to 40 feet below, the Brazilians were lying flat or crouched behind rocks, some of them watching the ridge above.

114

The Death Merchant pulled back his head as three of the commandos below opened fire with P-ARs. *Ba-zingggggg! Baa-zinnnngggg!* Dozens of 765-millimeter slugs crashed into the rocks at the edge, sending a shower of dust and chips toward Camellion. More projectiles split the air on their way upward, in front of him.

Camellion pulled the pin from the first grenade and heard terrified shouting from below. The Brazilians were trapped and knew it. All they could do was try to retreat in a southern direction. Camellion heard gunfire from still farther down, from his own people, who were doing their best to hinder the Brazilians in their efforts to hold onto life as long as possible.

"Business is business," muttered Camellion, and tossed the first grenade far to the south. "Nothing personal, boys. Sorry, but die you must."

Die they did. Camellion threw the grenades as quickly as he could pull the pins. He spaced them so that each grenade fell 20 feet or more from the one previously thrown.

Screams and explosions sang a duet of death. The symphony of violence ended as quickly as it began, the nine grenades leaving nothing but battered rock, pools of blood, and crushed and broken bodies, plus a series of dying echoes that bounced, like ping-pong balls, back and forth between the hills.

Camellion crawled back to the edge and looked down at the still smoking ridge. The strong fumes of burnt nitro flooded his nostrils.

How about that? Four Brazilians were still alive. Two of the commandos had tied white handkerchiefs to the muzzles of their P-AV4 carbines and were waving the flags of surrender back and forth. One fellow was signalling the Zero-Zero force below; the other man was facing the Death Merchant.

Twenty minutes later, a sad-faced Lt. Col. Eugene Ormenente was explaining to Camellion and Graff & Co. why he and his men had set an ambush. Speaking in broken English, Ormenente said very sincerely that the Brazilians had thought that Camellion and his men were—of all things—bandits!

The Death Merchant shook his head sadly from side to side.

"Colonel, since when do bandits use helicopters?"

Ormenente gave a weak smile.

115

"Colonel, we don't have the time to fence back and forth with liars," Camellion said. "Go with whatever God you believe in. . . ."

Rudolf Graff raised the Colt Commander .45 autoloader in his hand and split open a surprised Ormenente's skull by putting a bullet through his forehead.

The three other Brazilians, sitting on the ground, stared in horror and disbelief at their dead leader, who lay on his back, his sightless eyes looking straight up at the cloudless sky.

Convinced they were to be the big man's next victims, they were afraid to look at the colossus glaring down at them, yet they knew that the real boss was the shorter man standing next to the giant, the lean man with the odd blue eyes.

Turning his head, Camellion watched Zero-Zero members stripping the bodies of the four Zero Zeros who had been killed. Two other Zeros were removing the clothes of the dead Dr. Bangold and placing the items in his pockets in a small bag.

The Death Merchant turned his attention to the three Brazilians. For a full minute he stared at them in tight-lipped silence. Finally, he said, "Lies will bring only instant death. Truth will give you life. I want the truth, and I want it now."

Truth is what he got, the three men starting to babble as one.

They confessed they were members of the *Halcon Comando Unidad*, The Falcon Commando Unit, a crack Brazilian outfit that specialized in fighting terrorists. The Falcons had crossed the border into Surinam in search of WINK-EYE-1. The radar and telemetry stations at Belem and at Manaus had detected the satellite going down and fixed its location. The Brazilian National Commission for Space Activities (C.N.A.E.) was very interested in the super space station. The Falcon Commandoes had come to get the tapes from WINK-EYE. What they wouldn't be able to carry, they would photograph.

"There were three men of science with us," one commando said nervously. "They were killed by grenades."

Further questioning of the Brazilians revealed that the Falcons had seen the two helicopters. They had sat back and watched the Americans descend on cable ladders. But they hadn't opened fire for several reasons. First of all, the Vickers machine guns of the helicopters had been firing, raking the close-in area with a rain of slugs, and "we didn't know how much more fire-power you had. We had no way of knowing

116

whether you had napalm. We couldn't risk the helicopters fire-bombing us."

Another Falcon commando explained, "Colonel Ormenente was afraid that if we fired and one of your helicopters escaped, the pilot would radio for reenforcements. We considered the possibility that all of you were here with the permission of the central Surinam government."

"We didn't even know if you were Americanos!" another Brazilian added. "But we had to fire. At all costs we couldn't let anyone discover us. You do understand, Senors?"

"Sure, we know how it is," Camellion said in an easy manner. "A man has a job to do for his country and he does it."

Colonel Lippkor seemed to be experiencing some kind of inner doubt. He looked apprehensively at Camellion, a .45 stainless steel Hardballer automatic held loosely in his right hand.

"We can't take any prisoners with us," he said. "We can't spare the men to watch them."

"As the KGB would say, 'executive action' will have to be taken against them," Camellion replied. He stared down at the three Brazilian commandoes, noticing how their eyes widened in terror at the realization of what he meant. But the three doomed men had little time to reflect on their fate.

The Hardballer automatic in Lippkor's hand roared three times in quick succession, the last man throwing up his arms and yelling "SENOR" a split-second before a .45 bullet struck him in the center of the chest and pitched him back across another dead Falcon.

"I never thought I would be a witness to such brutality, to such cold-blooded killing!"

No one, certainly not the Death Merchant, had expected Dr. Calvin Leitch to express disapproval, at least openly.

"Mercy can be a passion with some men, Doctor," Camellion said. "With others it is good diplomacy or good manners. Then there are those other times when mercy can be stupidity. This is one of those times."

Graff glared contemptuously at Dr. Leitch. "In case you don't know it, we happen to be fighting a war with the Soviet Union, a silent but very real war!"

"I'm aware of the race we're in with the Soviets," said Dr. Leitch, "and this trip has taught me that fighting that war is a lot easier if one has a streak of cruelty."

"Yeah, it comes in damned handy," Graff snapped right back.

Watching Tony Flecher trotting toward them, Camellion said peaceably, "There are two kinds of people in the world, Doctor. The spectators and the performers. We're the performers. We're the people who do what must be done. Good or bad, moral or immoral, doesn't enter into it."

"It's all relative, Doctor," Kenneth Sedgwick intoned. "Look at it this way: Many men are making friends with death for lack of love alone. I can't remember who wrote it, but I've never forgotten it."

Dr. Leitch, a pained expression on his scraggy face, looked for a moment as if he might say, "Aw, shucks." He didn't. He only looked away. He was not a verbal match for these men and he knew it.

The Death Merchant reflected that Sedgwick was a kind of human anachronism. Any S.I.S. agent was. The British Secret Intelligence Service certainly wasn't needed to protect the 'empire!' The sun had set on the British Empire right after World War II. The value of S.I.S. lay in its worldwide contacts and the centuries of experience the British had in the field of intelligence and espionage. *Good judgment comes from experience*, thought Camellion, *and experience comes from bad judgment. The British have been through it all.*

Tony Flecher looked first at Graff, then at Camellion. Flecher was six feet tall, had very high cheek bones and gray-green eyes, and wore his sandy-colored hair rather long.

"The five bodies?" Flecher's voice was as calm as the eye of a hurricane. "We've undressed them and have taken all their ID. We can't bury them in rock. We leave them lying there or what?"

Camellion opened his mouth but Graff was faster, speaking scornfully, with the rapidity of a machine gun. "Damn it. Tony. Do I have to do all the thinking around here? There's only one thing we can do. I know Camellion will agree."

"If you're thinking of using TEA, I'll agree," Camellion said briskly. "Because that's what we're going to use to cremate the bodies." He said to Flecher, who was yawning, "Use two TEA grenades and a timer. Set the timer for five minutes. We'll have more than enough time to get out of the way."

"Uh-huh. I was going to use TEA," Flecher said and turned to go.

"Get on with it," Graff called after him. "We have to get out of here."

Flecher walked a little ways off and crooked a finger at

118

Terry Lemmons. The two men hurried to the aluminum litter and opened two metal cases that resembled ammo boxes; that is, each case was longer than it was wide and deep and had a removable lid, hooked firmly at each end.

Flecher opened one box and took out two red TEA grenades. Lemmons unhooked the lid of the other box and pulled out a roll of detonating cord and two PETN electric blasting caps. Then he took out a roll of friction tape and a Mertex battery timer and checked the batteries by pressing a small button and watching the tiny flashlight bulb light up in his cupped hand.

The Death Merchant and the rest of the men watched as Flecher and Lemmons strode over to the five corpses that had been laid out side by side, the clothes of each dead man piled on top of him.

"Hell, since we're going to reduce them to a handful of ashes, there wasn't much sense in stripping them," grumbled Lemmons. "It was all a waste of time."

They lay flat on a ridge, 400 feet away, watching and waiting. It is not easy to find material which, when ignited, will utterly consume flesh and bone. Ordinary fire will not do the job. Human bodies burned in fires of 2,000 degrees Fahrenheit, even for seven or eight hours, still retain recognizable bones, identifiable as human in origin. It requires temperatures of over 3,000 degrees to melt or volatilize bone.

TEA would do the job. TEA was a part of a U.S. advanced incendiary weapons system. Called Controlled Chemical Fireballs, the weapons system used triethylaluminum, or TEA, which burns at a fantastic 4,350 degrees. When mixed with 1 percent polysobutlene, TEA burns at 4,900 degrees. The TEA carried by Camellion & Co. was mixed with 1.4 percent polysobutlene.

Roy Bolinger looked at his wristwatch—8:24. "Another minute or so to go," he said, to no one in particular.

"Tony, are you sure that you and Terry wired up the TEA grenades okay?" asked Graff. Not for a second did he remove his eyes from the bodies in the distance.

"We could have done the job with our eyes closed." Flecher was annoyed. "It's just too bad we couldn't have shipped the bodies back to the States. It's a hell of a thing to have smoke for a grave!"

The two TEA grenades, underneath the two center bodies, detonated. They didn't explode like ordinary grenades. There

119

was only a short, loud hissing and a bright flash of blue-white fire that expanded, puffing out in all directions, to a 50-foot-diameter fireball, within a few seconds. Slowly the fireball began to shrink. Within half a minute it receded to an area confined to the five corpses on the rock. The bodies could not be seen. There was only the blue-white fire, burning with an eerie luster, a radiance which, while it was bright, did not hurt the eyes.

The Death Merchant stood up. "They'll be ashes within ten minutes. Let's move out. We're going to push and push hard. We're going straight to the satellite."

"All things come to him who waits," Graff joked, winking at Kenneth Sedgwick. "I don't remember who first said it."

Richard Camellion wasn't smiling as he shouldered his Colt M1.

"Sometimes, though, there are only leftovers from the other fellows, who got there first," he said. "I don't intend to have us pick over the Russian leftovers of WINK-EYE."

Chapter Twelve

To the southeast they moved, on a 111.45-degree course, the Death Merchant checking the compass every 10 minutes. With Camellion at the point, they moved in a T-formation, the cross of the T at the rear. An ideal formation, it enabled the force, now reduced to 33 men, to move with firepower on all sides.

The hills were bleak and barren, but there were places that possessed an occult kind of beauty. At one time, as they moved closer to the edge of the foothills and the beginning of the rain forest, they passed through an ancient riverbed that was a soft carpet of sand, shifting and as white as limestone. On either side were tiers of rocks and boulders , . . silent, like two rows of black-cowled monks. Around these mute sentinels were patches of ferns and grass, burning in the merciless sun, except in those places ruled by shadows; here there were areas of yellow-green half-darkness in the sunlight.

Other areas were uglier than blasphemy. Camellion led the force over layered rock that—how long ago?—had been raised by subterranean pressure to create hogback ridges and monstrous batholiths of granite. He led the men around or between rock spires with tops that clawed at the empty blue sky—spires and ancient pinnacles, weirdly sculptured over the ages by wind and rain, by heat and time itself.

The Death Merchant kept a fast, steady pace, as though possessed by demons demanding speed and still more speed. Now he no longer paused to consult his compass, but read it as he moved.

Graff, 30 feet behind Camellion and to his left, called him at one point on the radiotelephone.

"Listen, buddy, how long are we going to keep up this pace?" Out of breath, Graff was almost panting. "The boys are helping the East Indians carry the litter, changing off every five minutes, but they're not supermen. Neither am I. You're not either, for that matter."

121

"Once in a while a guy has to write the ticket for a thousand others," Camellion replied. "And he can do it if he loves his country enough. But you're right. We'll take a ten-minute break."

"Good enough."

Camellion turned and saw Graff signal a halt. Sitting down on a chair-high rock, Richard recalled an old Yiddish expression that Moshe Brosh was fond of using: *One notices a flea on someone else, but one doesn't recognize an elephant on oneself.* By the same reasoning, Camellion realized that he couldn't expect the other men to keep up with him. He had trained for years, using deep breathing exercises. *I doubt if they ever heard of Bhastrika and Kapalabhati breathing. If I told them about such techniques, would they believe me?*

The Death Merchant, noticing Graff coming toward him, pushed back his bush hat, reached into the sportsman's carry-all bag and pulled out a can of English wheatmeal biscuits. He pulled off the lid as Graff walked up to him, took out a biscuit, and held out the can to Graff, who took two biscuits and sat down next to him.

Graff took a huge bite and talked as he chewed. "The danger zone is going to be the area between the last of the hills and the edge of the forest. There's a strip about two hundred feet wide there; it's fairly flat. I know you've thought about it."

Nodding in understanding, Camellion swallowed the mouthful of biscuit. "An enemy could conceal himself at the edge of the jungle and waste us when we crossed. We'll use half a dozen TEA grenades to burn out the edge of the jungle. We'll make a run for it, with all weapons firing. Can you suggest anything better?"

"We both could." Graff bit into the second biscuit. "We could go around the flat strip if we had the time to spare, but we don't." His black eyebrows became one huge questioning V. "What the hell! You're the X.O.[22]! We'll do what ever you say. Those are my orders." A sly note of stubbornness crept into his low voice. "You know as well as I do that if we bypass the strip, we'll lose a couple of hours—a hundred and twenty minutes we can't afford."

Camellion dropped the tin of biscuits into the carryall bag

---

[22] Slang for Executive Officer.

and buckled the two straps, pleased with the big man's verbal strategy.

He's as anxious to get to WINK-EYE as I am, and he's afraid I might change my mind and order our boys to skirt the strip.

"We're going to cross the strip," Camellion reassured Graff. He got to his feet. "And kill anyone who gets in our way. Clear enough?"

The trek to the southeast resumed, the Death Merchant moving at a furious pace, the other 32 men, many of whom were angry, determined to keep up with him.

After another mile passed, Camellion called a halt. While most of the force rested, Camellion and Graff and Bolinger, as well as Colonel Lippkor, Sedgwick and Flecher, consulted a military grid map of southwestern Surinam. This time, Camellion did the calculations. With a compass he first determined the magnetic declination, doing so by computing the difference in degrees between true North and magnetic North. He next placed the compass on the eight-figure reference map and turned the map until the map's magnetic north was aligned with the compass needle. Good. Now the map was oriented. Yes, everything was as it should be. The bearing checked, each and every contour line in verification with the "roamer" in Camellion's hand, in this case, a matchbook cover.

"Not bad," said Bolinger, lighting an L&M. "We're damned close to WINK-EYE. At most, we're two and half miles from the satellite."

"Or a mile to a mile-and-a-half from where Doctor Leitch can begin using the Alphaometer," Colonel Lippkor said. He rubbed a fleshy cheek and stared again at the map, at the spot marked by a triangle around a dot and with the words RDF RAD FIX.

"We could be getting excited over an empty dream," Tony Flecher said. "If the Russian plane landed at Havana on time, the Russians could be at WINK-EYE right now. They could have the tapes and be getting ready to be sky-hooked out."

"Thank you for your vote of confidence," Sedgwick said cheerfully.

"It's what we're all thinking," Flecher said defensively, "and we can't brush aside facts." He looked around at the sweaty faces, as if wondering who might agree or disagree with him.

Richard Camellion said, "There are some deductions we can make. If the Russians have beat us to the satellite, the strip up yonder is the only place they can use to be lifted out, although they could use any large hilltop."

"Yeah, and there's something else," interjected Bolinger. "If the Charger flew in from Cuba, it had to have arrived quite a while ago or we would have heard it."

"All right. If the Russians are still around, then we still have a chance." Colonel Lippkor sounded hopeful. "The Ilyushins couldn't have lifted the Russians out yet. If the Starlifts fly in now, from any direction, we're so close we'd hear their engines."

"The unknowable can be an intolerable bore," grumbled Sedgwick, tugging at one ear. "I think it's even worse than that miserable muck that passes for coffee in Georgetown."

The Death Merchant put the compass in his pocket, folded the map, and stood up. "Speculation is useless. All we can say is 'maybe' and a lot of 'ifs.' We'll know when we get there."

He nodded to Graff and Flecher. Tony Flecher raised both arms above his head and signaled the rest of the Zero-Zero force. The march resumed.

By degrees the hills became fewer in number, the land more level. Little by little, the area became less impotent, the ground less rocky. Here and there were tall lacca ferns. Small trees began to appear, such as *quebracho*, a hard redwood. Instead of dull gray rock, there were patches of red soil and coarse grasses.

Because Camellion and his people were so close to their destination, he did not cross any hills. It would be a capital error to risk being seen by any spotters perched in trees at the edge of the rain forest. Camellion went between the hills, taking a winding course which would not permit anyone up ahead to see them.

They came to a narrow, long ravine in which grew ferns and evergreen birch and pine trees. In places, the route was impassable, the way littered with dead limbs and other rubble of nature. All this and more had been indicated on the map, so Camellion and the others knew they were on the correct heading, knew that beyond the ravine would be rocks large enough to use for cover and trees scattered around the region.

Several hundred feet onward, up a slight rise, was a long but narrow pass. A danger point! Here an ambush was possible, with little defense against it. The Death Merchant weighed the odds. The only other way out was 4.9 miles to the south. *We don't have that much time.*

Camellion raised his arms above his head and gave a warning X-signal by crossing his wrists. He pulled the Colt assault rifle from his shoulder, pushed off the safety and stared toward the pass, going into a trot as he drew closer to the entrance.

The cut was not an object of tropical beauty. Scored clean of vegetation, the pass looked as though it had been gouged from the earth—an ugly gap that had never grown together and healed. Here and there the ugly purple granite bluffs had sheared off, leaving the 30-foot-wide path, 60 feet below, strewn with small boulders and broken rock.

Panting, the men ran through the pass, fearfully watching the tops of the cliffs. No one shot at them. No one dropped grenades. Nevertheless, every man, Camellion included, was relieved when the opposite end was reached and the force merged onto a large, gently sloping region covered with patches of *glum* grass and marred by low, rocky mounds, and boulders of various sizes and shapes. In places there were tiny islands of cacti, scanty clumps of eucalyptus, and an occasional pine. It was a landscape of despair. The harsh climate of Surinam—muggy heat, chilly nights and crashing rainfall during the rainy season—the unfriendly earth and the *soroche*, the mountain sickness that clamps an iron band around your head and squeezes your heart into your mouth, all explain why the Indians are so miserable, so sad that even their dance and carnival music resembles laments punctuated by monotonous rhythm of three-toned flutes.

Richard Camellion crept behind a long, tonguelike slab of granite with a red color that revealed the presence of minerals, and took out a pair of Bushnell 10 × 40-millimeter binoculars. The rest of the men hurried out of the pass and wearily squatted behind the boulder. Lek Landa, a roly poly East Indian, screeched at Kenneth Sedgwick, "More pay we want for this kind of work. We carry boxes like mules and be made to run like ostriches. More money we want."

The S.I.S. agent didn't argue. "Double pay when we get

125

back," Sedgwick agreed. "But I don't want you chaps annoying me before we return. Got it?"

"Okay with double pay," responded Landa in his Guyanese English, his almond eyes lighting up. "Remind you when we get back."

If we get back! thought the Death Merchant, who was crawling up the side of the rock slab. Bolinger was on one side of him, Graff on the other. Lying flat, the three studied the forward region through powerful binoculars. The land was unfriendly, yet the air was sweet with the aroma of resinous shrubs.

There it was! A thousand feet to the fore was the strip . . . deadly if any enemy—Russian or Anacunna—were watching. To the north, the strip curved out of the jungle for several thousand feet before turning and vanishing in a mass of low boulders far to the south.

"Crap. It's an old riverbed," said Graff. "In some places it's two hundred feet wide. It sure must have been some river a couple of thousand years ago."

Bolinger's indrawn breath was wavy with pent-up tension. "We can get up there without too much effort. There's enough rocks and grass to give us all the cover we need. That leaves only the problem of the riverbed and the jungle."

"Problem, hell!" said Graff. "The jungle is just beyond the riverbed. We can burn the whole area with TEA without any trouble."

Bolinger lowered the binoculars and, wondering why Richard Camellion hadn't spoken, turned and looked curiously at him. Bolinger thought for a moment. He opened his mouth, paused, then closed his mouth, sensing that Camellion did not want to be disturbed.

Staring at the rain forest, Richard had the impression of a monstrous green grave, the highest tier of trees serving as the mound. Unlike temperate woods, with their clearly defined layers of vegetation—shrubs, ground herbs and trees—the rain forest presents a complex and bewildering facade. Here forests mount on forests like clouds on clouds. High above the lowly ground layers of herbs and shrubs, the crowns of the trees themselves form three or more superposed stories, creating shade above shade. Amid the profusion of leaves and climbing plants, the puny human being on the ground is a prisoner, for the true rain forest is indeed a many-storied mansion whose architecture can only with difficulty be discerned. Though ever present, the three strata are never clearly defined, for the forest is continually growing. As a result, one sees only shades and heights of tangled greenery.

Just beyond the far side of the riverbed, at the edge of the forest, were small flowering plants, matted and tangled vines, and the dangling roots of air plants. Further back the trees began, some of them truly sight-stunning. A strangler fig encased a host tree in a shiny red-brown sheath that had grown from small dangling roots when the young fig was an air plant. Close by stood the stilt-roots of dozens of palms dressed in vines and orange flowers.

It's not been killed by civilizations and buried under concrete; in a fire-fight that green hell would bury all of us. Hmmmmmm. . . .

He thought of what he had seen on the map. A fifth of a mile inward, a fifth of a mile past the edge, was another open area, another grassland. Beyond this space the map revealed solid rain forest. *What a mess! The DD/P is expecting miracles.*

The Death Merchant eased himself down from the top of the rock. He was putting the binoculars into their case as Graff and Bolinger came down on either side of him.

"What about Dr. Leitch?" Graff gave him a level stare. "We can forget the tapes if anything happens to him. Even if we find the damned space station!"

Camellion readily supplied the answer. "We'll leave Dr. Leitch and the four East Indians right here. The rest of us will go ahead. When we're sure there isn't any danger, we'll radio them to come ahead."

"Good idea," agreed Graff. He scratched his pillarlike neck. "We'll leave two Zero-Zeros with them. The East Indians did their part when the Brazilians attacked. They kept cool and didn't waste ammo. But four aren't enough. Two Zeros are worth a dozen of them."

Bolinger tossed a hard stare at Graff. "Leave two of them here!" he objected. "I don't consider it wise to cut down on our fire-power."

William Henderson, listening to the conversation, spoke up.

"Gentlemen, I should like to point out that we have triple, if not quadruple, the fire-power you think we have!" The strapping CIA weapons expert flipped sweat from his heavy mustache with a forefinger.

"Let me show you what I have in the case. My 'little' friend' might influence your attack plans. I think it will."

In the center of a sea of curious eyes, Henderson opened

127

the case and carefully took out a weapon which looked like nothing so much as a Buck Rogers death-ray. About 30 inches long, the weapon was made of stainless steel. Half of the body, the forepart, resembled a deeply grooved cylinder. The other half of the gun was semi-round. On one side was a small lever. On the same side was a slot above a 4-inch long feed bed. In the rear, on the underneath side, were a handle, a trigger and a trigger guard in front of the curved plastic. There was a forehandle attached to the underneath side of the grooved cylinder. A foot-long barrel protruded from the front end of the cylinder.

"Yeah, it's a machine gun," Camellion said. "How did the CIA steal it from 'Carbine' Williams[23]?"

For a moment alarm flashed over Henderson's deeply tanned face. Without answering Camellion, he explained in his quiet manner that the machine gun was called the X1-B and that there were only two in existence.

"The one I have here and the one at the Center," Henderson said. His gray eyes darted to the Death Merchant. "In a sense you're right, Camellion. The X1-B was patterned after Williams Model Seven machine gun. But this one is an improvement."

Roy Bolinger asked, "Why the designation X1-B? The 'X1' is self-evident. But why the 'B?' "

" 'B' for *Bombus*. *Bombus* is Latin for 'buzz.' The X1-B makes only a buzzing noise because it works too rapidly to produce the *bang* of less advanced guns."

"I say, that's somewhat difficult to conceive!" Sedgwick stared at the gun and rubbed his chin thoughtfully.

Everyone but the Death Merchant looked amazed. Graff stuck out his mountain of a chin and asked, "What about the Williams Model Seven deal? I heard that the Israelis were interested in his chatterbox."

"The Model Seven fires two-thousand rounds a minute, or thirty-three bullets a second, using either .20 or .30 caliber

---

[23] David M. "Carbine" Williams invented the M1 carbine, used by U.S. soldiers in World War II, while serving a prison term for shooting a U.S. Treasury agent who discovered his whiskey still. Williams designed the Model Seven machine gun; when he died in North Carolina in 1975, he left the working parts of the weapon to his best friend, L.E. Lisk. Lisk is the owner of the Model Seven machine gun.

rounds," Henderson said. A slight smile twisted his lips and he patted the barrel of the X1-B. "Our baby is better. It fires conventional .22 longs at the rate of fourty-two rounds a second. That's two-thousand-five-hundred-and-twenty rounds per minute—either automatically or semi-automatically. Not only that, the X1-B's barrel won't burn out from heat. It weighs sixteen pounds, four pounds more than the Model Seven. Have a look at it."

Henderson handed the X1-B to the Death Merchant, who took the weapon, then glanced in irritation around at Dr. Leitch, who was peering over his right shoulder. Camellion inspected the weapon briefly and handed it to Graff to keep him and Bolinger and Lippkor and the others from crowding around.

"Has it been tested?" Richard asked. "And what's the function of the threaded hole in the underneath side. It's for a tripod, right?"

Richard instantly gleaned that he had touched a sensitive nerve in Henderson, whom he trusted as much as he would a tiger shark.

"The tripod is in the ammunition case, with five thousand rounds of ammo," Henderson said slowly, as if weighing something in his mind.

Camellion inclined his head, his eyes glued to Henderson, who proceeded, "However, there is a flaw to the X1-B."

Bolinger made an I-told-you-so noise in his throat and said, "Now comes the bad news!"

"It's not what you're thinking!" Henderson's voice was brittle and hostile. "The machine gun works perfectly. The trouble is that it requires three men to fire it. One man to hold it and work the trigger, another to feed the belt into the breech, and a third to keep the empty belt tight as it comes out on the opposite side. Otherwise the X1-B will jam."

Rudy Graff guffawed outright. "Some weapons expert you are!" he said bluntly to Henderson. " 'Breech' is an imprecise term. Almost anybody knows that!"

Colonel Lippkor jumped in with both feet. "Henderson, you're suggesting that we take the X1-B with us when we advance? I'm all for it."

Henderson stared coldly at Graff. "Very well. The firing mechanism then, if that suits you better." His voice was as frigid as his gray eyes. All during the trip, as short as it had been, it had been evident that a natural antipathy existed between Graff and Henderson.

derson swung to Bolinger, but he didn't get the oppor-
to speak.

The Death Merchant looked at Graff. "Two of the Zero-
Zero boys can carry the box of ammunition to the riverbed.
There's plenty of cover out front and—"

Richard paused and, listening, cocked his head to one side.
The rest of the men then heard the faint sound coming from
the fiery sky to the north.

"I feel that I'm about to open a box of Crackerjacks that's
without a surprise inside!" whispered Herschel O'Connor.

"Shut up!" Graff snapped, staring at O'Connor unwink-
ingly. He took out his binoculars and, with the others, began
searching the north sky.

The noise grew louder, a sound that was very familiar: the
roar of a supersonic aircraft descending to lower altitude.

Chapter Thirteen

The most unhappy citizen of the Soviet Union in the entire Western Hemisphere was Colonel Valarian Agyants, who now was weighed down with grenades, weapons, and other equipment of death and survival. A padded crash helmet, the green visor turned up, was on his head, and a parachute pack on his back. With the webbed straps of the parachute pack around his chest and shoulders and thighs, the KGB colonel felt imprisoned, restrained, as though wrapped in a spider's web.

Keeping his expression emotionless, Agyants stood only 10 feet from the rear hatch to his left. In a very short while, the hatch door would be swung open, rip-lines would be attached to the main stretch cable, and Agyants would jump from the Soviet Concorde with Major Lyalin and the 90 men of the Sixth Direction.

Agyants reflected that the supersonic airliner was the best airplane in *Aeroflot*[24], even if its design had been initiated by the launching of the Concorde by Britain and France in 1963. The Soviet Concorde could carry 140 passengers and be operated by a crew of three—two pilots and an engineer. Separated from the flight deck by a narrow corridor, the cabin could be divided into three; however, movable bulkheads made other arrangements possible. The forward cabin usually seated 11 at first-class standards. The center and rear compartments, separated by galleys, toilets, and cloakrooms, seated 30 and 99 passengers at tourist-class standards. The 90 men of the 13th Direction were in the rear compartment, which now included the center compartment, the bulkhead

---

[24] *Aeroflot,* the Soviet airline, is a vast undertaking that cannot be compared with any Western airline. It is really the whole of "civil" aviation in the USSR. Its name is a hybrid contraction from *Grazhdanskaya Vozduzhnaya Flot,* the Civil Air Fleet.

between the two having been removed. Most of the seats usually five abreast, had been removed before the airliner ha left the USSR.

Agyants felt as if he were going to his execution. The would jump at 400 feet. This was the reason why each ma wore only one "short-range" chute. If the stretch cable didn open the chute automatically, there would not be time to pu the ripcord of a second chute. More precisely, by then th victim would be too close to the ground for a second chute t open.

The voice of one pilot came over the loudspeaker: "Fiv minutes."

Five minutes! Like a sentence of death to Agyants, wh remembered some advice an old KGB man had given hir years ago: *Never speak the truth to one's superiors. Look fo graft and useful connections instead. Have a good 'sense o smell.' Don't make the same mistake as one officer, wh never got beyond lieutenant in 20 years of service. Where h should have licked, he barked, and where he should hav barked, he licked. A very dangerous mistake to make. I you're given an important job and fail at it, be prepared fo the worst. The higher-ups will get you. Sooner or later, you' be 'unmasked as an anti-Soviet.' The moment you fail, "Ko" dossier—with the title of demagogue—will be starte on you. Remember my words!*

Valarian Agyants remembered only too well! He wa jerked back to the present by Major Lyalin's shaking him b the shoulder and saying in a commanding voice, "Colone didn't you hear my order? Snap your line to the cable."

Jerked from his melancholic reverie, Agyants said weakly "I was thinking of other matters, Major." He snapped the en of his chute line to the cable, giving the snap-link a tug t make sure it was secure.

"Keep your mind on the business at hand. We'll b jumping in five minutes," Major Viktor Lyalin said, but n unkindly. "Remember what I told you. When you hit, l your legs serve as a spring. Double them. Let yourself rela and roll with the motion."

"Yes, I understand," Agyants said. Trying to keep himse inwardly calm, he thought of the jump arrangements an looked forward at the line of men, in the front of the plan stretching into the first-class section. Half the force woul jump from the outside hatch that opened to the first cla compartment, the other half from the rear door of the touri section. He heard Major Lyalin speak into a pocket-size walkie-talkie and give orders to Captain Petyr Kuznessov and Captain Felix Mikolatah, the two officers in charge of the two jump groups.

"Open the hatches," ordered Lyalin

Chapter Fourteen

For several minutes Camellion and his group, staring at the slim and sleek Russian plane flying in low from the north, felt an intense elation, a happiness that must have been a first cousin to orgasm.

"We have them!" Graff's heavy voice quivered with excitement. "Once they're on that riverbed, we can fry them like bacon!"

"God! That pilot is fantastic!" yelled Bolinger, wanting to make himself heard above the noise of the Soviet airliner. "He's good. But the risk he's taking! One mistake and they'll all go up in smoke!"

"They're going up in smoke, anyhow!" sneered Colonel Lippkor.

The blue and white airliner was no more than several miles away. Second by second, its altitude dropped, the roaring of its turbofans slowly increasing from reheat boost.

But the pilot did not fly the aircraft toward the riverbed. Instead, he dropped to 400 feet or so, and the airliner roared straight south over the rain forest, its distance from the Zero-Zero force slightly over 2,000 feet to the east.

"They're not going to drop on the strip!" Bolinger's voice was small. He sounded like a child who had not found a filled stocking over the fireplace on Christmas morning.

Shaken with momentary defeat, Graff exclaimed, "I knew it was too damned good to be true. Those clever bastards have gone inward. They're going to jump over the grassland just inside. Come on!"

Feeling a firm hand on his shoulder, Graff turned and glared at the Death Merchant. "What's wrong?" he demanded.

"We must wait," Camellion said. "A man floating down on a chute will have a panoramic view of this entire area. We're staying put behind this hunk of rock until the last Russian has jumped. That's an order."

Graff considered for a moment, staring straight at Camellion. The mammoth of a man flexed his biceps and pushed out his Charles Atlas chest, both of which belonged on a baking soda can. Then he nodded vigorously. "You're right. I'm letting my enthusiasm get the better of me. It will be close, but they'll have to regroup and get organized."

You mean 'the better of me,' thought Camellion, glancing upward at the low sky over the rain forest. "Here come our friends from the Workers' Paradise!"

The Soviet Concorde roared over the rain forest, the sound of its turbofans, in re-heat boost, ear-shattering. Because the aircraft was flying south, the Death Merchant and his people couldn't see the Russian fighters stepping out of the front and rear hatches on the port side. They could see the parachutes opening, one after another, blooming like a species of flower bursting into full glory. Within a few minutes the sky was filled with slanting horizontal lines of huge mushrooms, a stem of a tiny figure dangling at the ends of the cords.

"I've already counted forty-two," said Colonel Lippkor unsteadily.

No one replied. The Death Merchant watched dispassionately as the Soviet Concorde roared up in a climb.

"I counted forty-six," Roy Bolinger said nervously.

"There'll be more. The plane is going to make a second run," Camellion said, biting off each word in bitterness.

As if responding to the Death Merchant's forbidding prediction, the pilot of the Soviet airliner climbed to 1,500 feet, then banked widely to the east. Within five minutes the aircraft was flying north and only a speck in the sky. Meanwhile, the last of the parachutes vanished into the rain forest.

When it seemed that the Soviet Concorde was about to become a memory in the hell-hot sky, the pilot banked to the west. The blue and white arrow turned and roared in once more from the north, losing altitude, its icepick nose pointing like a needle toward the rain forest.

Wayne Loos muttered, "I guess this beats watching paint dry."

"Or listening to your beard grow," added Arvel Frager.

"You two motor-mouths zipper it," Tony Flecher growled.

Again the Soviet *Concordskii* skimmed low over the tangled mass of green below and men tumbled out of the two hatches on the port side. As before, the sky was suddenly filled with white parachutes floating gently to the ground, the

Russians tugging at the lines to correct guidance and t'
prevent coming down on top of the green canopy.

The Death Merchant turned and called out, "Get set—an'
leave the two Sonder shortwave sets here." He stabbed a fin'
ger at Gordon Willet and Jackson Nipier. "You two stay wit'
Dr. Leitch and the East Indians. If none of us come back"—
Camellion shrugged—"you're on your own."

"But don't come ahead until you hear from us," Rudo'
Graff ordered.

The Tupolev-144 again climbed into the sky, the pilot be'
ginning the bank to the east at 1,500 feet; this time he con'
tinued to climb, taking the plane to the east. By the time th'
sound of the engines were fading, the Death Merchant an'
25 men were moving out onto the 1,000-foot region that sep'
arated them from the riverbed and the last Russian chute tha'
had disappeared into the green hell ahead.

In groups of two and three and four and more, Camellio'
and the small force moved in a twisting, crooked route, a'
times almost scrambling on their knees to the nearest rocks o'
clump of lacca ferns. There were times when they droppe'
and slithered on their bellies across the sun-baked groun'
This snakelike movement was particularly irritating to Wayn'
Loos and Arvel Frager, both men wishing they had kept thei'
mouths shut. It was they that Flecher had assigned to lug th'
ammo crate of the X1-*Bombus* machine gun. Tugging at th'
long crate, at times pushing it, the two men cursed with in'
tense discomfort as they were forced crawl with their freigh'
of ammunition.

Out in front, Richard Camellion estimated that the odd'
so far, were in his favor. The Russians weren't apt to hea'
west, to the strip of riverbed, after they regrouped. They to'
would be on a tight schedule. Their only goal would be t'
reach WINK-EYE, get the tapes, then get their Slavic selve'
back to Castro's Cuba.

Sodden and sticky with sweat, their clothes full of thorn'
and burrs, the Double-Zero men ran across an area wher'
coarse fragments of rock had, over the years, been laid dow'
by water and planed by winds, leaving a "pavement" neat'
fitted, as though by man.

Once they had crossed this *hammada*, Camellion and th'
entire group panted to reach an angular conglomerate of ada'
mantine shore boulders, streaked with blue veins of vermicu'
lite. Not much protection. The largest boulders were only fiv'
feet high. But there wasn't anything else close to the riverbed'

From this vantage point, the nearest side of the riverbed as 10 feet away, a long, winding ribbon of white sand shimmering in the sun. Pasted against the rock, Camellion looked cross the riverbed. It was 100 feet wide at this section, the opposite side, or "bank," sloping upward for a dozen feet into short, thick *glum* grass and some scattered and scraggly eucalyptus. A little ways inward was the beginning of the rain forest . . . vines and ferns and saplings that gradually merged with taller secondary trees, until finally there was only a wall of solid green-black foliage—or so it appeared.

"DAMN!," Camellion heard Graff say in resignation. "Don't ask me if there's a better way to get in there! There isn't and we both know it."

The ends of the big man's straight, black eyebrows dropped more, and his owl-shaped eyes jumped to four of the Double-zero men who were loading their CGL-4 launchers with TEA grenades from one of the crates.

Graff turned back to the Death Merchant, his manner quick, but urgent and impatient. He reminded Camellion of God's original angry man.

"Any special ideas on how to go in after the TEA starts to chew? And what about Henderson? I'm thinking that Loos and Frager can't make like winners of the hundred-yard dash, not with that crate of ammo between them!" He stared fiercingly at Camellion, who was so unnervingly calm that he might have been going to Sunday dinner with the Waltons!

Camellion said, "We'll lob a dozen TEA grenades into the forest. Then all we can do is go in, thirteen of us on one side of the fire storm, thirteen on the other side. Henderson and Loos and Frager will go with our group. All we can do is go fast as we can—and do a lot of hoping." Richard paused, grinned, added, "You're an 'almost' minister. You might try praying."

Graff snorted in disgust. "Have you ever heard of a prayer stopping a bullet?" His eyes poked at the Death Merchant. "We'll take two of the guys with launchers. There's no use putting all four in one group."

"Yeah, what's going down is too heavy. We'll need two of the launchers ourselves." Richard scooted around on his knees and looked down the crooked line of dirty-faced men, his icy stare finally coming to rest on the square-jawed Olin Maxton and three other Zeros with grenade launchers attached to their assault rifles. The four men were only eight feet away.

"Now?" asked Maxton hopefully.

"Keep a brake on your finger; I'll tell you when." Camel'
lion beckoned with his finger at Tony Flecher, who was a
the end of the line. Flecher started crawling toward him
Sedgwick and Colonel Lippkor, anxious to know what wa
going on, followed Flecher. Roy Bolinger crawled afte
Lippkor and Sedgwick.

Camellion said to Flecher, "When it's time for us to go in
take twelve men and go to the left, to the north. Graff and
will take eleven and go to the right. We're going to includ
two of the launcher boys and Henderson and Loos Frager in
our group."

"A straight-in plunge, then a link-up?" asked Flecher.

"What about us?" The dissatisfied expression on Colon
Lippkor's freckled face made it all too clear that he was n
enthused over Camellion's deciding in which direction h
would go—and with whom.

"Straight in," Camellion answered Flecher. "Kill any Ru
sian you see. Either Graff or I will contact you by RT for th
link-up." He glanced at Lippkor, who, with Bolinger an
Sedgwick, was watching him with narrowed eyes.

The Death Merchant turned back to Flecher. "Tak
Lippkor and Sedgwick with your group. I don't want the CI
and N.S.A. in the same group." He turned his head towar
Oliver Lippkor and the two other men. "With any luck, yo
both might live. We're walking into the worst kind of fir
fight. Some of us are going to be fatally burnt."

Lippkor, Sedgwick, and Bolinger stared tight-lipped at th
Death Merchant, all three realizing that he was not bein
pretentious; he had only spoken the cold-blooded truth.

"Flecher, have you got it all down?" asked Camellion.

Rudolf Graff said, "Tony, don't let you and your boys g
captured. I don't have to tell you about Directive-Four-Two.

"Check," Flecher said. He nodded to Oliver-Lippkor an
Kenneth Sedgwick. "Let's go to the other end and get orga
ized." Then he said to the Death Merchant. "I'll send Hei
derson and Loos and Frager up this way."

Flecher moved off with Lippkor and Sedgwick. Roy Boli
ger was as grim as death as he gazed steadily at Camellic
and whispered, "Directive-Four-Two? I wasn't aware of th
order from the Center."

"Neither was I, until now," Camellion said acidly, his ga
pouncing on Graff, who blinked rapidly in slight confusion.

138

"The DD/P didn't tell you?" asked the big man, pushing his head forward. "He should have!"

"He didn't!" Bolinger was firm. "I suspect it has something to do with the Oval Office."

The Death Merchant only smiled, then called over to the four men with grenade launchers. "Each of you put three TEA babies into that wall of green. Space them out so that we have a wall of fire four hundred feet long. Do it."

They did it. They sent grenade after grenade across the riverbed into the rain forest, each silent "explosion" resembling a colossal pale blue flower bursting into full bloom. The difference was that these petals were triethylaluminum and 1.4 percent polysobutlene, burning at more than 4,900 degrees. At such a fantastic temperature green leaves, vines, bark, and even wood-pulp ignite with the sudden explosiveness of tissue paper soaked in gasoline.

The edge of the forest became a roaring inferno, an incredible barrier of fire more than 100 feet high, its length increasing at each end with the bursting of successive TEA grenades. Olin Maxton and Terry Lemmons lobbed TEA to the right, Virgil Mild and Jose Meridias to the left.

"If hell exists, it must be something like that!" Bolinger mumbled, an awed quality to his voice.

"Don't forget the sulphur and brimstone!" mocked Graff.

There was a constant crackling and popping and other tell-tale sounds of Earth's materials being consumed by the man-made conflagration that could not be extinguished, that would have to burn itself out. Enormous tongues of flame and rolling clouds of white-gray-black smoke tumbled upward to heaven, some of the smoke whipping across the river bed, and with it came the odor of burning leaves and vines, of wood and vegetation and resins being boiled into nothingness. At times Camellion and his men caught the distinct stink of burning flesh. The cremation of Russian—or of animals trapped in the flames?

A very efficient Jose Meridias shot off the twelfth TEA grenade and it burst into a hideously beautiful ball of burning death a few moments later, adding the last length of fire to the wall of flames.

"Feel that heat?" Graff sounded pleased. He got to one knee and prepared to move out from behind the boulder, a trace of fear on his face. The odds were against them; ahead were almost 100 Russians. *And we're only 26! We're outnumbered more than three to one!*

139

The Death Merchant called out, "Mild! Maxton! You're going with me. Make sure you have TEA in your launchers. But before we make the run, check your trigger-locks."

Richard searched the faces of the men around him, the members of his and Graff's group. Roy Bolinger, a cigarette dangling from one side of his mouth, might have been an overly-large midget getting ready to play soldier. He held an assault rifle tightly in his hands, rivers of sweat running down his cheeks. He stared back at Camellion, his eyes saying, *I'm ready. I'll do my best.*

Bill Henderson's face was devoid of expression: *He's about as cheerful as a sponge!* The CIA weapons expert lounged on his left side, the X1-*Bombus* case in front of him. Camellion was positive that this kind of quick-kill action was not new to Henderson. The man was too calm, too composed to be a newcomer to extreme violence. And the way he carried his equipment marked him as a pro with experience. He had his sniper's Rifle and an M1 strapped in an X to his back.

To the left of Henderson, Wayne Loos and Arvel Frager waited mournfully with the X1-B's crate of .22 ammo, Loos puffing on a long, black cigar. Close by, five other Zero-Zeros were hunkered down, resting on their heels, their demeanor a mixture of quiet fear and impatience to get the job done and over with.

The Death Merchant's finger stabbed out. "The five of you will be with me and Graff. In a line. The seven of us will serve as the main fire section."

"Fire only short bursts and count your rounds," Graff broke in. "By the time we cross the strip and skirt around the fire, we'll have covered almost four hundred feet. There won't be any time to reload."

Camellion faced Roy Bolinger. "Roy, I want you with Henderson, Loos, and Frager." To Virgil Mild and Olin Maxton he said, "The two of you stay behind us and form the blunt protection point for Henderson and the three with him."

"We won't be able to fire with the seven of you in front of us," Amandus Warehime said, scratching the end of his nose.

"That's right," agreed Camellion. "When you birds have to fire, then we'll be dead. Or we'll be down and wounded or down and dying. Anyhow, we'll be out of the action."

"Do we stop for a man if he gets smacked and falls?" inquired Bruce Colminsky. From force of habit, he snubbed out his cigarette on the ground.

140

"We do not," responded Camellion. "If one of us stop [a]
bullet—tough. I don't like it that way any more than you do.
But that's how it's got to be. If you want to stay alive, get to
the forest as quickly as possible. Run like hell! Flap your
arms! Pray! Do anything. But get there."

Camellion turned to the right, looked down the line of
boulders and mixed rubblerock and found Tony Flecher and
his group of 12. If Flecher was afraid, he didn't show it as he
met Camellion's gaze squarely. *Another war-lover!* thought
Camellion, *like Graff. Or worse, like me!*

The Death Merchant nodded. Very suddenly he thought
of "The Charge of the Light Brigade"—and wanted to laugh.

Thirteen to the left!
Thirteen to the right!

Across the riverbed charged the 26 men, racing at an angle
that would take each group well past either end of the monstrous wall of fire. Their feet dug into the soft white sand of
the river bed, the smoke and the stink of burning jungle slap-
ping at them.

Yet not one shot was fired at them from the rain forest!

They crossed the empty riverbed, scrambled up the short,
uneven bank, and charged toward the steaming rain forest.
Gasping for breath, each man at this point was an island
unto himself, a soul alone in his own private universe of uncertainty, free to indulge in his own version of reality. Man is
born alone and he dies alone. Between these two extremes, he
hopes and dreams and makes a fool of himself.

The two groups reached the rain forest. One moment there
was sunshine and smoke, the next, only deep gloom and
smoke, the sunlight obscured by chaotic masses of verdure,
vast dimensions of tangled greenness which made many of
the men feel that they had invaded the very special world of
some very special primitive god.

Camellion and Graff led the men of their group 300 feet
inward, as it was vitally necessary that they penetrate deep
enough to have a solid background of green against their
backs. Outside in the sunlight, silhouetted against the outside
light, they would have made perfect targets.

Snuggled like curled-up fetuses in the moist leaves and
rank vegetation of the undergrowth, Camellion and his men
no longer had any doubts about the enemy. If the Soviets had
not previously known of their presence, the pig farmers now

141

o well aware that they were under direct attack; guess the aggressors were Americans.

afe for the moment," Graff whispered. There was ind of comfort to be found in lying on the forest floor; yet it was a flase security, for there were enemies other than the Russians. There were those crawling things. Poisonous insects. Poisonous spiders. Poisonous scorpions. And venomous snakes, such as the South American rattler and the *Vibora de la cruz*, an extremely dangerous viper. Prepared, each man carried a first-aid kit with hypodermics of antivenom serum ready for instant use.

Behind, to the west, the fire was dying down, the crackling less intense. The air was smoky but cool and filled with strange odors, a mixture of destruction and sweet, growing flowers . . . of life versus death.

From their positions of concealment, Camellion and the men with him surveyed the forest, staring ahead, determined to beat the force of the Soviet Union. Between the straight, unbranching boles of high trees were dark, roomy corridors, their floors thick with leaves. There were numerous places where the twilight was pierced by slanting shafts of sunlight that had succeeded in stabbing through the leafy fabric of the sheltering canopy. The sunlight was pale and diffused, due to the drifting smoke.

Graff, who had just finished talking to Tony Flecher, shoved the RT into the leather case on his belt and whispered to Camellion, who lay to the right of him. "They have to be less than 800 feet in front of us, unless they've moved to the other side of the grassland. What's your opinion?"

"The same as yours," said Camellion. "Let's wait a little and see what happens—if anything."

Hearing the rustling of leaves slightly behind him and to his right, Richard turned and saw that Bill Henderson had opened the case of .22 cartridges and was inserting a belt of shells into the X1-B machine gun.

"All we need now is an organ playing 'Nearer My God To Thee,'" mumbled Roy Bolinger, who was to the left of the Death Merchant.

An ironic smile slid across Camellion's mouth. "We may be closer to God than you think! Or maybe closer to pandemonium!"

Bolinger stole a quick sideways glance at Camellion. 'For my money, this is pandemonium."

Camellion prefaced his reply with a low laugh. "I was thinking of Milton's *Pandemonium*—the capital of hell."

As hard as he tried, the Death Merchant could not see the grassland far to the east, in front of him. The forest was too thick.

Graff stared at the mess of jungle ahead. "You heard Flecher," he said. "He's going to send out three scouts—point and flanks. The Russians will no doubt do the same."

"Not necessarily," said Camellion. "The pig boys might try to wait us out. It all depends on the nerve and the experience and the patience of the Soviet commander—the KGB wouldn't send anything less than a pro. The Russians are in the same position we're in. They're wondering where *we* are!"

"I think we should go out and find the Ivans!" Graff said, fully expecting Camellion to resist his proposal. To his surprise, the Death Merchant agreed.

"I'll bore a couple of hundred feet to the right, straight south, then turn and take a due-east route," Camellion proposed. "You remain here with the men and act as a relay station between me and our group and Flecher. The moment I spot a moron from Mother Russia, I'll give you a buzz on the RT."

Bolinger suggested, "Why doesn't one of us move straight out? Two scouts are better than one!"

"No. I don't want anyone in front of Henderson's weird machine gun," Camellion explained. "If we're going to win, we're going to have to whack out a lot of Russkies in one helluva big hurry."

"There's the TEA," offered Bolinger. "But I suppose it's too dangerous in here. The flames could jump back to us."

"It would be like sitting on a limb while sawing it off!" Camellion said; then, as an after-thought, "At least we can't use TEA in this immediate vicinity."

Graff scratched the top of his head through his short hair. "I'll pass the word to the rest of the men about what you're going to do."

The Colt M1 assault rifle behind his right shoulder, the Death Merchant traveled to the south, creeping from tree to tree, at times dashing across tiny open places. Under a different set of circumstances the rain forest, totally unspoiled by man, would have been beautiful in a primitive way. There were balconies and mezzanines between the various stories of the trees, trees of many kinds—broad-leafed evergreens, oaks

143

gwoods, poplar, willow, cedar and oak, jacaranda, id ombu. Draped over limbs and curled around trunks was bougainvillea, the vines alive with red and purple leaves. Everywhere, close to the ground, as well as in the upper heights, were orchids. A thought came to Camellion: *It's ironic that "orchid" is derived from the Greek word for testicle, because of the shape of the root tubers in some species of the genus Orchis. But such information from the File of Useless Facts won't do me any good here!*

Estimating that he had covered almost 300 feet, Richard turned and set a new course straight east. He pushed forward with caution, his eyes and ears alerted to any movement or sound ahead.

He didn't expect what he got! He was congratulating himself on having advanced 200 feet when the grenades started exploding. One right after the other! Ten explosions in all—150 feet to his left, to the north!

The tenth explosion was followed by the snarling of automatic weapons—Colt M1s, and Russian AKM assault rifles and Degtyarev submachine guns!

Camellion dropped down and crawled into a thick mass of orchard grass. He was grinning from ear to ear.

The Russian Commander has made his first mistake.

Chapter Fifteen

Curiously enough, Col. Valarian Agyants found himself enjoying the experience of floating down to earth at the end of a parachute. He touched ground without any difficulty, doubling up his legs and rolling over as Major Lyalin had advised him to do.

As he freed himself from the parachute harness and watched other men coming down, Agyants saw that he and the others were on a veldt thick with straw-colored grass and dotted with thorn and spicebushes. Per instructions, he pulled in his chute, rolled the silk into a large ball and hurried over to where the other men were placing their chutes. The chutes would go back with the men when the Ilyushin cargo plane lifted out the force for the return trip to Cuba. Nothing that was Russian must remain in the rain forest.

Smoking a cigarette and feeling somewhat more confident, Colonel Agyants joined Major Lyalin and they looked as the *Concordskii* roared in over the region and the second wave of men jumped from the airliner.

The Major patted Agyants on the shoulder with the hook that served as his left hand. "Efficiency! You are witnessing efficiency, Colonel. We are on schedule and proceeding as planned!"

An arrogant sneer on his almost-handsome face, Lyalin looked around at the surroundings. A hundred and twenty-five feet to the east was the rain forest; more towering green 75 feet to the west. The savanna was only 400 feet long—more rain forest on each end.

The men quickly formed into squads. Major Lyalin conferred with Captains Mikolatah and Kuznessov. In turn, Mikolatah and Kuznessov barked orders at the men, who quickly began to check their equipment. Two troopers ran to the west and began to climb a large oak at the edge of the rain forest, going up the trunk by means of pole-climbers attached to their boots.

For some reason the men were edgy. Everyone sensed that something was not quite right. There was something missing. It was Capt. Petyr Kuznessov, a squat man with a pushed-in face, who solved the puzzle.

"There's no animal life!" His voice was strained. "There's no birds singing. No rustling in the bushes."

"It's as if they've fled!" Lieutenant Biskib said, a muscle in his cheek quivering.

Colonel Agyants debated whether his imagination was playing tricks on him. *Nyet!* Other men were also sniffing the air.

From a short distance away, one of the Soviet scientists called out, "Major! I smell burning wood and leaves."

"*Da.* I smell it, too," nodded Captain Mikolatah in agreement.

High-pitched to begin with, the voice of the scientist rose even higher. "There's a fire in the forest, a fire close by."

The same instinct that had enabled Agyants to survive in the KGB now nudged him, the same intuitive reasoning that had let rise to the rank of colonel.

"It's the Americans," he said with a ring of certainty. "They're using incendiaries."

Major Lyalin gave him a quizzical look, then turned and looked upward as one of the men in the tree yelled down, "The forest to the west is burning!" There was fear and disbelief in the man's voice. "Some of the flames are higher than the tops of the trees!"

"How far away is the fire?" Lyalin called back. Agyants noted that he did not appear to be too concerned.

"About three hundred and fifty meters, sir. Maybe four hundred," the man bellowed.

The Major motioned with his hand. "Both of you come down," he ordered. To the other men he said, "The Americans have come down from the first layer of hills and think they are being clever. They have ignited the end of the jungle to give them cover while they move in around the fire and attempt to sneak up on us." He paused, then jeered, "The fools!"

An amazed expression burst over Captain Mikolatah's face, pock-marked from smallpox when he was a child. "More than fools, Major!" he exclaimed. "They have to be crazy. They

146

ad to see us come down. They have to know we outnumber hem. They are not being brave, they are being suicidal!"

Captain Kuznessov laughed and spit into the grass. "All we ave to do is wait. Ambushing them will be child's play." He aughed again, louder this time. "What is the expression the Americans use? Yes—a 'turkey shoot.' We will have an American 'turkey shoot.'"

Colonel Agyants suggested, "My opinion is that we should wait for them on the other side of the savanna, just inside the ungle. When they cross this open space, we can cut them lown!"

Major Lyalin shook his head, with a smile of superior amusement.

"No, Colonel. We will not wait. In the Soviet Union it is not our custom to wait for traitors. We go after them! And we shall go after the Americans and their stupid British helpers."

"You're in command," said Agyants generously, hating Lyalin more than ever. He unbuckled the Degtyarev submachine from across his back, the weapon giving him a feeling of security.

Speaking rapidly, Major Lyalin outlined his plan. Captain Kuznessov would take thirty men and go to the right. Kuznessov would send three scouts down the center, straight west. When the three men were half the distance between the veldt and the western edge of the rain forest, they would use grenades in an attempt to force the enemy to expose themselves—"although I'm convinced that the Americans will split nto two groups, with each group coming at us from the side."

Lyalin said to Captain Mikolatah. "You and I and twenty men will go to the left. We'll send three men in front to do reconnaissance. Lieutenant Biskib, take the rest of the men and the scientists and go into the eastern edge of the forest. We'll keep in touch by radio." He nodded to Kuznessov and to Mikolatah. "Chose the men."

Earlier, on the airliner, Major Lyalin had taken the two stainless steel knives from their case, put them into holsters and attached the holsters to his belt. Now, as his staff officers organized the men into groups, he used his right hand to remove the hook and its harness from his left wrist and arm. He put the hook and harness into the shoulder bag, then expertly screwed the 10-inch, three-edged blade to the metal platform of the wrist stump.

"In a very short while, this blade will taste the blood of an American," he said, leering at Colonel Agyants, who watched him in concealed hate and honest fascination. "Yes," mused Major Lyalin, "I'm going to enjoy myself."

Chapter Sixteen

A foot in the door is always worth two on the desk, Camellion told himself. *And I have both feet in.* He brushed an insect from his face and listened to the gunfire splitting the air to his right—the crack of M1 Colt ARs, the rapid *duddle-duddle-duddle* of the Colt AR-10 light machine gun intermingled with the deeper coughing of Russian AKM assault rifles and Degtyarev submachine guns.

It doesn't make sense! Why, the Death Merchant asked himself, had the Russians attacked straight down the slot? Why hadn't the Soviet commander employed basic tactics that demanded he send out probes to either flank? Any private in any army wouldn't be stupid enough to use a direct frontal assault, not under present conditions.

The Russains are too logical to make such a basic mistake.

There was only one answer that made sense: scouts had tossed the grenades, both to draw out the Americans and as a diversionary tactic while other comrades attempted flanking movements. There would be scouts ahead of each Russian group.

The scouts on this side must be very close.

Camellion's eyes narrowed as the firing intensified, as more weapons—farther to his right—began roaring, proof to Richard that he had analyzed the situation correctly. The Russians had found Tony Flecher and his 12 men.

Time to go hunting! He put down his two Auto Mags and slung the Colt assault rifle across his back, so the barrel was pointed to starboard. He picked up the AMPs, got to his feet and moved out of the large patch of orchard grass. His eyes darted ahead and from side to side. Single-line file? He hoped not. Jungle tactics of recon always emphasized either a wedge formation or a horizontal line approach.

Dressed in camouflage suits as the Russains were, it might take three or four seconds to separate them from the tangled wilderness. A gap of a single second could mean the difference between life and death. If one of the Russians saw him first, Camellion would end up feet first. Yet the same danger was also a protection: the Russians were faced with the same disadvantage. They wouldn't be able to see him.

It was impossible to move 10 feet without making some noise. Either dry leaves rustled or twigs cracked and snapped. The gunfire to the north was sporadic as each side, angling for some advantage, fired only to keep the other side down.

The Death Merchant tried to move through the leaves and other debris on the forest floor while the guns were firing. It couldn't be done. There wasn't any way he could keep in step with the intermittent roaring. *Taking a chance was part of the job, but committing suicide by letting some pig farmer blow me away is ridiculous!*

He got behind a thick lignum vitae tree and squatted down, keeping a nothofagus between him and the forward area. A species of evergreen, the nothofagus fern matched the green-brown pattern of his clothing and bush hat. Then again it was possible that the Russians were to the right of him, to the south, in which case he might not make contact with them. The Soviets might even get lucky and whack him out from the rear.

Richard reached into the game bag, thumbed out five .44 cartridges from one of the magazines and held them in his hand, listening and staring through the leaves and spines of the nothofagus.

He tossed one cartridge far to the right and, between bursts of firing, heard it land in the leaves 50 feet away. He ducked down, watched and listened. A few minutes passed. Without exposing himself by rearing up, he tossed two cartridges, in an overhand throw, to his left. However, just as he threw, a dozen machine guns roared to the north and he didn't hear the cartridges disturb the leaves. But he did see the slight movement 50 feet forward and slightly to his left—*or did I?*

He peered intently at a large viburnum bush growing intertangled with myrtles that had woody stems as thick as a man's ankle. In the rain forest all plants attained enormous stature. It was the large white flowers of the viburnum bush that revealed the green-brown clothing of the Russian. Flowers and camouflage pattern didn't blend.

The Death Merchant reared up slightly on both feet and fired the Auto Mags, the two tremendous roars drowning out all other sound, including the cry from the Russian, who dropped his AKM assault rifle, threw up both arms, and fell backward, dead. The .44 slugs had hit him squarely in the chest and blown him wide open.

More movement to Camellion's right. While he was swinging the two powerful autoloaders toward the area, a second pig from pigland paradise revealed himself as he stepped out from behind an acacia tree to rake the nothofagus bush with a storm of slugs. Camellion caught a flash of brown-green, a stark, staring face, and the barrel of the AKM, the muzzle jerking in his direction.

Silly Slavic Superman! Both Automags thundered. One .44 bullet hit the Russian just below the right knee and ripped his leg off, the vicious impact—kicking out his leg from underneath him—knocking him forward as the blown-off leg tumbled backward. The second .44 hit him in the right shoulder and spun him around. With his right arm almost severed, the dying Russian looked like a ridiculous puppet as he fell one way and spun another. Gravity won and he fell on his face and lay still, one arm entangled in a thick *malunna* bush, some of its orange flowers spotted with crimson blood.

Never stay in one position .Move and stay alive—maybe! The Death Merchant sprang to his feet, the flutter of death's wings loud in his mind. He flattened himself against the side of the lignum vitae tree a few seconds ahead of Boris Wenchez, the third Russian scout, who was convinced that he was killing the enemy by peppering the nothofagus with half a magazine of Degtyarev machine-gun projectiles—40 rounds. The banana-shaped magazine of the Model D-77 held 80 rounds, each cartridge slightly larger than a .25 caliber shell.

The rain of lead tore through the nothofagus bush. Bark flew from the side of the tree. *Thud! Thud! Thud!* Bullets buried themselves in the front of the tree. The Russian was taking no chances.

Now all he has to do is keep firing and creep up on me. Or throw a grenade. Oh fudge!

Ditto to being dead, but Camellion hated losing. He shoved full magazines into the AMPs and holstered them, then unslung the M1 assault rifle from his back. Thinking that he wouldn't be able to cover much distance with a backward throw, he took two grenades from the shotgunner's bag. But the explosions would give him "breathing room," enough time to use the Colt M1.

He pulled the pin from the first grenade and, with his left hand, tossed it around the side of the tree, doing his best to flip it forward and to his right. The grenade exploded only 20 feet away, stinging the tree with shrapnel.

This will never do! For a moment the Degtyarev stopped firing. Richard dropped the second grenade, picked up the Colt M1, stuck the barrel around the south side of the tree and fired a four-round burst. He pulled back quickly, just as the Russian began to slam lead at the south side of the tree. The Death Merchant picked up the grenade, his anger mounting. He pulled the pin, stepped out to the left from behind the tree and this time threw the grenade with his right hand. No sooner had the grenade left his hand than he was back behind the tree, the M1 in his hands.

The grenade exploded 40 feet away. The Degtyarev ceased to chatter. *He could be playing possum!* Camellion dropped to his knees and looked around the north side of the tree. The smoke from the two grenades, layed thickly in the air, was barely moving. WAIT! He detected faint movement in ferns to the north of the viburnum bush, where Camellion had spotted the first dimwit. This Russian was trying to get to a new position, to get in closer to Camellion and to escape a third grenade, in case he threw one.

"Bye, Brother!" Camellion stepped from the tree, opened fire with the M1 and raked the ferns with a five-second burst, 24 5.56-millimeter bullets tearing into the large rubbery leaves.

"AIIIEEEEeeeee!" Boris Wenchez screamed in torment. Three of the 5.56-millimeter bullets had found his perspiring flesh. One buried itself in his left thigh, another hit him in the pubic region. The third bullet broke the left side of his pelvis, shattering the bone. A giant roaring tortured his brain. With the world ending around him, Boris Grogonavitch Wenchez crumpled to the grass, unconscious from shock, bleeding to death internally.

The Death Merchant was reloading the M1 when Rudolf Graff contacted him on the RT.

"Il-gi-ga chot-sum-ni-da. Ku-rot-ch'i-yo?"

Camellion chuckled. The wily Graff, afraid that Russian communicators might be tuned to the same wavelength, was speaking in Korean. Then— *"Tsi redt ir Yiddish? Parla Italiano? Parlez-vous Francais?"*

Camellion replied in Korean. "Yes, indeed, it is a nice day. But I don't speak Yiddish. I do speak and write Italian and French. Let's stick with Korean. What's happening on your end?"

"We've advanced a hundred feet and the Russkies are falling back. It's that *Bombus* baby of Henderson's. All it does is 'buzz,' but that damn machine gun has made it impossible for the Russians to advance. Naturally our light machine gun has helped."

Speaking rapidly, Graff explained that the main Russian attack, on his side of the forest battlefield, had been directed at Flecher and his men. "But the Ivans attacked down the center of the slot after Tony and his guys rejoined us. Tony figured there were too many Russians for him to handle alone."

The big man sounded worried. "What about the firing on our side?"

"I've neutralized three of them," Camellion replied in Korean. "I think they were only scouts. The enemy has too many men to have sent only three on this flank. I'm caught with diarrhea and no corncobs in sight."

"I'm coming over and help out," Graff said. "So switch on your beeper. Over and out and see you later."

The Death Merchant pressed the button of the small box banded around the radiotelephone. The homing device—it was both sender and receiver—was now broadcasting a continuous tone of 48 MHz. Graff could hear the signal through the earplug connected to his own RT set. The stronger the signal, the closer he would be to Camellion.

Lying flat in the grass behind the lignum vitae tree, Richard Camellion waited. *I should have become a dentist!*

The three Russian scouts sent out by Capt. Petyr Kuznessev were dead, riddled with X1-B .22 slugs. Soon after the three scouts had thrown the grenades, Captain Kuznessev tried to contact them by walkie-talkie. Astonished when they did not reply, he had ordered his men to set up a heavy fire and to move forward. Tony Flecher and his group had returned the fire, all the while retreating in the face of the Russians' fire-power. Thirteen guns against 27 guns were not even odds.

Captain Kuznessev had commanded his men to spearhead southwest and follow the Americans, whom he thought to be only a tiny force. Too late did Kuznessev realize that, instead of chasing a tiny force, he had led his men into the line of fire of a much larger one. American assault rifles and a light machine gun had sent hundreds of slugs tearing through the leaves and vines and other green growing plant life of the

153

rain forest. Never had Kuznessev and his men experienced such a devastating tornado of lead. Three Russians were dead within a matter of minutes. Then a fourth man, crawling to a new position, had yelled and rolled over. Cutting all the way through his body, the bullet had penetrated one side of his canteen and made a loud ringing sound as it hit the other side, unable to pierce the metal because it had lost its power. Curious about the caliber, Kuznessev had taken the water-dribbling canteen from the corpse and removed the bullet. He could hardly believe it was a small-caliber .22.

Disheartened and angry, Kuznessev had called Major Lyalin, giving him the report that the Amerikanskis were throwing out such a tidal wave of lead that forward movement was impossible.

"My scouts are dead," Kuznessev had said sadly. "I think that the enemy is using some kind of machine gun that fires small caliber bullets. I found such a bullet. It's smaller than a twenty-five caliber. I think it's a twenty-two. Sir, I suggest we retreat."

"*Nyet!* Stay where you are!" Major Lyalin had been so enraged that Kuznessev heard the air whistling through his nose over the walkie-talkie. Lyalin, his voice shaking with anger, had said, "We have only encountered one or two of the swine. They've killed our scouts. But we're going to advance. As soon as we eliminate whoever is ahead of us, we'll move behind the American force and kill every single one of those spineless weaklings."

Captain Kuznessev and his men had not retreated an inch; they didn't advance an inch either. For a short time there had been silence. Then the light machine gun had begun firing again, the gunners raking the area, bits of leaves and vines almost forming a cloud as bullets became as thick as sand on a beach. Such a hurricane of lead had convinced Kuznessev and his frightened men that the Americans had three or four machine guns with noise suppressors attached. No single machine gun—the Colt AR-10 they could hear firing—could possibly spit out slugs with such fantastic rapidity. At the time, Captain Kuznessev had not suspected that there were only four men and two machine guns pinning down the Soviet force—Elton Heubach firing the Colt AR-10 light machine gun and Bill Henderson, Wayne Loos and Arvel Frager working the incredible X1-*Bombus*, which was firing 42 rounds a second each time Henderson touched the trigger.

Tony Flecher and twelve other men snaked their way for 50 yards. To a man, they were hot, tired, and sh[...]pered. They itched from chigger bites and their cloth[...] full of *zibque* bugs. Yet each man had that kind of fear that makes brave men daring, yet still cautious.

They turned east and crawled to a position that placed them opposite the Russians' right flank. Ever so slowly, Flecher, Lippkor, Bolinger, and the others began to belly-crawl south, stopping and ceasing all movement, hardly even daring to breathe, when Heubach ceased firing to put another belt into the receiver of the Colt light machine gun. Then, when the machine gun resumed its roaring, Flecher and the rest of the Americans—and one British S.I.S. agent—continued tunneling through the undergrowth. They were able to judge their distance from the Russians by an occasional burst from an AKM assault rifle.

They stopped when Flecher estimated they were about 50 to 65 feet from the Soviet force. Flecher whispered to Oliver Lippkor and Roy Bolinger, who were lying on either side of him, "Tell every man to make sure his M1 and side-arms are fully loaded. When I fire, that's the signal to charge in and give them everything we've got."

"Why not use grenades?" grunted Lippkor. "Why go like a bunch of gangbusters? You have some kind of death wish?"

"Don't you see what is in front of us?" pointed out Fletcher, half-angrily. "There are too many branches and vines, too much overhang. If only one grenade hit a tree and bounced back to us, we'd fail before we even got off to a good start—and no, I don't have a death wish."

"He's right," Bolinger whispered to Lippkor. "Grenades are too risky. Not only that, but we'd lose time. We'd only warn the sons of bitches."

Flecher inhaled deeply—honeysuckle and sweet-smelling *flamboyan* flowers mixed with smoke and acrid fumes of cordite. Ironic! Moonlight and roses! A garbage dump crawling with filth-covered vermin and scurrying rats.

When Bolinger and Lippkor passed word back to Flecher that the men understood, he inhaled again and sprayed the frontal area with a three-second burst of 7.62-millimeter bullets. Then, like a human bulldozer, he charged ahead. Moments later the other men were crashing through the brush, their assault rifles snarling.

The Colt AR-10 light machine gun and the X1-bombus became silent. There was now too much danger that their projectiles would hit Flecher and the other Americans.

Caught with their vodka bottles turned upside down, the Soviet force was at a deadly disadvantage. Captain Kuznessev realized immediately that he and his men had been tricked. Even so, by the time Kuznessev and his force realized the full implications and had swung around to face the attack, half a dozen Russians had stopped slugs and were dead. Another disadvantage for the Soviet force was that the unexpected assault disorganized its members. The instinct of self-preservation was automatically triggered, the urge to live forcing the Russians to be more concerned with finding new positions than with standing up and shooting from sites that left them exposed to enemy slugs.

Time for both sides became suspended. Now there was only life versus death, force against force, and the ear-splitting roar of automatic weapons. A Russian, his entire face a raw gaping wound, spun and fell toward Captain Kuznessev, who jumped back in horror and looked around in panic and confusion. It was difficult to tell friend from foe, at least at glance. Both Americans and Russians were dressed in identically patterned camouflage, although each side had different weapons and headgear, the Russians wearing fatigue caps, the Americans, bush hats.

Neither side had time to weigh any kind of odds. Americans and Russians became machines, flesh and blood and bone machines dedicated to killing. Feet smashed down on leaves and dead limbs. Sweat-bathed bodies crashed through ferns and bushes or ducked and dodged behind trees. The two forces came together.

A Russian screamed and crashed against a comrade as Kermit Bunton stitched him across the chest with 5.56-millimeter slugs. Bunton was next. He cried out in pain, dropped his M1 and looked skyward for a moment before he sank to his knees, both hands over his stomach. He sighed, died, and toppled forward, his head coming to rest in a spicebush.

Amandus Warehime was next to be stung by death. An average-looking man with a thin neck sunk within sharp collarbones, Warhime felt a terrible stab of pain in his left side. Another violent blow! A big steel fist, so it seemed, had smashed him in the chest. Warehime felt himself falling, felt an umbrella of blackness opening in his mind. He remembered Laddie, a collie he had had when he was a boy, and he wondered why he should be thinking of Laddie at a time like

156

this. *Hell! I'm dying! I—* Then there was no more thought. Warehime felt nothing at all.

Neither did Kasmir Patushlov and Miroly Opatrny. Both Russians had been made instant-dead by Kenneth Sedgwick, who was standing with his back to an oak, A Colt Python magnum revolver in each hand. One .357 bullet scattered Opatrny's skull. Another .357 tore through Patushlov's left side, making mush of his lungs and turning his heart into an unoperable pump.

Jolly good! thought Sedgwick. *These Pythons are certainly better than a P-38K.*

By now, Americans and Russians had exhausted the ammo in their automatic weapons. Since there was no time to re-load, each side resorted to side-arms, some men even using their empty assault rifles as clubs.

Tony Flecher, his bush hat hanging by its strap on the back of his neck, stood in a wedge formation with two other Zero-Zeros, a .45 Colt pistol in each hand. Flecher triggered shots with his back to Eugene Gurley and Bruce Colminsky. Three men! Three pairs of hands filled with Colt .45 autoloaders.

There were shouts, screams and curses, groans and grunts, as men fought to live and killed to win.

Colonel Lippkor, his lips fixed over his teeth in a snarl, got in close to a beaked-faced Russian who had a Stechkin machine pistol in his right hand. As the Russian tried to swing the MP around, Lippkor grabbed his right wrist, pushed the Stechkin to one side, shoved the muzzle of his .45 Hardballer into the Russian's belly, and pulled the trigger. There was a muffled explosion and a long "Uhhhhh" crawled from the Russian's mouth. His face went blank and, as he started to sag to mother earth, Lippkor jerked the machine pistol from the dying man's hand, then spun to the left to neutralize a Russian he had spotted from the corner of his eye. But the N.S.A. agent wasn't fast enough to stop Yevgney Ivanov from putting three 7.62-millimeter Tokarev bullets into Herbert "Hubbie" Boston, who had just fired two shots at Captain Kuznessov. Boston missed, because Kuznessov had seen him and ducked behind a tall acacia.

One percent in this world and 99 percent in eternity, Boston pitched sideways only a few moments before Yevgeny Ivanov jumped from the terrific impact of two .45 Hardballer bullets that Lippkor put into his body. Lippkor didn't know it at the time, but Tony Flecher saved his life by putting a .45 slug into the chest of a Russian who, 20 feet from Flecher, had been aiming at Lippkor with a Tokarev automatic.

The Russian cried out, spun as if cut loose from a coiled top, his Tokarev firing one last shot from pure reflex of his trigger finger. It was that one chance in a million, but that was how Herchel O'Connor was fated to die. The 7.62-millimeter bullet bored through O'Connor's right eye, tunneled through his brain, and made its exist through the back of his skull, taking bits of gray matter, bone, and hair with it. Dead, O'Connor dropped over a Russian who was unconscious and dying from a bullet that Bruce Colminsky had put into his hip. The red-haired Colminsky didn't live much longer. A 9-millimeter Stechkin bullet struck him in the left shoulder and knocked him away from Flecher and Gurley. A second 9-millimeter smacked Colminsky in the right side of the neck. A third smacked him in the right rib cage. Colminsky crashed to the ground, blood spurting from his neck and side.

Yelling curses at the Russians, Eugene Gurley jumped away from Tony Flecher, dodged, and killed the Russian who had put lead into Colminsky, the 255-grain .45 projectile smashing into the Russian's chest and knocking him back against Andrew Ryzenko, another member of the 13th Direction force. Ryzenko tried to get off the first shot at Gurley, but Gurley was a second faster. His .45 slug caught Ryzenko in the hip and knocked him to the ground. Yet Ryzenko was a tremendously powerful individual. Even as shock began to drape blackness over his brain, Ryzenko managed to get off two rounds, pulled the trigger twice in hate. The first 9-millimeter bullet missed. The second 9-millimeter struck Gurley just below the chin. The bullet blew out his throat, shattered two cervical vertebrae, and departed out the back of his neck. His throat pumping out a stream of red, Gurley hunched forward, dropped his .45, and toppled on his face, his blood coloring the purple and vermilion leaves of a bougainvillea vine.

Tony Flecher didn't take a lunch break; he didn't take time out to look around him. An ex-Green Beret Special Forces officer who had held the rank of major, Flecher was too battlewise to take inventory while he was exposed to enemy fire. He dropped to the ground and quickly crawled between two *obu* trees, bullets passing over his head. The Russian firing at him dropped his Tokarev and jerked first one way and then another as Roy Bolinger kicked him into infinity with two Smith and Wesson slugs.

Flecher, who was finding it difficult to believe he was still alive, snuggled down in thick orchard grass and hurriedly reloaded his Colt autoloaders, a quick look on his part revealing that most of the Russians were dead. The Russkies had a lot of company. A lot of Zero-Zero members were also dead! Those Americans and Russians still alive continued to fight with the desperation of men who knew that one mistake meant instant anihilation.

Holding both hands around the barrel of a Degtyarev submachine gun, Stephen Kordoskniv tried to use the weapon as a ball bat to cave in the side of Terry Lemmons' head. Kordonskiv swung with all his might. Lemmons, an empty Colt .45 in his hand, ducked, stepped back to deliver a power kick to the Russian's gut, then caught one foot on a vine. Unable to catch himself, Lemmons fell heavily to his back as Kordonskiv—snorting and loudly cursing Lemmons in Russian—tried again for another swing.

His arms upraised with the machine gun, Kordonskiv stopped snorting and cursing when Jose Meridias, ten feet behind him, threw a Tomahawk hand ax into him. The blade cut through several leather straps and cloth and buried itself in Kordonskiv's back. All kinds of funny sounds poured out of Kordonskiv's mouth. While his eyes bugged as though attached to invisible stalks, the Russian moved back and forth from side to side, blood flowing from his mouth. Then he gurgled, closed his eyes, twisted around, and fell.

As for Jose Meridias, his Colt .45 was empty. Just in time Meridias saw an ugly Russian lean out from behind an acacia and aim a machine pistol at him or maybe at Colonel Lippkor who was to Meridias' left. Meridias dropped to the forest floor as the Stechkin roared and four 9-millimeter slugs passed close to his body. Before Captain Kuznessev could correct his aim, Meridias crawled behind a Brazilwood tree, hoping he didn't get wanged out while he was reloaded the .45 auto.

Colonel Lippkor, who had also seen Captain Kuznessev, threw himself to one side and fired four quick shots at the Russian with the machine pistol he had grabbed from the Russian who had reminded him of a parrot. The four bullets clipped bark from the acacia and Kuznessev jerked back. Lippkor landed in the center of a virburnam bush, consumed with a sudden, fierce hatred of Kuznessev—*The son of a bitch is so ugly his mother must have even diapered his face!* Determined to kill Kuznessev, Lippkor began crawling to the right. He'd angle one way, then crawl another, and jump in from the side on the damned Russkie!

In the meanwhile, Kenneth Sedgwick had managed to reload his two Colt Python Magnums. He raised one and fired at a Russian who was behind Olin Maxton and getting ready to cave in Maxton's head with the barrel of an AKM assault rifle. The .357 JFP projectile caught the man in his right side, just below the armpit, and punched him off his feet. His body quivering, the Russian hit the ground only a short distance from Virgil Mild, who, hearing the noise, stepped to one side and looked toward the corpse, the motion saving him from the slugs of another 13th-Direction killer. Both 9-millimeter projectiles, fired from a Makarov PM pistol, were near-hits. One cut half an inch to the right of Mild's head, going through his bush hat and twisting it around on his head; the second hunk of lead clipped leather from the strap of a shoulder bag. Wild dropped to the ground and crawled into a rise of grass. The Russian did not have the time to fire into the grass. Roy Bolinger's .45 bullet struck him in the temple and exploded his head.

Due to his position by the side of a dogwood, Bolinger didn't see Lieutenant Leonid Purkinokov, who was 30 feet to one side of him, any more than Kenneth Sedgwick was aware that he was being targeted by Captain Petyr Kuznessov. For that matter Purkinokov didn't know that Sedgwick was only waiting for him to move out a bit more from behind the crooked trunk of a vochysia tree covered with lichen. Purkinokov took another step in order to get a better bead on Bolinger. He was lining up the back sight with the front sight and starting to squeeze the trigger when Sedgwick fired one of his Colt Magnums. The .357 bullet hit Purkinokov above the waist, a shard of a second before the Russian pulled the trigger of his Tokarev automatic. The big Magnum bullet did more than tear out Purkinokov's insides, it spoiled his aim. His 7.62-millimeter round-nosed bullet didn't bang into the middle of Bolinger's back. Instead, the bullet plowed through the top of the occipitalis muscle, between Bolinger's neck and shoulder, chopping in three-fourths of an inch below the skin. Bolinger yelled, thought of a red-hot poker and attempted to turn around, but the shock was too great.

I'll be damned! Bolinger felt a warm wetness flowing down his back and over his chest. He tried to keep the cobwebs

160

from piling up in his mind. He couldn't He sank into unconsciousness, his last thought of Richard Camellion— *He's right! Peace on earth, goodwill toward men! Bullshit!* His body relaxed. He lay unmoving.

Captain Kuznessev had finished moving 10 feet to the north of the acacia tree which had protected him during most of the short, bloody battle. Now he had a clear view of Kenneth Sedgwick's back. His homely face now twice as repulsive since it was twisted with hatred, he raised the Stechkin and fired.

The British S.I.S. agent did not even feel the first hint of pain. One! two! three! four! holes appeared in his back as the 9-millimeter slugs cut into his heart and lungs and knocked him forward face down in the leaves.

Captain Kuznessev's smile of victory vanished from his face at the sound of weight on the underbrush to his right. He spun and fired point-blank at Colonel Lippkor, who jumped to one side as the Russian pulled the trigger. The bullet didn't miss, but it didn't go where Kuznessev had wanted to put it. It grazed Lippkor's left side, the chunk of lead cracking a rib in its passage. His anger greater than his pain, Lippkor charged straight at Kuznessev, who again pulled the trigger of the machine pistol. Clink! It was empty.

Lippkor pulled the triggers of the Hardballer and the Stechkin. *Double click!* He, too, had miscalculated. Both autoloaders had exhausted their ammo!

Kuznessev jerked a knife from his belt and attempted an upper rib-slice directed at Lippkor's stomach. Growling "You Russian son of a bitch!" in English, Lippkor neatly sidestepped and slammed the butt of the machine pistol down on Kuznessev's thick wrist, grinning like Lucifer himself when he heard the bone snap and the Russian screech in pain. Lippkor wasn't finished. He slammed the side of the Hardballer against the side of the Russian's head. Unconscious, Kuznessev fell back and sideways behind a thick liana vine that had grown into a crazy pattern of knotted loops and spirals. He dropped and fell, the movement pushing his head forward through a half spiral of vine as his body sagged. Petyr Kuznessov hung there, looking ridiculous, his chin resting on the thick liana, his arms hanging loosely at his sides.

A single shot rang out—from a Colt .45 auto.

Tony Flecher had killed the last Russian, who had been creeping up on Lippkor.

The rain forest was suddenly very quiet. . . .

161

Chapter Seventeen

Lying side by side behind a large ageratum bush, and covered with leaves, Richard Camellion and Rudolf Graff listened to the roaring of gunfire to their left. They both realized that Tony Flecher and the Zero-Zero men were clashing eyeball-to-eyeball with the Soviet force that had approached on the northern flank. The Death Merchant and Graff were also very much aware that if they didn't stop the Russians on the south flank, the result would be disaster. The Soviet Union would gain possession of WINK-EYE-1.

"We had better be right," Graff whispered. "But I think that maybe we should have moved farther back."

The Death Merchant stared through the traceries of stems and leaves and crooked twigs of the ageratum, his eyes pacing back and forth across the frontal area. The naves of the forest did not reveal any trace of human life. Could the Russian force on this side have retreated?

"By now, they know I killed the three scouts," Camellion said. "The officer in charge will do what we would do. He'll do the only thing he can. He and his men will creep forward firing short bursts to keep us down. When they can, where there's at least a fifty-foot clear area, they'll use grenades. That's why we're back here. Our only hope is that our grenades do the job."

Camellion's fingers tightened around the six fish-lines, each line of which was high tensile strength Trilene. While waiting for Graff to join him, Camellion had fastened six grenades to low-hanging branches, tying the grenades five feet apart from each other. He had tied the end of a fishline to the ring of each grenade. After Graff had arrived, the two men had crawled back, moving 75 feet to the west, playing out the lines, and covering each one with leaves.

Camellion and Graff had discarded their back packs and bags of grenades. The two packs and the bags lay to one side, covered with leaves. Their Colt assault rifles were fully loaded and so were their side-arms. There wasn't anything the two men could do but wait.

"It's been almost ten minutes." Graff's muffled voice was not without concern.

"The Russian commander is being cautious," said Camellion. "It's only that the Russians are moving toward us very slowly."

"If they move any slower they'll have moss growing on them!"

"Be patient. We'll get a message from Ivan!"

The message arrived a few minutes later. Machine guns and automatic rifles began firing 175 feet ahead of Camellion and Graff, 100 feet in front of the nothofagus bush behind which the Death Merchant had previously hidden. It was in the area of the nothofagus that Camellion had spaced out the grenades.

"They're coming," Camellion said quietly.

"I hope one of their slugs doesn't hit one of our grenades and that none of the fishlines gets snagged," mumbled Graff.

The Russians, crouched, zigzagging, and weaving, advanced in a U-formation, the bottom of the U forward. They fired methodically and alternately, first the front of the U, followed by the left side, then the right side, then back again to the front line of men.

AKM and Degtyarev bullets chewed through leaves and vines and bushes, thudded into trees, and ate their way over Graff and Camellion's head. With each step, the Russians moved closer to the vicinity of the nothofagus bush. The Death Merchant, staring through the ageratum, tightened his hands around the lines, three in his left hand, three in his right.

"I see four or five of them in the first line," hissed Graff. "They're only a short distance from the bush."

"We've got to wait until the whole bunch is around the bush and the lignum vitae tree," replied the Death Merchant.

Watching the advancing Russians, the Death Merchant tensed, his impatience mounting as he waited for the Russian force to get closer. He didn't have to wait very long. The first line of the enemy, firing three-round bursts, weaved and dodged first one way and then another. A minute more and they were past the nothofagus and the lignum vitae tree. At either end of the line were the rest of the men who composed the sides of the U-formation. When the Russians of the first line were fifteen feet west of the nothofagus bush and the lignum vitae tree, Camellion pulled the six fishlines. One of the Russians happened to be stepping on the fourth line and it failed to pull the ring-pin of its grenade. The five other lines tightened. Five rings were pulled from just as many grenades. Five grenades exploded simultaneously.

An immense explosion! Five very brief flashes of red and a stupendous wave of concussion!

Four Russians were instantly killed, the mammoth explosion tossing three of the men high into the air. They came down like rag dolls, most of their bones pulverized. The fourth Russian was killed by a blown-off limb that stabbed through his chest. The concussion, a wall of pure force, knocked the rest of the Russkies to the ground, including the yo-yo whose foot had been holding down the line of the fourth grenade.

"Not yet!" snarled Camellion and pulled the fishline. He and Graff, who had picked up his assault rifle, then buried their faces in the leaves. Six seconds later there was another roar and more shrapnel joined the thousands of tiny pieces of jagged metal junk still raining down from the other grenades.

The *ping-ping-pings* were still sounding as the Death Merchant yelled "Let's go!" grabbed his Colt M1 and jumped up, leaves and twigs falling from his body.

Together Camellion and Graff stormed toward the members of the Soviet force.

The shock wave from the explosions had stunned the Russians into a kind of stupor, the enormous concussion not only knocking them to the ground but leaving them dazed, deafened, and unable to think clearly.

Maj. Viktor Lyalin and Capt. Felix Mikolatah had been at the end of the left side of the U-formation. Pitched eight feet to the butress roots of an *andira* tree, Lyalin, Mikolatah, and other men were unhurt, only benumbed, stupefied to the point that every single movement required a great effort of will.

Col. Valarian Agyants, who had been at the end of the other side of the U, lay on his face in a patch of viburnum, part of his psyche spinning around in a pit of morose helplessness. One word was born in his mind and grew to monstrous proportions: *AMBUSH!* Another thought came to him as he rolled over. *Why not defect? But will I have a chance to?*

Only a few minutes had passed, but to the Russians, their

minds wrapped in semitransparent shadows, it seemed that a hour had vanished into the stream of time. Slowly the mechanisms of sensation began to function with their former smoothness. Brain circuitry and synaptic joints jumped back to normal levels of efficiency and minds were no longer paralyzed.

But the damage that had been done was beyond repair. The Death Merchant and Rudolf Graff had used those 120 seconds to bulldoze their way through the forest and move in on the Russians. The 16 men were picking themselves up when Camellion, charging in on one side, and Graff, zigzagging in on the other side, opened fire.

Triggering his Colt M1 at hip level, Camellion fired short five-round bursts. One Ivan, getting to his feet, cried out horribly from the impact of two 5.56-millimeter slugs that tore through his midsection and pitched him backward to die against a dangling liana. Another Russkie was trying to get behind a tree. Camellion's bullets stabbed him in the right hip, each projectile travelling at 2,860 f.p.s. and with a muzzle velocity of 2,730 foot-pounds of energy. This kind of power pulverizes bones and flesh. The three projectiles exploded the Russian's pelvis with such force that he was actually lifted several inches off the ground.

Although disorganized and still in a state of partial shock, the highly trained Russians responded with twice the speed of ordinary men. Grabbing their ARs and submachine guns, they either dropped down into the orchard grass or scrambled frantically for tree trunks.

Major Lyalin and Captain Mikolatah crawled behind the trunk of a fallen Brazilwood which was very close to the giant *andira* tree, Lyalin trembling in blind rage. Everything had gone wrong. Now this! Only two men had inflicted all this damage! Worse, the group had walked into an ambush by grenades! Three scouts murdered! How many men killed by grenades? And already two more men butchered by American bullets! How could he report such a disaster to Moscow?

Major Lyalin screamed at his men, *"I want them alive! There are only two of them. Take them alive!"*

He saw one of the attackers, a tall, muscular man with a lean, hard face—*he's actually smiling!*—look his way and swing the assault rifle. Lyalin dropped back down behind the Brazilwood, the slugs from the American's weapon chipping bark from the side of the tree, other slugs thudding into the

165

ree behind the Russian major. "He'll come closer," Mikolatah said. "We'll get him."

n might as well have ordered his men to wrap up the tissue paper. Most of the Russians had not heard the order above the firing. Those who had, ignored it. When two crazy men are trying to kill you with assault rifles, you don't try to capture them. These *Amerikanskis!* Devils! Devils who fought like demons!

Graff, zigging and zagging to a new position, blew away a Russian with a domed head and a pasty white face. The stream of 5.56-millimeter slugs dissolved the man's features, exploded his skull and brain, and splashed two other pig farmers with bloody bits and pieces of what had been a part of their 13th-Direction comrade.

Anton Garshin started to gag in revulsion, staring down at the parts of brain and bone dribbling down his chest. Maxim's head had exploded like a watermelon. Next to Garshin, Aleksandr Stulyev swung his Degtyarev machine gun to one of the attackers, who had just gunned down Vladimir Ermalova. A giant of a man, the American had a barrel-like body and a small head in which huge dark eyes were framed by drooping eyebrows. The American walrus dived behind a large oak as Stulyev fired a volley of slugs at him. But Stulyev couldn't be sure if he had hit the man. He would never know. The Death Merchant killed him and the vomiting Garshin with the last nine rounds of his Colt M1.

Camellion dropped the empty assault rifle, pulled both Auto Mags, and charged straight for the Brazilwood tree.

Colonel Agyants and four other Russians close by attempted to get off streams of AKM projectiles at the American who was coming in with the big shiny pistols in his hands. But the other attacker leaned out from behind the tree and sprayed the entire region in which they were hiding. Georgi Tabriz howled in pain as a bullet tore off the flap of his right ear lobe. Some of the projectiles came within a few centimeters of the men. More pieces of lead popped off bits of bark and snipped leaves that fluttered down on the terrified Russians, who began to crawl frantically to the south end of the huge buttress root. The root itself was a ponderous pedestal nine feet high and spreading to a diameter of 50 feet. Agyants and the rest of the men found refuge behind the huge root, all save one, Pavel Gargarin. He raised his head only once and Graff put a bullet into the top of his brain.

Now advancing, Graff fired the last four rounds of his M1,

dropped the weapon on the run, drew his Colt Commander .45 autoloader, and sprinted for the south end of the big *andira* root, leaping nimbly over small bushes and plants. Twenty feet to Graff's left, the Death Merchant headed for the Brazilwood, which lay horizontal on the forest floor.

Other than Felix Mikolatah, there were three men with Major Lyalin crouched behind the Brazilwood. There was a narrow opening in the buttress root and Lyalin, who had seen Colonel Agyants and three other men crawl behind the south end of the root, sent Dmitri Tersch through the opening to tell Agyants and the three other men that "when you hear me fire three shots with my pistol, that will be the signal for all of us to charge out. But I want those two men alive. *Alive!* There are nine of us and only two of them. Remember, three shots!"

Major Lyalin didn't realize it at the time, but that order was the biggest mistake of his life. He raised his Stechkin with his right hand and pulled the trigger three times when Camellion and Graff were only 20 feet away from the Brazilwood and the *andira* trees.

Unaware of the take-them-alive order, the Death Merchant and Graff put on the brakes and began firing the instant they saw the Russians leaping out at them, each Russkie weaving and jumping as though he had springs in his feet.

'Pon my soul! thought the Death Merchant. *One has a knife instead of a hand! I'll bet that pig farmer thinks of me as a stick of butter!*

The twin 200/International Auto Mags roared simultaneously!

Dmitri Tersch and Nicholas Comdin looked very startled and very very hurt. The two Russkies were also very dead. The powerful .44 Magnum slugs hit Comdin in the chest and Tersch in the stomach, tore through their bodies, and knocked them all the way back to the Brazilwood, to Major Lyalin.

Clever and treacherous, Lyalin had hung back, not that he was a coward. But like all KGB officers, he was practical. Let those of lesser rank do the fighting. *Should the situation get out of hand—how could it, with three against one—I can always kill the American with my Stechkin!* Major Lyalin began to have a few doubts when the .44 bullet that had passed through Comdin cut through the end of the left sleeve of his combat fatigues, grazing the leather-and-aluminum platform

167

knob fastened to his wrist. The other .44 slug thudded into the Brazilwood.

Lyalin felt better when he saw Alexander Zerbst and Captain Mikolatah rush the American before he could again pull the triggers of those strange-looking weapons.

Those guns, thought Lyalin smugly. *Two nice trophies for me to take home. The Center will want to inspect them.*

Colonel Agyants, even more of a survivor than Major Lyalin, was also lagging behind. But unlike Lyalin, who was still behind the Brazilwood, Agyants had not stayed behind the buttress root.

What would the Center think if Lyalin reported that I did not do my part? 'Lack of duty,' they would call it, or 'Factionalism! I'm in enough trouble as it is. If the worst happens, I can always kill the big American. The hell with Lyalin and his stupid order!

Agyants dropped low and rushed to the left of the enormous American while the three other Russians charged straight at him, ducking and moving from side to side. Ilya Zepin didn't duck fast enough! A .45 Colt autoloader bullet struck him in the chest and knocked him to the leafy floor. Graff fired again, but Georgie Tabriz, his right ear dripping blood, dodged to one side and the bullet skimmed over his left shoulder.

Graff tried to step back and trigger off another round with the Colt Commander auto. He was too slow or Ivan Rolstov was too quick. Rolstov grabbed Graff's right wrist with his left hand and then attempted to slam his Tokarev against the side of Graff's head. Tabriz, darting in very low to the other side of Graff, intended to end the fight in a hurry. *Take him alive—Da! But why not wounded?* Tabriz intended to shoot the big American in the foot!

The Death Merchant had double trouble. Capt. Felix Mikolatah seized the Death Merchant's right wrist with his left hand, pushed the Auto Mag away from him, and used the Stechkin machine pistol in his right hand to swing at Camellion's head, sneering in broken English, "Got you, you sonabitch!"

Alexander Zerbst, a fleshy man with a bulldoglike physiognomy, tightened the strong fingers of his left hand around Camellion's left wrist, jerked the AMP to one side, and tried to use his pistol to cave in the Death Merchant's left rib-cage.

Neither Mikolatah nor Zerbst expected Camellion to react with such speed. With one well-coordinated motion, Camellion ducked the deadly machine pistol aimed at his head and jerked his body to the right. Mikolatah's Stechkin swung harmlessly over his head while Zerbst's weapon only skimmed his left side. Yet the duck-and-sidestep movement had relaxed the strength in Camellion's arms and Zerbst and Mikolatah succeeded in disarming him, the pain in his wrists forcing his fingers to open around the butts. Both AMPs fell from his hands.

Confident that they were winning, the two Russians renewed their attack with greater speed and renewed strength. Eight feet away, Major Lyalin watched with satisfaction. Nonetheless, he was ready to fire his own Stechkin.

The Death Merchant now realized that the two men were not trying to kill but to capture him, their purpose giving him a slight edge but only for the moment. Taking several deep breaths and trying to watch the good-looking Russian behind the Brazilwood—*He must be the ranking officer!*—he knew he would have to act quickly or die. Capture would be even worse.

Their missing Camellion's head and side had thrown Mikolatah and Zerbst off balance. Recovering first, Captain Mikolatah again tried to use Camellion's head as an eggshell. Zerbst made another effort to use his Stechkin as a club, this time endeavoring to bring the barrel down on the Death Merchant's left collarbone. In his try, Zerbst stepped slightly to one side, his fingers relaxing on the Death Merchant's left wrist.

Quick to take the advantage, Richard pulled his left arm free and in the next instant, with his left hand, captured Zerbst's right wrist and smashed Mikolatah squarely in the testicles with the tip of his right boot, the foot-blow so vicious that Camellion could feel cloth and skin grinding to pulp.

Captain Mikolatah didn't scream. The instant agony, stabbing out like chain lightning from his groin to every cell of his body, drained him of every particle of strength and left him as helpless as a baby. The machine pistol dropped from his hand and he sank to his knees, the fire in his manhood eating at his consciousness. His eyes went wide. Bile and slime poured from his mouth. Moaning, he fell to his side, his hands pressed against his groin, wishing that he could die or at least pass out.

Alone now, Alexander Zerbst lost his nerve. He changed

cs. He tried to kill the Death Merchant by swinging the machine pistol in his right hand. He couldn't force the barrel toward Camellion whose steely grip was too strong. Zerbst tried a side-hand chop against Camellion's neck. Again he scored zero. The Death Merchant blocked the attempted blow with his right forearm. During the same moment he raised his left foot and brought his heel crashing down on the Russian's right instep.

There are 52 bones in the human foot and Richard's pile driver stomp broke 41 of them in the Russkie's foot. Zerbst howled in agony, his body going rigid with astonishment. He snorted, his mouth going slack, his eyes bobbing around in their sockets. In hidious pain, the Russian tried to scream. He couldn't because the Death Merchant stabbed him in the side of the neck with a *Yon Hon Nukite* four-finger spear thrust. More agony! There was another blur and this time Camellion stabbed him directly below the Adam's apple with a four-finger spear thrust. Choking to death, gagging and gasping and fighting waves of nausea and a tidal wave of onrushing blackness, Zerbst dropped his machine pistol. He would have fallen if the Death Merchant hadn't caught him, spun him around, and shoved him toward the Brazilwood, just as a frantic Major Lyalin pulled the trigger of his Stechkin.

Rudolf Graff ducked the Tokarev that Ivan Rolstov had aimed at his head, the pistol creating a stiff breeze as one side of it swished through his short crew-cut. In concert with his dodging the intended blow, Graff heard a pistol shot—*It was a Colt .45!*—followed by a high-pitched scream, far to the north. He also tried to keep his eyes on a Russian who seemed to be trying to get behind him.

Ivan Rolstov, not about to make the same mistake twice, now attempted to clip Graff's Goliathlike chin with the end of the Tokarev. He felt like a fool as the big man's left hand shot out and grabbed his wrist, the grip tightening with the force of a steel vise.

Almost jerking the now terrified Rolstov off his feet, Graff sidestepped at the same moment that Georgi Tabriz, in his attempt to shoot Graff in the right foot, pulled the trigger of his machine pistol which he had switched to semiautomatic. The pistol discharged, the 9-millimeter bullet missing Graff's right foot but coming very close to his left ankle, the slug cutting a deep groove in the leather of the Moc-Toc field boot only a shave of a second before Graff's left foot lashed out and kicked the Stechkin from Tabriz's hand. The MP went sailing, landing seven feet away.

Snorting and cursing in anger and agony from his mashed fingers, Tabriz, who was stooped over in a crouch, attempted to turn to retrieve the machine pistol. Very quick for a large man, Graff kicked the Russian in the face, an experienced, flat-footed smash that shattered the Russian's nose, broke his upper and his lower jaws, and tore out his upper and lower front teeth.

Tabriz thought that a grenade had exploded in his face. Choking on blood and teeth, he did his very best to move toward the precious Stechkin. The pain was too great, the shock too immobilizing. From far far far away, like the voice at the end of a very long tunnel, Tabriz heard the American laughing. Then the laughter began to grow faint and fainter still . . . dwindling into the silence, into the purple shadows, of unconsciousness.

Ivan Rolstov—poor fool—was in the same position as an idiot who has grabbed a Bengal tiger by the tail. His fingers were around Graff's right wrist, and so far he had succeeded in keeping the muzzle of the .45 Colt pointed upward, away from him. Yet Graff's left hand was wrapped tightly around Rolstov's right wrist, making it impossible for the Russian to use his Tokarev. Worse, Rolstov's grip was weakening while Graff's was firm. Any moment now, Graff would succeed in freeing his right hand.

Rolstov's only hope was that Colonel Agyants would succeed in getting behind Graff and knocking him in the head. A few seconds later, Rolstov's hope faded into a mist of misery.

As Agyants tried to get in behind him, Graff exerted himself with tremendous effort. Taking Rolstov with him, he spun halfway around and kicked Colonel Agyants in the stomach just as the KGB officer was swinging the barrel of the pistol downward. The Stechkin didn't come close to Graff's head; it even missed his shoulder. But the kick in the stomach forced Agyant's finger to contract against the trigger. Set on full-automatic fire, the Stechkin spit out five 9-millimeter bullets. Three missed Graff by several inches, the fourth by half an inch. The fifth cut through his combat fatigues and raked his right hip, cutting a quarter of an inch into the skin. Graff yelled in pain, lost his temper and, with another gigantic effort gave Rolstov's wrist a tremendous twist. The Russian groaned in pain, his fingers jumped open, and the Tokarev dropped to the leaves.

The pile-driver kick that Graff had given Agyants had been a long one. Graff's foot had fallen short, hitting Agyants with only enough power to severely agonize, but not with enough force to create the necessary shock which would have put him out of action.

In severe pain, tasting bile, Agyants tried to swing the Stechkin toward Graff. *Kill him! There is no other way!*

Graff's left hand shot out, the large fingers clamping around Agyant's wrist and jerking the surprised man closer.

In the meanwhile, Ivan Rolstov aimed a Sambo two-finger spear thrust at Graff's drumlike neck. The strike would have landed if Graff hadn't smashed Rolstov in the belly with a savage knee-lift. Rolstov groaned loudly. The color drained from his face. Easily now, Graff freed his right wrist from Rolstov's grasp, shoved the .45 Colt Commander against the horrified man's chest and killed him with a slug in the heart, the muffled roar echoing throughout the rain forest.

"No! No! I surrender!" screamed Colonel Agyants in perfect English. He lifted his left arm above his head and opened the fingers of his right hand, letting the machine pistol fall. *"Don't shoot! I'm a KGB colonel in the Mokryye Dela! I can tell you much! Don't shoot! Please don't shoot!"*

Sweat pouring down his cheeks and from his upper lip, Agyants stared at the huge muzzle of the Colt .45 pointed at his face. He gaped, as if seeing a Martian, at the huge black eyes glaring at him from behind the Colt. Without a word, Graff flammed the automatic against the side of Agyants' head. The Russian Colonel's legs turned to wet straw and he wilted.

Graff glanced toward the north and saw a man crawling on his knees toward a machine pistol. In great pain, the Russkie was gasping, spittle dribbling down his mouth. Graff raised the Colt Commander and performed surgery on Captain Mikolatah's head with a .45 bullet. The dead Mikolatah flopped flat on his face, the top of his head missing.

There were groans on the otherside of Graff. He turned and looked at Georgi Tabriz who was lying on his side, his face a demolished red mess. Semiconscious, Tabriz was trying to raise himself. The Colt Commander roared again and Georgi Tabriz was dead.

Major Lyalin's 9-millimeter slug did not strike the Death Merchant. Instead, the projectile went all the way through Alexander Zerbst's dying body and sizzled the air several inches to the right of Camellion, who was leaping over the Brazilwood. Too late, Lyalin realized his mistake.

He had switched the Stechkin machine pistol to semi-automatic before he had fired the three signal shots. But he had forgotten to change the MP back to full automatic. Now, the weapon had fired only a single round. For a few moments, Lyalin stood there, his finger pressing down the trigger. During those few seconds, the Death Merchant turned and came at him.

Stumbling back, his eyes darting to Camellion, Major Lyalin attempted to push down on the lever with his thumb. At the same time he stabbed out at the Death Merchant with the 10-inch equiangular blade securely attached to the stump of his left wrist.

Lyalin failed. The Death Merchant succeeded. Camellion twisted sideways just in time, and the knife, missing his stomach, cut through the right side of his fatigues, the three-edged blade drawing blood from a shallow gash. With all his strength, Camellion chopped down with the edge of his right hand on Lyalin's wrist. The Russian yelled in pain and rage, dropped the machine pistol and pulled back the knife-blade—all at the same time.

Camellion kicked the Stechkin to one side and leaped back to avoid the sinister three-sided blade, his right hand darting to the back of his neck, his fingers seeking the weighed handle of the ice pick he carried in a holster strapped to the top center of his back. It was impossible for him to retreat. He was already flush against the buttress root of the andira tree. In a large enough area, fighting a man with a knife for a hand—and winning—would not have been too difficult. In a closed area, the odds were against him.

His face twisted into a demonic snarl, Lyalin shook with rage when he heard Camellion laugh and sneer, "Germ, where's the rodent that's been carrying you around?"

Lyalin's right hand darted for a second weapon he carried in the left breast pocket of his fatigues, a small .21 caliber Trevoga pistol. The same instant that the Death Merchant threw the ice pick and dodged to one side, Lyalin fired the Trevoga and rushed forward, holding his knife-arm forward like a sword.

The .21 Trevoga slug struck the holster on the Death Merchant's right hip, cut through both sides of the leather, and buried itself in the "wall" of the buttress root.

The Death Merchant also missed his target. The ice pick did not stab Major Lyalin in the throat. The blade shot into his partly opened mouth and bored all the way through the back of his throat, so that several inches of the blade protruded from the back of his neck—not at all surprising since the handle of the pick was a one-inch-diameter steel pipe filled with lead, which meant a lot of carrying power behind the blade.

Lyalin's body jerked and rippled with a giant shudder. The Trevoga pistol fell from his right hand. However, he had charged and the momentum of his body continued to carry him forward. He tottered and crashed against the buttress root and the equiangular blade, at the end of the stump of his left wrist, buried itself almost its full length into the half-rotted wood. Lyalin fell then, his eyes wide and staring, great rivers of blood flowing from his mouth and dripping from his chin. One of his knees was on the ground, his other leg pulled out crookedly behind him. There he hung and there he died, fastened to the andira tree.

"Too bad, Russian!" murmured the Death Merchant. "You should have had an agreement with the Cosmic Lord of Death."

Camellion picked up the Trevoga, pushed on its safety, and dropped the pistol into his pocket. He had spent almost three hours fitting the blade of the ice pick to the handle. There had to be a precise weight to the handle. Richard didn't intend to leave the pick in the dead Russkie. He reached around and pulled the bloody handle from the throat of the corpse, wiped the ice pick on the fatigues of the dead man, and shoved it back into its holster.

Taking a deep *Ujjayi* breath, Camellion looked all around him. The rain forest, with all its various stinks and smells, had been turned into a green graveyard, a cemetery in which Rudolf "Preach" Graff was speaking into a RT and standing in front of a stark-naked man, who had his hands above his head. The Russian's clothes lay piled beside him.

Drawing closer to the Zero-Zero commander, Richard saw him switch off the RT, shove the set into its case, and glance with a broad grin in his direction.

"You have opened a nudist camp?" joked Camellion, eyeing the Russian, a straw-haired man with a powerful torso

174

and narrow waist. There were several long scars on his hairy chest. An appendicitis scar gleamed dull-white in the gloom.

Colonel Agyants gazed back at Camellion with arrogant confidence, yet with a trace of embarrassment over his nudity.

"This yahoo here is Valarian Agyants," said Graff, sneering at the Russian. "He claims he's a colonel in the KGB and the boss of all the 'blood-wet' boys in the Caribbean and South American. I think he's full of goatshit! Big shots in the KGB don't go on kill missions!"

"They do if they're in trouble with the 'Center!'" Agyants said coolly. "Both of you are professionals and no doubt in counterintelligence. You know how the internal apparatus of the KGB functions."

"And that's why you were so quick to surrender?" Graff motioned toward Agyants with the Colt Commander. "If you're lying, I'll blow your balls off. OK, you don't have any concealed weapons. Get dressed. You look ridiculous!"

Graff's expression grew serious. "I've news for you, Camellion."

At the mention of the Death Merchant's name, Colonel Agyants, who was reaching for his striped shorts, paused and looked up at the lean American with the odd blue eyes.

"So! You are Richard Camellion!" Agyants said curiously. He stepped into his shorts and pulled them up around his waist. He looked again at the Death Merchant, smiling in defeat. "My best *Mokryye Dela Spetschasti* agents did their best to apply 'executive action' to you in Paramaribo and in Georgetown. You are either very lucky or very good, American. Which is it?"

"I doubt if you would believe if I told you, Colonel," said Camellion. "Now shut up and put your clothes on." His eyes skipped to Graff. "Tell me about Flecher and the others."

With one eye on Agyants, Graff whispered the report. Twenty men were still alive, that number including Dr. Leitch, the four East Indians, and the two Zero-Zero men with them.

"And us!" Graff whispered. "But Bolinger's got a muscle wound. It's not serious, only painful. Lippkor has a bad graze and several cracked ribs. We suffered a lot of damage, but Flecher got the job done."

Camellion's expression was scornful. "We wasted maybe twenty-three, twenty-five at the most. Flecher couldn't have neutralized sixty-five or seventy of them. There has to be a

175

third Russian force somewhere. You should have asked our Russian friend about that!"

"I didn't have to! Flecher persuaded the Ivan they captured to tell him!" said Graff triumphantly. "A Captain named Kuznessov. The Russkie tried to play it dumb, but Tony shot off one of his fingers and turned him into a parrot."

Graff explained that the rest of the Soviet expedition was in the forest beyond the small savanna into which the Russians had parachuted.

"They're in that part of the forest, them and their equipment. It's like we figured. They intend to be sky-grabbed after they find WINK-EYE." Graff scratched the side of his face with the muzzle and of the Colt and continued in a normal tone of voice, "Flecher and six Zeros have gone to burn them out with TEA." The Death Merchant could see the doubt in Graff's eyes. "TEA will do the job and the strip will keep the fire contained. But if the Russian commander ordered the third group to advance—God help us!"

"He didn't!" spoke up Colonel Agyants, zipping up his fatigues, and smiling faintly at Camellion and Graff, who were looking at him with hard eyes. "Maj. Viktor Lyalin was the commanding officer. That's him over there, stuck to the big tree root. I was with him, and he didn't call for any reenforcements. He was too proud to. The man was a fool! He didn't know the difference between peasants in the middle of the Soviet Union and highly trained combat fighters."

"I hope you're not lying, you Russian son of a bitch!" warned Graff. "Your longevity hasn't increased with us, not yet."

Colonel Agyants wasn't smiling as he answered Graff. "I realize you can kill me, I can't stop you. But my position does not give you the right to insult my mother. I was born in wedlock, as I'm sure you were."

Agyants sat down and began to pull on his boots, ignoring an amazed Graff and an amused Camellion.

"He has nerve, hasn't he?" Graff said, frowing, "and he scored a Brownie point, too." He winced slightly and moved his hand to his right hip, to where the fatigues were ripped and blood had congealed.

"It's nothing more than a bad graze," he said to Camellion and reached for his cigarettes with his left hand. "It's not bleeding any more. I'll have a nice long scar."

"I'm going to pick up my Auto Mags and our M1s and go

back and collect our stuff," Camellion said. "Did Flecher tell you where Bolinger and Colonel Lippkor are?"

"He said they were going to link up with Henderson and Heubach. Heubach was manning the light machine gun. What have you got in mind?"

"Get on your RT and call your two boys with Dr. Leitch and the four East Indians. Have them join up with Henderson and Heubach and the others. They can use the beeper system. Then call Henderson and the men with him and tell the four to turn on their beepers for Leitch and his crowd—and hope that Flecher finishes the job."

"If he doesn't, we will," Graff said with certainty. "I don't intend to die in this stinking forest." He waved the Colt at Colonel Agyants. "Not with that son . . . not with that damned communist!" He seemed to study his cigarette. "Frankly, it's the Indians that worry me."

"We're safe from the Anacunna, as long as it's daylight," Camellion replied. "They very primitive, but they're not stupid. They know what the 'big-bang fire sticks' of the white man can do. If any were around, the first series of TEA grenades set them scampering."

"And when night comes?"

"By then we'll be headed for home," Camellion said. He turned to Colonel Agyants, who had put on his other boot and was getting to his feet.

"Colonel, what is the nucleus of the plan to lift out the Russian force? I should suppose that Major Lyalin was to radio Havana?"

"Yes," admitted Agyants. "But I don't know the code. Lyalin and his officers had it."

"I'm not concerned with any code," Camellion said. "I only want to make sure that your people won't arrive from Havana until they're called. Realize, Colonel, if you're lying, you'll die. You'll die slowly and painfully."

"I spoke the truth," insisted Agyants. "I'm your prisoner and I couldn't gain anything by lying. I don't want to die any more than you do. May I smoke?"

"If you have your own cigarettes," said Graff grudgingly. He and Camellion watched as Agyants reached into his fatigues and took out a lighter and a pack of American Kents.

The Death Merchant said, "As soon as we find out how Flecher does, we'll establish the L-and-L and full coordinates of the savanna up ahead. Then we can radio the Hut and S.I.S. can send a chopper for us while we're searching for

WINK-EYE. By the time the Vickers gets here, the fire will have burned itself out."

"It's a good plan." Graff reflected for a moment. "But only if we can locate the satellite before dark."

"Whether we do or don't, we're not going to be around tonight. We can't defend ourselves against the Indians in this jungle. Even in the foothills, twenty of us couldn't do the job. We can't help Uncle Sam by getting ourselves killed."

The Death Merchant picked up his Auto Mags and moved south where he and Graff had lain in wait for the Soviet force. He was picking up the back packs when he heard the faint screams to the northeast, in the direction of the savanna.

Hurrying back to Graff, the Death Merchant smelled that peculiar kind of smoke, the kind that is given off when vegetation is being consumed by triethylaluminum to which 1.4 percent polysobutlene had been added.

It was all very simple: either Tony Flecher and the six Zero-Zeros had succeeded in burning the remainder of the Soviet force or they had not. . . .

Chapter Eighteen

The Alphaometer did not work; yet there wasn't anything wrong with the sensitive instrument.

"The Alphaspectro-generator inside WINK-EYE isn't functioning," Dr. Leitch explained in his nervous manner. "It's not sending out any low-frequency signals."

Despite the useless Alphaometer, the Death Merchant and his hot, tired crew of 19 found the American satellite.

By accident!

Four hours after they had begun the search!

The satellite had come down by parachute. Therefore, it was logical to assume that the enormous chute could have been caught in some of the highest trees.

The Death Merchant had Gordon Willet and Ram Fakhruddin climb one of the tallest trees in sight, a *quebracho*, a hard redwood. It was Ram Fakhruddin who, peering through binoculars at 100 feet up, found the parachute, 2,000 feet due east of the burned-out strip. Part of the chute had snagged in the upper limbs of a giant lignum vitae.

Tony Graff and his six men had done a thoroughly hellish job on the last one-third of the Soviet Force. A dozen TEA grenades, shot from CGL-4 launchers, had incinerated all of the Russians but five. They had run out onto the savanna and had been cut down by M1. fire. The TEA had turned most of the strip and a goodly portion of the rain forest beyond into an area as bald as a coconut. Not a single vine or flower, not a single blade of grass or tree had been spared. There were no skeletons of partially burned trees. There was nothing but acres and acres of gray-white ash.

When they reached the site, they found that the satellite had freed itself from the parachute and fallen to the ground, coming to rest against a redwood. There it lay, looking as out of place in the rain forest as a legless man at a skiers' convention.

179

They stood there looking at the satellite, soaked in their own sweat.

"So this is what we've been risking our necks for!" said Arvel Frager in disgust. "I hope it was worth it."

"Funny-looking contraption, isn't it?" offered Olin Maxton.

A silver-colored ball, 12.4 feet in diameter, WINK-EYE had numerous pole antennae and four booms extending from its rounded surface. From one side protruded a cylinderlike affair—the radioisotope thermoelectric generators, explained an excited Dr. Leitch, as happy as a teen-age boy who has just discovered sex!

"A marvelous piece of instrumentation!" he said proudly. Speaking quickly, he began to lecture. See those two knobs? They were part of two TV cameras with 1,500-millimeter f/8.5 and 200-millimeter f/2 optics, multiple filters, variable shutter speeds, and variable scan rates. Wide-angle field of view, 56 × 55 millirad. There was a spectrometer measuring ion, atomic, and small-molecule gas abundances; its spectral range was 400 to 1,600 angstroms. And there! The arm for the dual plasma detectors; two dual, rotating solid-state detector sets, covering various ranges from 10 Kev to more than 30 Mev/nucleon.

"What you see on the other side are the 'eyes' for the two high-field triaxial fluxgate magnetometers," said Dr. Leitch.

"Doctor, I don't care if WINK-EYE has a built-in popcorn popper," Camellion said severely. "We came here to get the tapes. I suggest you get them. You do know where they are, don't you?"

Doctor Leitch drew back, insulted. "Of course I do! The removal procedure is not at all difficult. All I have to do is open the TRW protective panel and—"

"Then do it," Camellion interjected sharply. "We've wasted enough time. Do you need help?"

Without replying, the scientist gave the Death Merchant a superior look and moved to the other side of the satellite.

Camellion mentally checked the present situation. Graff had stationed the nine Zero-Zero men in a wide circle around the satellite, each man positioned behind a tree or concealed in a bush or fern. An attack by the Anacunna was not possible, not a successful attack.

Colonel Agyants sat on the ground between Colonel Lippkor and Roy Bolinger, his hands securely tied behind his back. Lippkor was in a good deal of pain from his cracked ribs, but tried not to show it. Bolinger was suffering even greater pain, evidenced by an occasional groan. The wounds of both men had been dressed, as much as had been possible with only the limited aid of the first-aid kits. Both men had been given shots of penicillin and, for pain, propoxyphene hydrochloride.

Tony Flecher sat by one of the Sonder shortwave sets wearing a pair of headphones.

Graff lit a cigarette, exhaled noisily, and looked up at the sky.

"Camellion, you are sure you gave the right position of the strip when you radioed S.I.S. at the Hut?"

"I'm positive," Camellion reassured him. "The chopper should be arriving before we're finished here. Tony will be the first to know. There isn't anything more to do. As soon as Dr. Leitch has the tapes, we'll move back to the strip and wait it out."

Graff glanced at Colonel Agyants, then lowered his voice. "We should have blindfolded him. Hes' seeing everything that goes on. I guess it doesn't matter. He's not a scientist and I'm damn sure he'll never be able to tell anyone what happened here this day."

The Death Merchant nodded. "Come on. Give me a hand with the COMP-Y."

Camellion paused. Dr. Leitch had come from around the satellite and was hurrying toward them. There was a disturbed expression on his thin face, his eyes disbelieving behind his glasses.

"The tapes have been destroyed," he said in a choked voice. "Please come with me."

Camellion and Graff glanced at each other and followed Dr. Leitch to the other side of the space station. They saw that he had removed a large outer panel, which had been at knee level, and two other steel panels from the interior of WINK-EYE-1. The three panels lay on the grass.

A foot above the opening of the first panel was a perfectly round hole, three inches in diameter.

"Gentlemen, you see this hole?" Dr. Leitch moved his finger around the smooth edges of the hole. "The hole was made by a laser beam. The beam destroyed most of the tapes and fused the rest of them together." He indicated the 30-inch-square opening. "See for yourselves." He handed Camellion a small flashlight.

The Death Merchant switched on the flash, bent down and shined the beam of light into the opening, Graff beside him.

Neither man knew precisely what he was looking at, but they could both see that the equipment had been fused into a mass of useless junk.

Camellion and Graff stood up. Richard switched off the flashlight and handed it back to Dr. Leitch.

"Cosmos, the Soviet Union's killer satellite," Camellion theorized. "I suppose we now have proof that it exists."

"It was the laser beam that interfered with the guidance system," Leitch said studiously, "although I can't be sure."

"But WINK-EYE didn't crash immediately," said Camellion. "It made numerous orbits around the Earth. Ah ha! It has a built-in defense of some kind against a laser."

"Yes," admitted Dr. Leitch. "But I don't know the details. I couldn't tell you if I did."

"I wouldn't expect you to, Doctor."

"What gets me is that all the risks were for nothing," Graff said bitterly. "All we've done is trade death for useless metal that's not even good scrap."

"We have Agyants," countered the Death Merchant. "He can tell us a lot about the KGB and GRU setup in Cuba and South America. That's not too bad of a monument to the Zeros who died."

Dr. Leitch said in a small voice, "My work is done. Destroy the satellite."

The three men walked to the other side of WINK-EYE and Camellion and Graff went to the case, which contained the 125 pounds of nitroglycerin.

They were opening the case when Tony Flecher called out, "Good news, men. Not one but two choppers are only 50 miles away. S.I.S. has brought reenforcements, just in case."

"That's a worry we can scratch," Graff said.

The Death Merchant did not reply.

Camellion's thoughts were on Japan.

THE INCREDIBLE ACTION PACKED SERIES

DEATH MERCHANT

by Joseph Rosenberger

His name is Richard Camellion, he's a master of disguise, deception and destruction. He does what the CIA and FBI cannot do.

Order		Title	Book #	Price
	# 1	THE DEATH MERCHANT	P211	$ .95
	# 2	OPERATION OVERKILL	P245	$ .95
	# 3	THE PSYCHOTRON PLOT	P117	$ .95
	# 4	CHINESE CONSPIRACY	P168	$ .95
	# 5	SATAN STRIKE	P182	$ .95
	# 6	ALBANIAN CONNECTION	P670	$1.25
	# 7	CASTRO FILE	P264	$ .95
	# 8	BILLIONAIRE MISSION	P339	$ .95
	# 9	THE LASER WAR	P399	$ .95
	#10	THE MAINLINE PLOT	P473	$1.25
	#11	MANHATTAN WIPEOUT	P561	$1.25
	#12	THE KGB FRAME	P642	$1.25
	#13	THE MATO GROSSO HORROR	P705	$1.25
	#14	VENGEANCE OF THE GOLDEN HAWK	P796	$1.25
	#15	THE IRON SWASTIKA PLOT	P823	$1.25
	#16	INVASION OF THE CLONES	P857	$1.25
	#17	THE ZEMLYA EXPEDITION	P880	$1.25

TO ORDER

Please check the space next to the book/s you want, send this order form together with your check or money order, include the price of the book/s and 25¢ for handling and mailing to:
PINNACLE BOOKS, INC. / P.O. BOX 4347
Grand Central Station / New York, N.Y. 10017

☐ CHECK HERE IF YOU WANT A FREE CATALOG

I have enclosed $_____ check_____ or money order_____ as payment in full. No C.O.D.'s.

Name_____

Address_____

City_____ State_____ Zip_____

(Please allow time for delivery.) PB-36

the Executioner

The gutsiest, most exciting hero in years.
Imagine a guy at war with the Godfather
and all his Mafioso relatives! He's rough,
he's deadly, he's a law unto himself —
nothing and nobody stops him!

THE EXECUTIONER SERIES by DON PENDLETON

Order		Title	Book #	Price
	# 1	WAR AGAINST THE MAFIA	P401	$1.25
	# 2	DEATH SQUAD	P402	$1.25
	# 3	BATTLE MASK	P403	$1.25
	# 4	MIAMI MASSACRE	P404	$1.25
	# 5	CONTINENTAL CONTRACT	P405	$1.25
	# 6	ASSAULT ON SOHO	P406	$1.25
	# 7	NIGHTMARE IN NEW YORK	P407	$1.25
	# 8	CHICAGO WIPEOUT	P408	$1.25
	# 9	VEGAS VENDETTA	P409	$1.25
	#10	CARIBBEAN KILL	P410	$1.25
	#11	CALIFORNIA HIT	P411	$1.25
	#12	BOSTON BLITZ	P412	$1.25
	#13	WASHINGTON I.O.U.	P413	$1.25
	#14	SAN DIEGO SIEGE	P414	$1.25
	#15	PANIC IN PHILLY	P415	$1.25
	#16	SICILIAN SLAUGHTER	P552	$1.25
	#17	JERSEY GUNS	P328	$1.25
	#18	TEXAS STORM	P353	$1.25
	#19	DETROIT DEATHWATCH	P419	$1.25
	#20	NEW ORLEANS KNOCKOUT	P475	$1.25
	#21	FIREBASE SEATTLE	P499	$1.25
	#22	HAWAIIAN HELLGROUND	P625	$1.25
	#23	ST. LOUIS SHOWDOWN	P687	$1.25
	#24	CANADIAN CRISIS	P779	$1.25
	#25	COLORADO KILL-ZONE	P824	$1.25
	#26	ACAPULCO RAMPAGE	P868	$1.25

TO ORDER
Please check the space next to the book/s you want, send this order form
together with your check or money order, include the price of the book/s
and 25¢ for handling and mailing to:
PINNACLE BOOKS, INC. / P.O. BOX 4347
Grand Central Station / New York, N.Y. 10017
☐ CHECK HERE IF YOU WANT A FREE CATALOG
I have enclosed $_____ check_____or money order_____as
payment in full. No C.O.D.'s.

Name_____

Address_____

City_____State_____Zip_____
(Please allow time for delivery.)   PB-3

THE PENETRATOR

by Lionel Derrick

Mark Hardin. Discharged from the army, after service in Vietnam. His military career was over. But *his* war was just beginning. His reason for living and reason for dying become the same—to stamp out crime and corruption wherever he finds it. He is deadly; he is unpredictable; and he is dedicated. He is The Penetrator!

Read all of him in:

Order			Title	Book No.	Price
_____	#	1	THE TARGET IS H	P236	$ .95
_____	#	2	BLOOD ON THE STRIP	P237	$ .95
_____	#	3	CAPITOL HELL	P318	$ .95
_____	#	4	HIJACKING MANHATTAN	P338	$ .95
_____	#	5	MARDI GRAS MASSACRE	P378	$ .95
_____	#	6	TOKYO PURPLE	P434	$1.25
_____	#	7	BAJA BANDIDOS	P502	$1.25
_____	#	8	THE NORTHWEST CONTRACT	P540	$1.25
_____	#	9	DODGE CITY BOMBERS	P627	$1.25
_____	#10		THE HELLBOMB FLIGHT	P690	$1.25

TO ORDER

Please check the space next to the book/s you want, send this order form together with your check or money order, include the price of the book/s and 25¢ for handling and mailing, to:
PINNACLE BOOKS, INC. / P.O. Box 4347
Grand Central Station / New York, N.Y. 10017
☐ Check here if you want a free catalog.

I have enclosed $_____ check_____ or money order_____ as payment in full. No C.O.D.'s.

Name_____

Address_____

City_____ State_____ Zip_____
(Please allow time for delivery)

PB-40